RULE

THE DRAAX SERIES
BOOK TWO

ELIZABETH KELLY

EK PUBLISHING INC.

Edited by
L. Nunn Editing

Cover art by
The Final Wrap

RULE

Three hearts, an uncertain future. Will love rule?

I never thought I would give up everything and sign up for a lifetime breeding contract with an alien race. Although, being mated to a big green alien is a far better fate than my perilous struggle here on Earth.

Being one of the lowers, I didn't expect to be matched with the Draax king. Who knew I would be what they referred to as a guaranteed breeder?

Only, there's been a mix up.

This is a farm, not a palace.

Waiting out a month-long storm with two surprisingly sexy Draax and one adorable little girl needing a nanny shouldn't be that bad, right? So, why am I craving both Bran and Court in my bed and wishing I could break my breeding contract with the king?

Except, violating my contract means life imprisonment back on Earth. When the storm ends and the king arrives, I'll have to go with him… or will I?

CHAPTER 1

Evelyn

"Congratulations, we've found you a mate."

I stared at the blonde woman sitting behind the desk. "You're kidding."

The woman laughed before leaning forward and tapping her pen against the shiny surface of her desk. "I assure you, Ms. Fisher, that I'm not. We have matched you with a Draax, and you'll be leaving for the Draax planet the day after tomorrow."

"I didn't expect it to be so quick," I said. "I just had the genetic testing last week and only found out three days ago that I carried the gene for breeding with the Draax. I haven't even looked through the database yet."

The woman shrugged. "We pride ourselves here at the agency on our efficiency." She hesitated and, this time, tapped the end of her pencil against her teeth. "Honestly, we rarely have breeding compatible women who sign up for the lifetime program, so we tend to fast-track their applications."

I swallowed heavily as the woman said, "Mind you, most

of the women we send to the Draax planet to breed never come back."

She paused, realized how that sounded and said hurriedly, "Because they're very happy with their new life and the Draax they are mated with. Not because they're forced to stay."

"I know," I said. "I did some research before applying for the program."

The woman gave me a fleeting look, and I tried not to blush. The woman sitting across from me was a middle, and the shirt she wore probably cost more than my entire wardrobe. I pulled at my too-tight shirt. I was so poor I couldn't even afford decent clothing for the breeding program meeting. I'd had to borrow a top and skirt from my neighbour, Candy, and both items of clothing were too small.

"Oh, I didn't realize you had a tablet. Most of the lowers don't," the woman said.

I squirmed in my seat. Like most middles and uppers, the woman didn't have a clue about lowers. "I don't. But the library has them."

The woman gave me a blank look – I had an idea that she had never once set foot in a public library – before nodding. "Oh, right, of course. The library."

She glanced at the tablet on the desk before me as a rush of uncustomary anger flooded me. I tamped it down immediately. It wasn't the woman's fault that I was a lower. It wasn't her fault that she didn't know what it was like to be hungry, cold, or on the verge of being kicked out of her home. It did no good to be angry with her just because she'd never laid awake at night in a closet of a bedroom, clutching a knife to her chest and hoping that her stepbrother and his friends didn't get drunk enough to try to rape her.

My stomach clenched, and I took a shaky breath. The

woman glanced up from the tablet and frowned. "Ms. Fisher, are you all right? You're very pale."

"I'm fine. What is the name of the Draax I'm, um, mated to?"

I supposed it was strange to ask the name of the alien I was about to be mated to for the rest of my life. In the old fairy tales my mother read to me as a child, the girl married her Prince Charming. He was handsome and rich and madly in love with her. He certainly didn't have green skin or a tail and was only interested in knocking her up with a baby. My stomach clenched again at the thought of having sex with an alien. What if he was rough with me?

He won't be. Candy has nothing but good things to say about the Draax aliens she slept with, remember? Besides, it's better than what will happen to you if you stay.

I shuddered all over and closed my eyes. My inner voice was right. In fact, I should be celebrating the fact that the agency had found a match for me so quickly, not worrying about how rough alien sex would be. Even if the alien didn't take his time or didn't care about my pleasure, it would still be better than being married to that scumbag Troy. Just the thought of sleeping with Troy made me want to vomit.

I realized the woman from the agency was speaking, and I said, "I'm sorry, what did you say?"

"I said I had even better news about who you were matched to for mating. You have been matched with a Draax named Quillan, and he," the woman gave me a look of breathless anticipation, "is the king of the western province of the Odias continent."

"I – what?" I said faintly. Did the woman just say I was matched to a king?

The woman nodded. "It's true. You're our number one match for him."

"Are you sure?"

"Positive. You've tested higher than any other human for breeding compatibility. You're a - what we like to call in the business - guaranteed breeder. You'll likely become pregnant on the first try. Because of this, we pull you from the general breeding database and match you with higher ranking Draax who are in the program, and you can't get much higher than a king. We like to give these," she paused, "Draax special treatment so we match them with the guaranteed breeders rather than making them wait to be chosen, but you didn't hear that from me."

"Right," I said.

The woman smiled at me. "And with you signing up for the lifetime program, it makes you extra valuable. The king is apparently very anxious for an heir."

"Right, of course," I said. "Um, he knows I'm a lower, right?"

"We have passed on all of your information but, frankly, the Draax don't care what class you are. They just want you to be healthy and able to breed. Now, you can, of course, say no to mating with the king and choose your mate from the breeding program, but I highly encourage you not to do that. You'll be a queen, afterall."

"I didn't care about being a queen. I just cared about getting the hell off of Earth. But I smiled at the woman and said, "I'm happy to be matched with the king."

"Excellent," she said happily. "Your payment of gallberry juice is waiting for you in the front room."

The woman pushed a few buttons on her tablet and then frowned. "This can't be right. It says you'll receive only a gallon of juice for a lifetime of service. Oh, for the love of God, the juice guys can't get anything right. I just knew they would screw this up some -"

"It's right. I only need a gallon."

The woman gave me a suddenly anxious look before speaking slowly and clearly. "Ms. Fisher, you understand you have signed up for the lifetime program, correct?"

"Yes."

"You will never be able to return to Earth unless your mate allows it. You will become the queen of the western province and will most likely bear the king more than one child."

"I get it," I said.

"But you only asked for one gallon of juice."

"That's all I need."

The woman hesitated. "It's for the rest of your life, Ms. Fisher."

"I'm aware."

"Very well. You are to be at the docking bay at eight-thirty Tuesday morning. We'll have someone from the agency pick you up at your apartment at eight to escort you to the loading dock. Please be ready to go by eight. The pilots don't like it when the cargo is late."

"I won't be late," I said.

The woman pushed the tablet toward me. "Your signature is required on the bottom line. Did you read over the terms of the contract like I asked?"

"Yes, I read it after I tested positive for breeding."

"Good. By signing, you agree to the terms of the contract. Breaking them is considered a first-class felony, and you'll be sentenced to at least twenty-five years in prison. Is that clear?"

"Yes."

"You will go to prison, Evelyn," the woman said. "There is no getting out of it once you sign the contract. Be very certain you wish to do this."

"I'm certain." I signed across the line with the tip of my finger and only felt a moment of panic before it subsided. I sat back in my seat as euphoria washed over me. I was free of him. By this time next week, I would be on a new planet, and my stepbrother would never be able to hurt me again.

You still need to get to the docking bay without him noticing. You're not free yet, and he's dangerous and unpredictable. Don't ever forget that, my inner voice cautioned.

"A copy of the contract will be sent to the email address you provided. Unless you have more questions, we're finished here," the woman said.

She stood and smoothed down her skirt as I stumbled to my feet. I hesitated and then held out my hand. The woman glanced at it before giving it a brief shake. "Nice to meet you, Ms. Fisher. Enjoy your new life. Don't forget to pick up your juice at the front desk."

"Yeah, I won't forget." Did the woman think I was that stupid? I could hear the disdain in my voice, and I automatically cringed. At home, that tone would get me a punch to the face if I were lucky or a kick to the kidneys if I wasn't.

The woman gave me a strange look before pointing to the door. "The reception is to the right. Goodbye, Ms. Fisher."

"Goodbye." I hurried out of the woman's office and down the hallway. At the front desk, I picked up the gallberry juice and tucked it into the backpack I had brought for that very purpose. I couldn't very well walk through my neighbourhood carrying a gallon of gallberry juice. My throat would be slit in the first two minutes.

I rode the elevator down to the front lobby and walked outside. I breathed in the warm air and the smell of the flowers planted in front of the office building before slinging the pack over my back and tightening the straps. An airtrain roared overhead, blotting out the sun momentarily and sending a gust of warm air over me. I studied its silver underbelly as it flew by, wondering for a moment what it would be like to travel in the air like that.

You'll find out in two days.

A little sprinkle of excitement bloomed in my belly. Yes, I would. In two days, I would fly in a spaceship to another planet, and my life on Earth would be a distant memory. I took another deep breath and started the long walk toward home.

CHAPTER 2

Evelyn

"Thank you again for letting me borrow your clothes, Candy."

"Don't mention it, sweetie." The curvy brunette sat at the table and watched as I folded the clothes she'd given me and placed them on the table. "How did the interview go?"

"Good," I said. "I got the job."

"Seriously?" Candy's eyes widened. "That's awesome. Congratulations, Evie."

"Thank you."

Candy studied her small and shabby apartment. "Just think, with a government job, you'll soon be making enough money to move out of this piece-of-shit building. Hell, you'll get an apartment in the city, and you'll never have to see your asshole of a stepbrother again. He won't be able to make you quit this job like he did the last one."

She reached out and squeezed my hand. "I'm going to miss you. You need to promise me that we'll still see each other. I can scrape up enough cash for Roden and me to take the airtrain into the city once or twice a year, and we can meet in the park. What do you say?"

Before I could reply, there was a low moan and coughing from the tiny bedroom just off the kitchen. Candy jumped up and hurried into the room. I could hear her soothing Roden, and a few minutes later, she returned to the kitchen with him.

Candy was on the shorter side, and Roden was eight years old, but the cystic fibrosis had ravaged his body to the point where she could still carry him easily. She sat him gently in the chair and wet a cloth before wiping his face and mouth. The young boy was sweaty and pale, but he gave Candy a small smile.

"Thank you, Mama."

"You're welcome, baby. Is your chest still hurting?"

He nodded, and a pinched look of worry came over Candy's face. She grabbed an amber-coloured bottle from the cupboard and poured a spoonful of liquid. "Take this, baby. It'll help."

Roden swallowed it obediently before smiling at me. "Hi, Evie."

"Hi, honey. How are you feeling?"

"Okay. Mama says I have another infection."

"I'm sorry."

"That's okay. I don't feel too bad."

I reached out and ruffled his dark hair. Candy had been our neighbour for only three years, but I loved her and Roden like they were family. The cure for cystic fibrosis had been discovered over fifty years ago. Unfortunately, the treatment was expensive, and only the uppers could afford it. The only other option was the gallberry juice from the planet of Draax.

A shiver went down my back. In two days I'd be on

Draax. Being bred by a big green alien in exchange for a gallon of gallberry juice and, more importantly, a place to live free of being beaten every time I opened my mouth or gave the wrong look.

You hope. What if this Draax king is as bad as your step-brother? As bad as Troy? You'll be going from the frying pan into the fire.

I shook off my trepidation. The Draax king wouldn't beat me. I was too valuable to him. If I were lucky, he would leave me alone except when he wanted to breed. Hopefully, as long as I spread my legs, let him have sex with me, and gave him an heir to the throne, I could live my life peacefully without worrying about being hurt. I'd even have a child or two to love. Being a mother was something I'd always wanted. Did it matter if the baby was alien instead of human or that I wouldn't love its father?

No, it didn't.

You'll still spend the rest of your life on an alien planet with a savage warrior race.

My stomach was churning, and I could feel that familiar fear and panic enveloping me. I hated being so timid and afraid of everything, but after years of living with my step-brother, I couldn't control it. It didn't help that the race I would soon live permanently with came across as merciless killing machines. Of course, if it hadn't been for them, Earth as we knew it would no longer exist.

The Draax race had saved Earth's bacon over forty years ago from an alien race called the Gokmards. The Gokmards were very close to taking over our planet when the Draax swept in with their swords flashing and destroyed over half the Gokmard army. The Draax's muscular green bodies and brutal fighting skills made them true warriors. Despite the Gokmards advanced technology, they were no match for the

Draax's viciousness and healing abilities. After watching most of their kind be cut to pieces, the rest of the Gokmards had fled in defeat to their own world.

The Draax saved us for a reason, of course. Females were rarely born on their planet and now females of breeding age were almost non-existent. Thanks to similar anatomies and our need to be rescued from the Gokmards, the Draax had chosen us to help repopulate their planet.

The gallberry plant they grew and harvested into juice only sweetened the pot, as the old ones used to say. After the war, the Draax revealed that their healing abilities were actually thanks to the pink juice extracted from the gallberry plant that grew on their planet. The juice healed every known illness and injury to man, from the common cold, to cancer, to genetic diseases like cystic fibrosis.

The Draax joined the United Space Coalition and quickly struck up an agreement with Earth's highest authorities. In exchange for saving us from the Gokmards and supplying us with limited quantities of gallberry juice, the Draax wanted to start a breeding program with us. It was entirely voluntary, but after a lack of female volunteers for the program, the Draax withheld the supply of gallberry juice that humans were already beginning to rely on.

I studied Roden's pale face as his mother set a glass of water before him. Desperate to save themselves or their loved ones from disease, the women had signed up for the breeding program in droves – mainly lowers and middles, of course. Once they provided a Draax male with a child, they were free to return to Earth. Not many did. Very few women wanted to leave their child. The Draax race's fear of extinction had disappeared in the last forty years thanks to humans.

I watched Candy lovingly stroke Roden's face before

studying the backpack at my feet. What I was about to give them would change both their lives.

"Mama, can I watch the hologram screen?" Roden asked.

Candy nodded. "Yes, but we only have three chits left. Are you sure you want to use up one today? Mama doesn't get paid again for another week."

"I'm sure. I wanna watch *Discovery World*. They have a special on the Draax and how they grow the gallberry plant." The young boy twisted in his seat to stare at the sad, drooping pink plant on the windowsill. "I'm gonna figure out how to save my plant."

"All right, baby." Candy picked him up and smiled at me. "I'll be right back."

She carried Roden back into the bedroom. I stared at the gallberry plant. It was given to Candy last week by a Draax male who had visited the bar where she waitressed. It was robust enough when she'd brought it home to Roden, and he had planted it in a small pot of soil and carefully watered and tended to it, but the plant was dying. Many people, from qualified agricultural specialists to hobby farmers, had attempted to grow the gallberry plant to no avail. I'd been reading a lot about the Draax race in the last few months, and in the *History of the Draax*, I had read something about the gallberry plant not growing in our atmosphere.

Didn't stop the humans from trying, though.

"Sorry about that." Candy had returned, and she poured us both more tea.

"What was the medicine that you gave him?" I asked.

"Just a cheap cough medicine I got at the pharm-aid. It helps ease the cough a bit, but…"

She blinked back tears and cleared her throat. "He's getting worse. The lung infections never really clear up, you know? Even with the bit of juice I can get him."

She gave me a pleading look. "Hey, do you think you could come by tonight? Roden's regular sitter can only stay until eleven, and normally, I would be home by then, but I'm, um, gonna try to get some juice tonight."

Her face turned red, and I could see the shame in her eyes. My stomach ached for her, and even though the Draax males she slept with in exchange for a bit of juice always treated her well, I hated what she had to do for the juice.

She won't have to do that any longer.

No, she wouldn't. Before I could show her the juice I was carrying, Candy squeezed my hand. "I know you disapprove of it, sweetie, but I have no choice."

"I don't disapprove of it," I said. "I just worry about you. If you get caught, you'll go to prison. What the Draax are doing is illegal. They're not allowed to give gallberry juice in exchange for sex unless you're in the breeding program."

"I know it's a risk, but I'm not breeding compatible. I have no choice, Evie."

Only about seventy percent of Earth's females were breeding compatible with the Draax. I knew that Candy had applied for the breeding program when Roden was only a year old, but she'd been incompatible.

The breeding program and the gallberry juice were strictly regulated, but like all things of value, a black market for the juice had quickly sprung up. Candy couldn't afford the juice even on the black market, but more than a few Draax males were willing to risk imprisonment by handing over a bit of gallberry juice in exchange for a night of sex.

I'd been to the bar where Candy worked, and there were always Draax there looking to convince a woman to sleep with them. Even with a language barrier, the Draax were amazingly good at seducing females.

Hell, Candy had told me once that half the Draax didn't

even need to bribe the women with a bit of juice to sleep with them. They were strong and handsome, if you didn't mind green skin and tails, and lots of women were willing to at least give sleeping with a Draax for fun a try. Apparently, their bedroom skills were legendary.

"I hate to ask because I can't pay you for it, but I really need to get him a little gallberry juice. If I don't, I don't think he'll make it past the month." Candy's voice hitched, and tears slipped down her cheeks. "I should be home by five or six in the morning by the latest."

I bent and opened my backpack. I pulled out the jug of gallberry juice and set it on the table before Candy. "I don't mind staying the night, but you don't have to do that anymore."

She stared at the jug of pink liquid. "What – is that what I think it is?"

"Yep. I looked up gallberry juice requirements for kids with CF, and while the exact amount varies, they never need more than half a gallon of it. I got a gallon, though, just in case."

"Oh my God..." Candy's voice was a whisper. "You got Roden some gallberry juice?"

"I did." I grinned at her.

"How? When?"

"I told you I got a new job."

Candy stared at me. "You said it was with the government."

I shrugged. "It sort of is."

"You got picked for the nanny program?"

I shook my head. About ten years ago, a secondary program opened up. Breeding incompatible women could sign up for the nanny program on Draax. Nanny positions varied in length from a year to five years, and three months ago, I applied to the nanny program. I hadn't been picked yet and probably never would. I loved kids, but I didn't have much experience with them.

"Then how..." Candy gave me a shocked look. "The breeding program. You signed up for the breeding program?"

"I did."

"But you said you would never do that. You said you didn't want to pop out alien babies while living on a strange planet with an alien you didn't love."

I shrugged. "I changed my mind."

"You changed your mind."

"Yes. Give Roden a glass of gallberry juice."

She stared at the juice for a moment. "I – this is an incredible gift, Evie, but I -"

"You're taking it, Candy. No arguing."

"Fucking right I'm taking it. I was going to say I'll never be able to pay you back for it."

"You don't have to. Give him a glass of juice."

Candy stood and quickly poured a glass of the juice before hurrying into the bedroom. I pulled the jug closer and sniffed the opening. It smelled vaguely of strawberries, and I pushed the jug away before I was tempted to try some for myself. I was pretty sure that a gallon would be enough to heal Roden completely, but I wasn't taking any chances.

Candy returned and gave me a delighted grin. "You should have seen the look on his face when I gave him the glass."

I laughed as Candy bent and threw her arms around me. She hugged me hard. "Evie, you have no idea what you've done for me. I will never forget this." She leaned back and cupped my face as tears ran down her cheeks. "You've saved Roden's life. You know that, right?"

She wiped away the tears running down my cheeks with

her thumbs before giving me a loud, smacking kiss on my mouth. "Now, let's talk about fucking the Draax."

I burst into laughter as she returned to her seat. "Are you serious?"

"Dead serious. Wait, maybe you should tell me first why you joined the breeding program. Did you do it solely for Roden? Because, sweetie, I -"

"I'm glad I could help Roden, but I didn't join the program because of him."

"Then why?"

I traced the worn wood of the kitchen table with my fingertip. "Alex is forcing me to marry Troy."

"Fuck." Candy scowled. "That fucking son of a bitch."

"Yeah."

She paused and then gave me a delicate look. "I thought that because you weren't a virgin anymore, Troy lost interest in you."

"He had at first but apparently changed his mind."

"Well, shit. So, you gave up your V-card to some random guy for nothing."

I winced, and Candy gave me a look of chagrin. "I'm sorry. I shouldn't have said that."

"It's okay."

"It isn't okay." Candy grabbed my hand and squeezed it again. "None of this is okay. You shouldn't have had to find some guy at the bar and sleep with him to avoid that asshole Troy, and you definitely shouldn't have to give up your life to keep from being married off to that scumbag."

I didn't reply, and Candy sighed. "I've heard that some Draax are allowing the women to return to Earth with their children. They either stay on Earth with them or visit like once a month or something."

"You know that's not true," I said. "If a woman joins the breeding program, she rarely returns to Earth. Besides, it doesn't matter. I signed up for the lifetime program."

"What?" Candy's mouth dropped open. "Why would you do that? You can't ever come back now, Evie. Not without the Draax's permission."

"Exactly," I said. "I don't want to come back. Once I leave, if I even step foot back on this planet, Alex will track me down and kill me. You know he will. Hell, I'm lucky he hasn't killed me yet. I need to get out of here before he beats me so bad that he puts me in a coma. I joined the lifetime program because if I didn't, knowing my luck, I'd end up with some Draax who only wanted me for one kid and then would force me back here without my baby."

"I don't think so," Candy said. "The Draax are actually pretty nice and love and respect females."

"How do you know that? You don't even speak their language," I said.

"Yeah, but," Candy glanced at the bedroom and lowered her voice, "I've fucked plenty of them, and they come across as really nice."

I laughed, and Candy blushed. "I know that sounds stupid, but it's true. I don't know how to explain it."

"It doesn't matter," I said. "I've already signed the contract for the lifetime program. If I try to back out, I'll go to prison."

"When do you leave?"

"The agency is picking me up at eight on Tuesday morning."

"What? So soon?"

I wiggled my eyebrows at her. "I'm what they call a guaranteed breeder. My bloodwork returned as highly compatible."

"Holy shit."

"Yeah, and get this. I'm being, uh, mated to a king."

"Shut the hell up!"

"It's true." I was terrified of leaving everything I knew, but I couldn't help but grin at the look on Candy's face. "I'm to be married or mated or whatever the heck they call it to the king of the western province. His name is Quillan or Killen… something like that."

"You'll be a queen," Candy said.

"Yeah. Weird, huh?"

"I can't think of anyone who deserves it more, sweetie. Even before you saved my son's life." She gave me a giddy look of excitement. "He's not going to die, Evie. He'll grow big and strong and live a good life."

"He will," I said.

"Because of you." She was starting to cry again.

"Don't cry, honey."

"You really have no idea what this means to me. I love you, Evie."

"I love you too, Candy." We sat in silence for a few minutes. "Anyway, the king needs an heir, and thanks to my superior baby making abilities, I was matched to him."

Candy grabbed a tissue and blew her nose before staring solemnly at me. "Listen, I know it will be difficult to leave Earth, but I promise you your life will be better with the Draax."

I picked at the fraying hem of my shirt sleeve. "Yeah, I know."

"Are you anxious because you're leaving Earth, or is there something else?" Candy asked.

"What if the Draax king is like Troy or Alex?"

"He won't be," Candy said.

"How do you know that?"

18

"I just do. I've been with a lot of them, and they're all very…kind in bed and out. They can be demanding and dominant during sex, but they would never hurt you, Evie. Women are special to them, you can tell."

"Do they think we're special? So many of them come to Earth just looking to fuck a woman."

"I know, but can you blame them? The breeding program has saved them from extinction, but it's not like women are just walking around on their planet, available to date or whatever. Women that are on the planet are already claimed by a Draax, so of course they're going to come to Earth to get laid. They have high sex drives."

I must have made a face because Candy smiled a little. "That's not always a bad thing."

"Isn't it?"

"No. Listen, your one and only experience with sex wasn't that great, so don't judge all fucking by that, okay?"

My cheeks were heating up. "It wasn't that bad."

"You didn't even come, Evie."

Now, my face felt like it was on fire. "He tried to make me come. I was just too nervous and uptight."

"Yeah, because the guy was a stranger, and you were only fucking him because you needed to get rid of your virginity in a hurry. Of course, you were going to be nervous. It'll be different with the Draax, I promise."

"You don't know that."

"I do," Candy insisted. "The Draax love women, and they love making you come. This king will be the same, I promise."

"I'll be fucking a stranger again. What if I can't relax enough to, uh, climax?"

"You'll have an orgasm, even if you are nervous. Trust me,

sweetie. The big green dudes have skills in the bedroom." She grinned at me.

"I can't believe I'm about to sleep with an alien," I said.

She shrugged. "It's no different from sleeping with a human. Well, except for the green skin and tails, I guess. But it's not like the tail comes into play during sex, so you won't even notice it. They do a lot of the same things that human men do."

"Like what?"

Candy grinned again. "Fall asleep and start snoring immediately after sex, rub their cum all over you, make -"

"Whoa, they do *what* with their cum?"

This time, Candy laughed out loud. "Okay, so I rarely use condoms with the Draax I sleep with -"

"Candy!"

"What? They don't have the sexually transmitted infections that we can get, and I'm breeding incompatible, so it's not like I have to worry about pregnancy, right? Anyway, after sex, almost every Draax I've been with will rub their cum on my stomach and tits."

"What? Why?"

"For the same macho bullshit reason that human men like to smear their cum on us."

"Gross."

"It's not really. They're almost sweet about it, to be honest. At least they don't shoot their load in my face when I'm giving them a blowjob, like most human males do. The Draax respect us too much to do that."

I stared into my now cold cup of tea. I knew Candy was trying to help, but she was making my anxiety worse. My biggest fear was that I would never be able to truly enjoy sex. The Draax loved fucking. What if my inability to come, my inability to just relax and enjoy the ride, so to speak, made the Draax angry? What if my frigidness infuriated him and made him lose his temper?

I cringed inwardly. Alex wasn't that big of a man, and his kicks and punches hurt like hell. What would happen if a Draax punched me? They were massive in size and built to maim and injure.

Candy was talking again, and I forced myself to focus on what she was saying.

"Just be prepared that your king might invite a friend to join you."

I gave Candy an uneasy look. "Those are just rumours, aren't they?"

She shook her head. "Girl, seriously, have you never watched Draax porn?"

"Of course not. We rarely can afford chits for the hologram screen, and when we can, we watch what Alex wants to watch."

"Right. Well, it's not just rumours. The Draax like to share."

"He's a king. He's not going to share his queen with someone else."

"He might," Candy said. "Most Draax love threesomes."

My unease was growing by leaps and bounds. What if I had to worry about pleasing two Draax males?

"Have you been with two Draax?" I asked.

"Yeah, quite a few times. They'll give you extra juice if you take two of them on at once."

I swallowed. "Uh, how was it?"

"Amazing," Candy said. "Like, change my life, amazing."

I gave her a doubtful look, and Candy nodded. "It's true. I mean, at first, I was a little worried because their dicks are so friggin' big, but they always go slow and use plenty of lube. If the king invites a friend, you'll want him to keep inviting one. Two is always better than one."

I didn't believe her for a second, but I kept my doubts to myself. It didn't matter if I was nervous or afraid, I had signed the contract and was about to be mated to a Draax male. It was too late to back out now. If I couldn't relax enough to come, I would just have to fake it and hope the Draax didn't notice.

CHAPTER 3

Evelyn

I woke slowly. My lower back and side throbbed, and pain radiated up and down my shoulder. I rolled onto my side, staring blearily at the wall of my small bedroom.

I was lying on the cold floor. Why wasn't I on my mattress?

I sat up, groaning at the agony it caused in my lower back, and tried to focus as I rubbed my aching kidneys. Why did I hurt so much?

The memory of last night came rushing back, and I pinched my lips shut against the moan that wanted to escape. Alex had come into my room late at night, drunk and looking to fight. He'd taunted me about marrying Troy, and when I refused to respond, he'd started punching.

I rubbed my shoulder and slipped my top down to stare at the bruise blossoming across it. I climbed to my feet and grabbed the wall for support when a wave of dizziness swept over me. Hot and intense pain shot through my side, and for a moment, I thought I would vomit all over the floor. I swallowed grimly and bowed my head, pressing my hand against my kidneys and waiting for the pain to subside.

After a while, a *long* while, it did. I raised my shirt and studied the bruise on my side. It was the exact shape and size of Alex's boot. I vaguely recalled him slamming his foot down on me while I was huddled on the ground with my arms over my head to protect it.

More nausea hit me, and I took a few deep breaths before shuffling to the full-length mirror against the far wall. I turned my back to the mirror and carefully twisted my head to study my back. A horrified groan snuck past my lips. No wonder my kidneys and lower back felt like they were on fire. My pale skin was covered in angry red welts and mottled purple bruising. The whole area felt swollen and hot, and I couldn't bring myself even to touch my lower back.

I had blacked out as Alex was punching and kicking me, and typically, that made him stop, but it looked like this time, he'd kept going. I lowered my shirt, wincing at even that pressure and quietly left my bedroom. I hobbled down the hallway, pausing at Alex's bedroom. I could hear his loud snoring through the door, and I stepped over the squeaky spot on the floor and continued to the bathroom. It was doubtful I would wake Alex up, not after how much he drank last night, but I didn't want to take any chances.

It burned and hurt like hell to pee, and I wasn't surprised when I stood up and saw blood in the toilet. It wasn't the first time I'd peed blood after being beaten by my stepbrother.

It'll be the last.

I blinked in confusion at my reflection in the bathroom mirror. Why would it be the last time? I was sure Alex would find a way to beat the shit out of me even after I was married to Troy and living...

My eyes widened. I was leaving. I was moving to Draax

and being married to their king. Alex would never beat me again.

Fuck! What time was it? I staggered out of the bathroom, forcing myself to walk quickly despite the agonizing pain, and looked for my PAR phone in my bedroom. It was shattered on the floor, Alex must have broken it, but I didn't have time to mourn its loss. I needed to know what fucking time it was.

I snuck back out into the small and messy living room. It didn't matter how often I cleaned, Alex and his friends were pigs and never picked up after themselves. I glanced at the clock on the hologram screen, and dismay filled me. It was ten to eight. The people from the agency would be here in ten minutes to pick me up. If I wasn't downstairs, they might leave, or worse – knock on the door. If they woke up Alex, who knew what he would do? Hell, he would probably try to kill me before he let me go.

I returned to my bedroom, avoiding the squeaky spot again, and grabbed the large backpack from my closet. I had very little clothes or personal possessions, but I still wouldn't have time to pack everything. I had planned to get up early this morning and pack – it was too risky to pack beforehand – but I hadn't counted on being beaten unconscious by my stepbrother last night.

I stuffed some clothes into the bag, my wallet, and my broken PAR phone. It was probably pointless, but it had a ton of photos on it. Maybe I could somehow get the phone working and transfer them to a memory stick or something.

I bent – God, did it hurt my back – and slid my hand between my mattress and the floor. The picture was still safely tucked under the mattress, and I studied my father's face before pressing a kiss against the photo and carefully sliding it into the backpack. It was the only picture I had of him, Alex and his mother had burned the rest when he died, and it was my most precious possession.

I slipped out of my bedroom. It hurt too much to lift my backpack and I had to drag it on the floor behind me. Distracted, I didn't avoid the squeak in the floor, and I froze when I stepped on it. Alex's snoring cut out, and I pressed my hand over my mouth, the tears dripping down my cheeks.

To my immense relief, he started to snore again. Shaking and shuddering, my entire body pulsing with pain, I grabbed my toiletry bag from the bathroom, stuffed it into my backpack and headed toward the front door, rechecking the clock.

Three minutes.

Shit.

I eased out of the apartment I had called home for the last decade without looking back. I closed the door, the latch click excruciatingly loud in the silence, and hurried down the hall, still dragging my backpack. I paused to press my hand against Candy's apartment door. I had said goodbye to her yesterday, but she was my only friend, and I would miss her terribly.

I wiped away the tears and dragged my backpack down the hall and the narrow, dirty stairs. Maybe the king would let me hologram with Candy from time to time. I stepped out into the street. A black vehicle was pulling up, and I knew it was from the agency. No one in our neighbourhood could afford a vehicle, not even a land one.

Trying not to look like I was in agony, I walked slowly toward the car as a man stepped out from behind the wheel. "Ms. Fisher?"

"Yes, that's me." I glanced behind me at the building door, half-expecting Alex to come busting out into the street.

"I'll need to see some ID, ma'am."

I rooted through my backpack for my wallet, glancing behind me again. Fuck. Where was it? I finally found it and yanked it out, showing the man my ID. He studied the picture carefully before studying me, and I tried not to give him an impatient look. I peeked behind me again.

"Good." He handed me my wallet, and I stuffed it into my backpack and zipped it up. He put my bag in the trunk before opening the back door. I climbed in, my breath hissing out between my teeth as pain sliced through my body, and breathed a sigh of relief when he shut the door. I'd never been in a car before, and as the man used voice controls to start the vehicle, I watched in fascination as the dashboard lit up. The man studied his phone and typed on the keyboard as the vehicle pulled out onto the street. I closed my eyes and rested my head against the back of the seat.

I was free.

"Evelyn, open your eyes, please."

The voice was loud and intrusive, and the hand on my shoulder was incredibly painful. I forced my eyes open and stared at the woman standing over me. She gave me an impatient look before walking away.

I sat up, my back and shoulder and kidneys screaming in protest, and stared around blearily. I was at the International Space Station and would never see Alex and Troy again. Deep relief swept through me, and I blinked back the tears before studying the woman sitting in the cot across from mine.

She had dark hair like me, gorgeous blue eyes, and a curvier body than mine. I'd always been chubby, but I knew enough about the Draax to know that was an asset. They liked their women to be on the larger side.

The woman was staring at my shoulder. My top had slipped, and I hurriedly pulled it up to cover the visible bruise.

The woman looked slightly embarrassed as she said, "Hi, I'm Sabrina. I didn't get the chance to introduce myself yesterday. It was pretty loud on the ship."

I didn't think telling her I was glad she hadn't spoken to me would be smart. It was my first time on a ship, and, in addition to the pain I was in from Alex's beating, I was fighting constant motion sickness the entire time. I'd also been terrified that when we got to the International Space Station, they would give us a physical, and I'd be rejected because of the bruising.

I didn't need to worry. We'd arrived late, and they'd simply shown us to a room with a dozen narrow cots. The woman named Sabrina had fallen asleep almost instantly, but I'd laid awake until nearly dawn, worrying and wondering if they would do a physical in the morning.

"I'm Evelyn," I said. "It's nice to meet you."

"Nice to meet you, too." She glanced at the cots around us. "Not many volunteers on this trip, huh?"

"Are you in the breeding program?" I asked.

"No. I have a job as a nanny. You?" Sabrina replied.

"Breeding program." I could hear the nerves in my voice. Sabrina must have as well because she reached across and touched my arm.

"You okay?"

"Yes. Just, uh, a little nervous," I said.

"Understandable, but I hear the Draax treat their females very well."

I tried to smile at her, and she squeezed my arm comfortingly. "I'm sure it will be fine."

"Yes," I said, but even I could hear the fear in my voice.

The woman who had woken us returned to the room. Sabrina studied my shoulder for a moment before turning to the woman. "Hey. Do you have any gallberry juice she can have?"

The woman scowled at her. "Of course not. Don't be ridiculous."

She seemed weirdly angry and impatient. I swallowed my apprehension as she yanked a giant syringe from the left pocket of her lab jacket and walked over to Sabrina.

"Whoa," Sabrina held up her hands, "what is that for?"

"It's your identification chip," she said impatiently. "It has all of your details as well as the details of the Draax male you're breeding with."

"Not breeding," Sabrina said in alarm, "nannying."

"Yes, yes." The woman gave her an irritable look. "Lift your sleeve."

Sabrina lifted her sleeve, and the woman injected her in the upper arm with the syringe. She wiped it with a cotton ball before taking another syringe from her right pocket and moving toward me.

"Arm, please," she said as the flag emblem on her lab jacket glowed brightly. "Oh for..."

She sighed and slapped her hand against it as I pushed up my sleeve. "Yes, what is it?"

A man appeared in a hologram behind me. "Are they ready for transport? A storm is brewing on Draax, and we want to get them there and drop them off before it gets too bad and we end up stranded."

"I'm just chipping them now, and then I need to put the translators in," the woman said.

"Well, get a move on it," the man snapped. "We're leaving in ten."

"Shut up, Gary." The woman slapped the emblem again. Gary disappeared, and she injected me with the syringe.

"There," she said. "If you get lost, they can scan you and know who you belong to."

"Oh, perfect," Sabrina said, "we've been microchipped like stray dogs."

The woman scowled, and I gave Sabrina a horrified look. She grinned at me as the woman in the lab coat said, "You might want to watch your mouth when you're on Draax. They like the women they sleep with to be submissive and quiet."

"Well, it's a good job I'm nannying and not fucking then," Sabrina said.

My mouth dropped open as the woman made a loud snort of irritation. I couldn't believe how bold Sabrina was, and for a moment, I wished I could be like her. Or, at the very least, be her friend and watch from the sidelines as she sassed everyone around her.

The woman was rummaging in the inside pocket of her lab coat, and she removed two small gun-like contraptions.

"What are those?" Sabrina asked.

"The translators. One is embedded in your skull here," she pointed to just behind my right ear, "it'll translate the Draax language into English for you instantly when they speak to you. The other one is injected here," she touched the spot above the hollow of my throat, "and it will translate your English to Draaxan when you speak."

"Right," Sabrina said.

"Is it going to hurt?" I asked.

"It's not going to feel like kisses, sweetheart," the woman said.

I flinched at the sharp bite of pain when the woman pulled the trigger on the gun.

"Lift your head," the woman said as she reached for the second device. She quickly injected the second translator into my throat. I could feel blood slipping down my throat, and the woman held a piece of gauze against the entry point on my throat and behind my ear. "Apply pressure for a few minutes."

She walked back to Sabrina. As she readied the translator guns, she said, "So, don't panic if these don't work immediately. Sometimes, the chips can take a day or two to start working and translating properly."

She pressed the gun behind Sabrina's ear as the curvy brunette said, "A day or two? Seriously? We'll be on a strange planet where we won't speak or understand the language for forty-eight hours, and you're just mentioning it – ow! Fuck, that hurt!"

She rubbed at the spot behind her ear and glared at the woman.

"Lift your head," the woman said. She implanted the second translator and slapped gauze on both spots. Sabrina scowled at her. "Seriously? A day or two? Why didn't you implant the damn things before we left Earth then?"

"Not my department." The woman pointed to the far door. "That's the bathroom. You've got five minutes, and then I'll be back to take you to the ship."

Court

"You are really not going to go to the ship?"

Bran finished cutting up the warracot and placed it on a

31

plate. He set the plate on the table and picked up Bella. He kissed her cheek, and she giggled as he put her in her booster seat and pushed the chair closer to the table. She crowed in delight and shoved a piece of warracot into her mouth as her father smoothed her long dark hair affectionately.

"Bran," I said impatiently.

"No, I am not," Bran said. "It is getting late, and I do not want to take Bella out into the storm. It will be past her bedtime by the time I return home with the human."

"I can stay with her," I said. "It was your idea to hire a human as a nanny. You should be the one to pick her up."

"You know that Bella cannot sleep without our bedtime routine," Bran said. "What is your problem, Court? It is not that far to the docking bay, and you have driven in bad weather before."

"We will be lucky to make it home before the storm really hits," I grumbled before glancing out the window at the dark clouds. "The pilots may not even be able to land the ship."

Bran shrugged. "If not, we will pick her up after the storm ends."

"It will last at least a moon."

"I know."

"I do not know why you even bothered to hire the human right now. The cold weather is here to stay, and we can care for Bella ourselves."

"I hired her now because this will give Bella time to grow accustomed to her new nanny." He smiled at the little girl who was still greedily eating the warracot. "You know she is shy and requires time to become comfortable with new people. It will be easier for her if we are around while she gets to know the human."

Bran had a point, but I still wished he had waited until the warm months. Mainly because I would be busy in the fields and spend very little time in the house. I had no wish to be anywhere near this new human, but the frequent storms during the cold months would force me to be in close contact with her.

I swallowed down my anger and disgust. Bella needed a nanny. We could no longer carry her on our backs while we worked in the fields. She was two, and being carried around in a hot field all day was not fair to her. She needed to have the opportunity to play and learn like other small ones.

"You agreed to this, Court. Do not forget that." Bran stared steadily at me.

"Do not forget that you agreed she would be a nanny and nothing more."

Bran scowled. "It will not be an issue. You, more than anyone, should know that. Besides, the female is breeding incompatible. She is of no use to us other than as a nanny."

"The female humans cannot be trusted, Bran. Remember that."

"You speak to me as though I am a child." Bran's temper was rising. "You are not the only one who suffered because of what she did."

"Papa, juice." Bella had finished the warracot and gave her father a large smile. "Juice."

Bran grabbed the plastic cup from the counter and checked that the lid was secure. "What do you say, meena?"

"Please," Bella said. She grinned when Bran handed the cup to her and brandished it at me. "Juice, Uda!"

"I see your juice, meena."

"Drink, Uda." She held her cup out to me.

"No, you must drink all of it to grow big and strong."

She giggled and drank from the opening in the lid. Pink liquid trickled down her chin and she placed the cup on the table before wiping her chin. She licked the palm of her hand and giggled again.

As much as I hated the human who had forever fractured my relationship with my best friend, I couldn't deny that we would not have our sweet Bella without her. I bent and pressed a kiss against her forehead.

"You need to leave now to get to the docking bay in time," Bran said.

I put on my cloak and buttoned it as Bran grabbed his tablet. "She has long dark hair, blue eyes, and large breasts and hips. Do you need to see her picture?"

"No. She will be implanted with an ID chip if I cannot find her."

Bran rolled his eyes. "Your unwillingness to even look at the human I have hired is tiresome, Court. You must treat her with respect when she is here. Do you understand?"

"I understand." I kissed Bella's forehead again before leaving.

Evelyn

I STUDIED THE LAST PLASTIC BAG TUCKED INTO THE SIDE OF the seat. I had already vomited twice into the other two plastic bags, and I was on the verge of throwing up again. The ride to the Draax planet was brutal, and the jolting and shaking of the ship made every part of my body scream in pain. My kidneys were jarred with every air pocket we hit, and I was dangerously close to just screaming in pain. I held the screams back with a grim determination.

Sabrina held the bottom of her seat and shouted, "It'll be okay."

I nodded and closed my eyes. The ship was going to crash, I knew it was. I didn't want to see my approaching death, so I kept my eyes shut as a deafening noise nearly shattered my eardrums. I put my hands over my ears as the seat belt dug painfully into my side. The ship dipped and then dropped with a terrifying speed that ripped a soft scream of fear from my throat.

"Almost there, ladies!" the pilot shouted.

He was laughing. Why was he laughing?

I clutched my seat, my stomach rolling and churning as the ship dropped again. We landed on the ground with a thud that made my body lurch up against the confines of my seat belt. My kidneys and back screamed at me, and I swallowed down the vomit rising in my throat before opening my eyes.

The ship slowed to a complete stop, but the hail hitting the metal ship made it impossible to hear anything. Sabrina smiled reassuringly as the outside doors opened. Cold air swirled in, plastering my hair against my face. I unclicked my seatbelt as two Draax males boarded the ship.

One of them approached me and took my hands, helping me to my feet. I winced, and he gave me a curious look before leading me to Sabrina. Three more Draax had squeezed into the ship, and my heartbeat went into overdrive. Which one of them would I be expected to sleep with?

All of them were tall and muscular with broad chests, narrow hips and black hair. I stared in fascination at the tails waving back and forth behind them. I moved closer to Sabrina, and we put our arms around each other without speaking.

An older male, a bit bent with age and threads of gray in his hair, spoke into the ear of the Draax standing beside him.

The Draax shrugged, and the older one removed a thin, silver box from his cloak and approached us.

He tugged us apart and I didn't resist when he pushed up my sleeve and scanned my right arm. He read the information on the screen before pressing a button and turning to Sabrina. He scanned her arm, read the information, nodded, and pointed to Sabrina. She was led toward the ship's door, and I felt a pang of loss even though I barely knew her.

"Wait!" Sabrina pulled free of the Draax and turned around. She hugged me hard, and I flinched and gasped with pain. I returned her hug as she pressed her mouth against my ear.

"It was nice to meet you, Evelyn. Take care of yourself, okay?"

"You too!" I shouted.

The Draax took her arm again and gently tugged her to the door. I couldn't hear her but saw Sabrina's lips moving as she stared at the Draax. I didn't know why she bothered to talk to him. It wasn't like they could understand us.

I watched in surprise as the Draax picked up Sabrina like she weighed nothing before walking out of the ship. The older Draax, as well as another, followed them out. I gave the two Draax standing in the ship a tentative smile.

The one stepped closer, and I held my breath when he bent and studied my face. He had thick, black, slightly curly hair on the longer side and copper coloured eyes. I stared in fascination at them as he frowned and scrutinized my eyes.

To my confusion, dislike radiated from him in a strong vibe. I swallowed down my nervous laughter as he continued to study my face. There was a brief flicker of confusion in his eyes, and he straightened and turned to the second Draax. The second alien had moved to the ship's doorway, and he nodded before disappearing into the storm.

I was already beginning to freeze in my t-shirt and jeans, and the shaking of my body was incredibly painful. I gave the Draax another timid smile as he studied my shivering body. He headed toward the door, and I glanced at the pilots before following him. He wore a drab brown cloak and if he was the king, then the Draax certainly didn't dress like they were royalty.

Don't be stupid, Evie. Do you really think the king would come to get you himself? He's probably a servant or something.

Yeah, that made more sense. Hopefully, he wasn't the king. I had no idea why, but the big Draax definitely didn't like me. Panic trickled down my spine. What if he was the king? He hated me on sight. He would hurt me and make me cry and...

I took a deep breath, trying to quell my rising panic. I was acting like an idiot, but truthfully, I was in an incredible amount of pain, exhausted, and scared to death. I would most likely be having sex with an alien tonight, and what would I do if he took one look at my bruised body and sent me straight back to Earth because I was damaged goods?

Ask him to keep the lights off. He won't see the bruising.

Good plan, but how exactly did I do that if we couldn't understand each other?

The Draax was waiting in the doorway, and he looked me up and down before staring at the hail falling. I was surprised when he took off his cloak and wrapped it around me. It was deliciously warm from his body heat, and I didn't object when he buttoned it and pulled the hood over my head. It was miles too big and dragged on the ground. For a moment, I half expected the Draax to pick me up like the one did with Sabrina, and my face turned red when he raised his eyebrows at me before making a 'come with me' motion with his hand.

I followed him out into the storm. A combination of hail

37

and snow was falling, and I winced when one particularly large piece of hail slapped me on the shoulder.

I flailed my way down the slick stairs of the ship, hanging onto the handrail in a tight grip. The Draax was moving quickly, and I couldn't blame him. His thick cloak was doing a pretty good job of protecting me from the brunt of the storm, but hail pelted his large body.

Ignoring the pain, I hurried after him as he headed to the back of the ship. Another Draax, who was wearing a uniform with the name of the docking bay, stood next to my backpack and a large trunk. One of the Draax who had left with Sabrina picked up the trunk and carried it toward a large land vehicle.

The Draax in the uniform handed over my backpack to the curly haired Draax. The possible king stared at my backpack and then said something to the other Draax, who shrugged and nodded. He turned and looked at me, and I nodded, too.

"Yes, that's mine." The wind whipped away the sound of my voice, and I watched as the Draax said something else to the one in the uniform.

The uniformed Draax shook his head and pointed at the backpack again. Bending his head against the hail and the snow, he headed toward the building about twenty feet away. The other Draax who'd been in the ship with us was opening the building door and slipping inside.

The maybe-he-was-a-king Draax held my backpack in one hand and walked toward a land vehicle. He opened the back door and threw my bag in before slamming it shut and opening the front passenger door. I swallowed nervously and moved past him to slide onto the seat.

He closed the door and moved to the driver's side. I stared in fascination at the steering wheel as he shut his door and pushed a button on the dashboard. The vehicle rumbled to life, and my eyes widened when the alien pushed a pedal on the floor, and we moved forward.

I never thought I'd be in a vehicle in my lifetime, and now, not only had I been in two vehicles, but one of them was a gas powered one that you steered yourself.

Despite how tired I was and the pain that wouldn't go away, I smiled in delight as I watched the Draax drive away from the ship.

We'd only driven a few minutes when he said something in his low voice. I had no idea what he said, it sounded like complete gibberish, but it made my stomach clench with something that was almost lust. I jerked in my seat and then bit back my groan as pain radiated across my back. I'd never had such a visceral reaction to a man's voice.

He was waiting for me to reply, and I cleared my throat. "Um, my translator isn't working yet. I don't understand you."

He stared at me before scowling and pointing to my throat. I nodded and touched the spots where the translators were embedded in my throat and behind my ear. "Yes, I have a translator, but it isn't working yet."

Feeling slightly stupid, I put my hands over both spots and shook my head. "Not working yet."

He scowled again, and while I was no expert on the Draax language, I was pretty sure he was spitting out an expletive.

"I'm sorry," I said as he gave me an angry look.

He stared out the windshield. I folded my arms across my shivering torso and stared at the falling hail and snow. Hopefully, it wouldn't take long to get to the palace.

CHAPTER 4

Bran

I shut the door to Bella's nursery and returned to the living room. My home was decorated similarly to the humans' dwellings, as were all Draax homes. My grandfather once told me that when our kind and the humans first made the breeding agreement, we'd mimicked the human's furniture and decorating choices to help the females feel more comfortable and entice them to stay even after bearing us a child.

I sat on the couch, picked up the remote and pushed a button. The fireplace lit, and I stared moodily at the flames. Not that it had made a difference with my female. Dana had never truly been happy living on the Draax planet, even though she chose to join me and Court. Her misery was not eased by similar housing décor.

I pushed the memory of Dana and her unhappiness out of my head. I'd become very good at not thinking of her in the last two years. It helped that Bella looked very little like her mother, but ever since I'd decided to hire a human as a nanny, thoughts of Dana kept creeping back in.

I stood and paced in front of the fire. The storm was getting worse, and I was worried about Court. We may have been pushed apart in the last few years and it felt awkward between us even though he'd returned home as soon as I needed him, but he was still my best friend and always would be. The thought of losing him was almost as bad as the thought of losing Bella.

I grabbed my tablet and logged in to hologram him when the front door slammed. My hands turned sweaty, and my tail flicked back and forth in nervous agitation. I remained by the fire, hoping I didn't look as nervous as I felt as Court's boots clomped down the hall.

"Bran? Where are you?"

"The living room," I called.

He stepped into the room. His cloak was missing, and his shirt and pants were covered in snow. "We barely beat the storm."

"Where is your cloak?"

"I gave it to the human. She was not dressed appropriately for the weather."

I peered around him. "Where is she?"

"She saw the bathroom and asked to use it. At least, I think she did."

"What do you mean?"

"The translator is not working yet."

I groaned. "Krono, are you serious?"

"Yes. She does not understand a word I say, and she speaks complete gibberish."

"The agency assured me she would have a working translator when she arrived."

"She does not."

41

I muttered a curse and rubbed at the back of my neck. "How does she look?"

Court shrugged. "Small and frail. She does not carry enough meat on her bones."

I frowned. In her picture, she'd looked curvy enough. Not that it mattered. I wasn't attracted to the human. I had deliberately chosen her both because she was breeding incompatible and because I did not find her pleasing to the eye. I knew I didn't need to worry about Court. After what Dana did, he hated all female humans, but I didn't trust myself, so I found a human I was not attracted to.

Does that matter? Even if you were attracted to her, you would not be able to satisfy her. Your ability to please a woman is gone and never returning.

I shoved my inner voice deep down as a flush covered my face.

Court gave me a curious look. "What is wrong?"

"Nothing. Does she seem healthy?"

"I guess. She," he paused, "flinches when you move too fast."

"She is probably nervous. She cannot understand you, and you do not give off a welcoming vibe."

Court frowned at me. "I was courteous to her. I gave her my cloak so she would not freeze to death. She did not even have a coat, Bran. She came here for a three-year job with only a small bag. Does that seem strange to you?"

I didn't want to admit it, but it was strange. When Dana moved in, she had three trunks and four suitcases. Her clothes alone had filled my closet and the guest bedroom's closet.

"Perhaps she does not care for material things," I said.

"Perhaps." Court studied me for a moment in the light of the fire. "Her eyes are green, not blue."

"What?"

"Her eyes are not blue. They are green."

"They are blue. In the picture, they are blue."

"I do not know what to tell you, Bran. You will see for yourself soon enough that they are green."

Something niggled at the base of my skull, and I flicked on my tablet. I pulled up the human's file from the agency and scrolled to the end, where her picture was. I studied it carefully. Her eyes were definitely blue. I glanced up at my best friend. "Court, her eyes are -"

The human was standing next to Court. She was wearing his cloak, and she had an anxious look on her face. Her pale cheeks flushed, and she bowed her head and, oddly, curtsied before smiling at me.

I studied her face, feeling a weird warmth burning in my gut as I stared at her soft pink mouth, high cheekbones, and light green eyes. Krono, she was beautiful.

I tore my gaze away from her, my heart thudding in my chest, and Court gave me a curious look. "Bran, what is wrong?"

"That is not the right human."

Court jerked in surprise, and the little human made a soft cry and cringed away. Her mouth trembled, and she stared wide-eyed at Court as he turned and studied her. "What are you talking about?"

"That is not the human I hired to be a nanny. That is not Sabrina Green."

"Of course, it is," Court said. "She was scanned at the ship, and I saw the screen. It said Sabrina Green."

I joined them and showed Court the picture on my tablet. "This is Sabrina Green."

Court's skin turned a light green. "That is the other female from the ship."

"Krono! The stupid humans mixed up the identification chips." My agitated tone made the human cringe again. I ignored my weird urge to soothe her and scowled at her instead. "What is your name?"

"She does not understand you. Remember?" Court said.

"Oh, for the love of Krono." My irritation at being given the wrong human and my unexpected attraction to her made my tone harsh.

I glared at the human, immediately feeling guilty when she wrapped her arms around her torso and backed away until she touched the wall and could go no further. She was making quick darting glances around the room, wetting her lips with the tip of her tongue, and I could see her body shaking even under Court's thick cloak.

"You are scaring her, Bran." Court's tone was disapproving, and I turned on him.

"What do you care? You hate her."

"I do not hate her."

"Please, you hate all female humans." I ran my hands through my hair. "We need to call the agency and tell them there was a mistake. Find out where my nanny was sent to and trade her for this one."

"Have you forgotten the storm?" Court said. "Communications with Earth will be impossible by now. And lower your voice before you wake Bella."

"So, what are we supposed to do?" I snapped. My gaze wanted to keep returning to the intoxicating human. I wanted to touch her skin and see if it was as soft as it looked, and it was making me even angrier.

"We wait out the storm. Once it is finished, we will contact Earth and inform them of their error."

"A moon, Court. This storm will last at least a moon.

What do we do with this human in the meantime? I do not want her anywhere near Bella."

"Why not?" Court asked.

"She is a stranger. Who knows what she would say or do to Bella."

"Bran," Court gave me a strange look, "what is wrong with you?"

"We have a human that we know nothing about living under our roof. What is wrong with you that you are not concerned for Bella's safety?"

I was overreacting, I knew I was overreacting, but the human's presence was making me feel strange and off balance.

"You know that I will allow no harm to befall Bella until the day I die," Court snarled at me. His own temper was hitting the breaking point. "But you are acting like a froden. The girl is harmless, and you know it."

I stepped back, breathing deeply as my tail flicked back and forth. Court was right. I was being a froden.

"I will take the human to her room and bring her some food. She can stay in her room until morning. No doubt the translators will be working by then. We can explain the mistake and send her to where she is supposed to be once the storm ends," Court said.

"Fine." I was suddenly extremely weary. "But I do not want her to have anything to do with Bella."

"All right. Come with me, human."

I watched Court make a 'come here' gesture to the human. She stepped toward him hesitantly and then made another strange curtsey in my direction before following Court from the room.

Evelyn

I POKED AT THE BLUE RICE AND THE WEIRD LOOKING MEAT ON the plate before setting my fork down and standing to pace the room. Ten minutes after the Draax brought me to the bedroom, he'd returned with a plate of food and a glass of water. He'd set it on the top of the dresser and repeatedly made a 'stay' motion with his hand until I nodded in understanding.

That was three hours ago. I wasn't usually a picky eater, and I was reasonably confident that no one in the palace was actively trying to poison me, but I couldn't eat a single bite of food. The pain in my side and lower back had made my appetite disappear.

That's not the only reason.

No, it wasn't. Like the Draax who had picked me up at the ship, the king seemed to actively dislike me on sight. I had no idea why or how I'd offended him, but I didn't need to understand what they said to know I had.

Evie, are you even sure he's the king?

I stared at my pale face in the mirror. No, I wasn't sure. Although the palace was much bigger than the tiny apartment I'd called home, it certainly wasn't very...palatial-like. I had seen pictures on the holograms at the libraries of the castles on Earth. Compared to those, this one was very modest. Humble, even.

I'd assumed a palace would have many servants, but I'd only seen the two Draax. Plus, the way the king dressed was very similar to that of his servant. Or employee? What did they even call them here?

I wished I'd had more time to research the king of the western province, but I couldn't sneak away to the library before I left, and my PAR phone had no access to the Info-

Net. I knew next to nothing about Draax royalty. Hell, for all I knew, both Draax I met tonight were servants. Maybe I would meet the king in the morning.

I sat down on the bed. The palace might not be fancy, but their beds were amazing. Of course, after sleeping on a lumpy mattress on the floor for years, maybe any bed would feel incredible. I bounced a little, hissing out a breath when it made pain rocket across my back and into my side. I pressed a hand against my side and tried to take shallow breaths until the pain subsided. When I'd used the bathroom earlier, there was still blood in my urine.

Fear tingled through me. I'd never peed blood for so long after a beating before. What if Alex had really hurt me this time? What if my kidneys were permanently damaged? What if it affected my ability to carry the king's child?

Panic was worming through my gut, and tears were sliding down my face. Stupidly, I was homesick for my tiny room and awful mattress. I despised living under my step-brother's cruel thumb but was still homesick for Earth. I hated that my only way to escape him was by whoring myself out as a baby-maker to some big, green angry king on an entirely different planet.

Still crying, I opened my backpack and pulled out a long t-shirt and shorts to wear to bed. It was late, I was tired, and the palace was dead quiet. With my translator not working, I was pretty sure I wasn't going to be having sex with the king tonight.

With any luck, my kidneys would be much better by tomorrow. The bruises would be horrible and very notice-able, but I would tell the king that I was in a vehicle accident before I left Earth and that I was fine. Hopefully, he would believe me.

I slowly undressed before turning and studying my back

in the mirror in the corner. Shit. The bruising on my back was so bad, and the one on my shoulder had spread until it was across my upper back as well. I tried lifting my left arm above my head and moaned in pain as hot tears leaked down my face.

I wished I could ask for an ice pack, but I wasn't sure if I should leave my room, nor did I even know how to begin to pantomime for ice. For all I knew, the Draax didn't even use ice.

Another wave of homesickness washed over me, and I eased into my t-shirt and shorts. I gingerly sat down on the side of the bed, pressing my hand against my side. The pain, the lack of sleep, and the realization that I would never see Earth again hit me like an airtrain, and I began to cry in earnest. I covered my face with my hands to muffle the sobs.

When the door to my room opened five minutes later, and the king walked into my room, I was still crying like an overtired toddler. I hurriedly stood, wiping my face with the palms of my hands as I stared wide-eyed at the Draax. His short, dark hair was wet like he'd just showered, and he wore only a pair of sleep pants that hung low on his hips. His upper chest was hairless, but I could see a trail of dark hair below his navel.

His body was incredible. All sinewy muscle and smooth green skin. His tail reminded me of a lion's tail with a tuft of black hair at the end of it. It waved back and forth in the air behind him. Unlike the other Draax, his hair was cut short, and he had dark brown eyes. When his gaze dipped to my braless chest, a flush of heat and nerves went through me.

I cleared my throat. I guess my question about whether he was king or not was answered. "So, uh, you're looking for sex, right?"

He scowled and closed my door before holding his finger to his lips.

"Sorry." I hadn't spoken very loudly, but obviously, the king didn't even like the sound of my voice. I had forgotten to curtsey when he entered and wondered if I was supposed to do it now. I decided not to. It made my back hurt too much.

You can't even curtsey, but you're going to have sex with him? Do you have any idea how much it's going to hurt?

My inner voice wasn't wrong, but I had no choice. I needed to play down my injuries. If the king thought I couldn't have sex with him, he'd send me back to Earth.

Evie, you're not thinking clearly. Candy said they were kind, remember? He'll give you time to heal. Show him your bruises, so he'll leave you alone tonight.

I couldn't take that risk. If they sent me back to Earth, Alex would kill me or worse... force me to marry Troy.

He was still standing across the room from me and staring at my legs. I was beginning to feel self-conscious. Why wasn't he undressing or undressing me? Was I supposed to make the first move? Maybe he found me so hideous that he had to work up the nerve to fuck me.

My cheeks flushed, and a wave of shame went through me. The guy I'd given my virginity to had been nice enough. He'd complimented me a lot when he got me naked and told me I was beautiful and sexy, but it was evident that the Draax king didn't like me.

Despair uncurled in my belly. We needed to have sex so he could have an heir, but could he even get it up if he found me ugly?

My gaze dropped to his crotch, and I took a deep breath. Like I'd just told myself - I was here for a reason – to have sex with the king and give him a child. If I couldn't do that, I would be useless to him, and he'd send me back to Earth. If I wanted to stay here, if I wanted to avoid being killed by my stepbrother or married off to Troy, I needed to use my limited seduction skills on the king. It was apparent that he couldn't make the first move. Maybe he would just close his eyes while we were fucking. I mean, a pussy was a pussy, right?

My cheeks reddened, but I took another deep breath and walked toward the king. He seemed almost frozen to the spot, and he didn't move when I pressed my body against his and put my arms around his waist. Steeling myself, I kissed his chest and then his collarbone before nuzzling his neck. I stroked his lower back and a bit of his middle back, but my throbbing shoulder wouldn't let me lift my arm any higher.

The king still hadn't moved a muscle, and feeling awkward and weird, I stood on my tiptoes and pressed my mouth against his. His lips were warm and firm, but his entire body went ramrod stiff. When I licked his lower lip, he made a startled noise and pushed me away.

Not expecting it, I tripped over my own feet and landed hard on my ass. It sent agony up and down my spine and through my kidneys, and I couldn't stop my sharp cry of pain.

For one terrible moment, I thought I would black out. I immediately lowered my head between my knees, breathing in long, slow inhales and exhales, counting seven beats for each breath.

I cringed when the alien's hands wrapped around my arms, and he lifted me to my feet. He wasn't rough, but I still scurried away from him and held my hands up in supplication as tears slid down my face. "I'm sorry. I'm so sorry. I thought that was what you were, um, here for. I'm very sorry."

He scowled, and my throat went dry. What was the punishment for angering a king on Draax? What if it was a beating? My kidneys pulsed in pain at just the thought, and I backed up again until my legs hit the side of the bed.

"Please, I'm very sorry."

The king turned and walked out of my room, closing the door softly behind him. My heart thudding in my chest, I sank onto the bed, holding my hand against my throbbing kidneys and trying not to cry.

I was so screwed.

Bran

I HURRIED DOWN THE HALLWAY TOWARD MY BEDROOM. Court's bedroom light was off, and there was no sound coming from his room, but I still snuck past it like I had done something wrong. I entered my room and closed the door behind me.

What in Krono's name just happened?

After my shower, I'd gone to Bella's nursery to check on her. She was sound asleep with her tiny fist curled around her favourite doll. I'd sat on the floor beside her bed for nearly half an hour, just staring at her face. Krono, I loved her.

The human's room was next to Bella's, and, at first, I couldn't identify the sound I kept hearing. Finally, I stood and pressed my ear against the wall that separated the rooms. It sounded like the human was crying.

I'd hurried out of Bella's room. I told myself I only went into her room to tell her to be quiet, not because I wondered why she cried. Bella was a real groden if she was woken up, and I had no wish to spend the rest of my night soothing a grumpy toddler.

I'd entered the human's room, and things went strange. I scrubbed a hand across my jaw. The human had changed her clothing, and I was almost mesmerized by the smooth paleness of her long legs. I was thinking about what they might look like wrapped around my waist when the human approached me. The feel of her soft lips on my chest and neck shocked me into stillness. When she'd pressed her mouth against mine, licking me with her soft tongue, I'd come to my senses and pushed her away.

I cringed and walked to the bathroom connected to my room to stare at my reflection. I hadn't meant to be rough, but I'd hurt the little human. No longer covered by Court's cloak, it was obvious that her body was small and fragile. When she'd landed on the floor, the cry of pain and the way her lovely face paled had made me feel lower than a glackenswine.

But it was even worse when I had helped her to her feet, and she had startled away from me like a terrified grundleswat. The way she cried, and her body trembled in fear... I groaned and returned to my room, climbing into bed and staring at the ceiling. I hadn't meant to scare or hurt her, and once her translator was working, I would tell her that.

CHAPTER 5

Evelyn

With my phone broken, I had no idea what time it was. The storm outside the window made it impossible to tell if their star keo had risen, but it felt like morning. The wind rattled the window, and I took a step back. It was cold in my room despite the heat blowing from the vent in the floor. I studied the thick snow that was falling and wondered how long the storm would last.

After a few minutes, I gathered my courage and left the bedroom, carrying my uneaten plate of food. I'd dressed in a t-shirt and jeans before putting a sweater on over my shirt. It was chilly in the palace, but mostly, I was embarrassed at how noticeable it was that I wasn't wearing a bra. I tried to put it on, but the pain in my shoulder made it impossible. Getting the t-shirt and sweater over my head was an exercise in agony.

I hadn't slept again last night. The pain, homesickness, and worry that I had somehow insulted the king made sleep impossible. I felt sick to my stomach, exhaustion was making my vision blurry, and I was on the verge of tears.

I moved slowly down the stairs and the hallway. I could hear noises coming from a doorway to the right, and I peeked into the room. It was the kitchen, and, again, while it was giant-sized compared to the narrow alley kitchen in my apartment, it didn't seem nearly large enough to feed an entire palace of people. Of course, the palace still wasn't exactly bustling with aliens. The only Draax in the kitchen was the one who had picked me up from the ship last night.

I tried to smile in a friendly way at him as I entered the kitchen. "Good morning."

Maybe the translator was working now. Please, God, let the translator be working.

He studied the plate of food in my hand before scowling and striding forward. He took the plate and said something that was gibberish before pointing at the food.

Shit. Still no translator.

"I'm sorry," I said. "I, uh, I wasn't hungry last night."

He frowned, and my heart lurched against my ribcage. I took a step back, my right hand automatically coming up to protect my liver – a favourite punching spot for Alex – and sputtered out another useless apology.

A strange look appeared on his face, and he backed away from me immediately. He turned and walked across the kitchen, dumping the food from my plate into the garbage as his tail flicked agitatedly back and forth.

He turned and pointed at the chair as he put the plate into what looked like the Draax version of a dishwasher. I eased my body into the chair, fuck did it hurt my kidneys and back to sit, and wiped away the sweat on my forehead as the Draax brought me a glass of water.

"Thank you."

I sipped at the water. Even though I knew I was dehydrated, I didn't want to drink too much. This morning, I discovered the door on the right wall of my bedroom led to a small bathroom. I'd used it, but peeing was torturous, there was more blood than before, and I'd nearly passed out on the toilet. I had no desire to pee again anytime soon.

The Draax was leaning against the counter, his arms folded across his massive chest. He wore a loose cotton shirt and dark pants that clung to his thick thighs. He was barefoot, and his hair was sticking up at the back like he had just rolled out of bed. It was both adorable and a little confusing. Wouldn't someone who worked for the king make sure he was more presentable?

Evie, something's wrong. Just try to think past the exhaustion and the pain, would you? Something is very, very wrong. This place isn't big enough to be a palace, and there aren't nearly enough servants around.

The Draax said something before pointing at his chest.

"I'm sorry?"

He pressed both hands against his chest before saying. "Court."

I blinked at him, trying to concentrate beyond the pain. Court. He was saying court. Did he mean the king's court? "Uh, we're in the court?"

He nodded and pointed to himself again. "Court."

"Oh!" The lightbulb went on. "Your *name* is Court."

"Court." He repeated before pointing at me.

I pressed my right hand against my chest. "Evelyn. My name is Evelyn."

He cocked his head at me before hesitantly saying my name.

I smiled and nodded my head. "That's right. Evelyn, but most of the time, I go by Evie."

He just stared at me, and I took another sip of water. "Which I shouldn't have said because it'll just confuse you until the translator starts working. God, I hope it starts working soon."

There was a noise behind me, and I shifted in my chair, pressing my hand against my throbbing kidneys to see who was behind me. My mouth fell open. The king had walked into the kitchen and carried a little girl. She had long dark hair and purple skin and stared as wide-eyed at me as I was at her.

The king gave me an irritated look before speaking to Court in a fast and angry tone. The little girl continued to stare at me, her chubby arm slung tight around the king's neck. I sat back in my chair. Why did the king have a little girl with him? I was sure the lady at the agency said he was looking for an heir. Maybe he needed a boy? Maybe he...

Evie! Think, goddammit! You know what this is!

"Oh no," I exhaled before touching the spot where the woman on the ship had injected me with an ID chip. "They mixed them up. They – *she* mixed up the chips, and they thought I was Sabrina. Oh shit. Oh shit, oh shit, oh shit."

The king – no, not the king – was staring at me, and my face flushed bright red. I had kissed him last night, I had kissed him and touched him and... oh shit.

My head was buzzing, and it was hard to breathe. I was on the verge of passing out, and I pushed back my chair and leaned over, crying out at the pain, and immediately stuck my head between my knees.

Shit. This was so fucking bad.

Court

"Why is she in here?" Bran glared at me.

"Do you mean to keep her as a prisoner, Bran?" I replied. "If so, lock her door if you do not want her leaving her room."

His skin darkened, and his tail flicked rapidly behind him. "Of course, she is not a prisoner. But I told you I do not want her around Bella."

"She has to eat," I said. "Not that she is."

"What do you mean?"

"She did not eat any of the food I brought to her last night. Not a single bite."

"She will eat when she is hungry enough," Bran said as an odd look of guilt flickered across his face. "I take it the translator is not working yet?"

"No, but I believe her name is Evelyn." The human name sounded foreign on my tongue.

"What kind of name is Evelyn?" Bran said.

I shrugged. "You know the humans sometimes have strange names. She -"

The human cried out with pain, and we both turned to see her leaning over with her head between her knees. I pushed past Bran and crouched in front of her. She ignored me, and I poked her lightly on the top of her head. "What is wrong, human?"

She straightened and stared at me. Her pale skin was even paler than usual, and her eyes were huge in her face. Little pain lines were etched around her mouth, and she was breathing much too quickly.

"Human – Evelyn, do you feel faint?"

"She cannot understand you, Court." Bran had placed Bella in her booster chair, and he stood next to me, staring down at the human.

"Does she look like she is in pain to you?" I asked.

"Yes," Bran admitted.

"Perhaps we should give her some gallberry juice." I studied the silent, sweating woman in front of me. "If she is sick, it will help."

The human began to talk, but it still made no sense to me. I glanced up at Bran. "Pour her a glass of juice, would -"

"I'm not here for the nanny job. Oh shit. How do I make them understand? Maybe I could pantomime it. Think, Evie. You've played charades before. How hard can it be to make them understand you're here for breeding, not nannying?"

The human was suddenly completely understandable. I heard Bran heave a sigh of relief behind me, and I poked the human, this time in the thigh, to make her stop talking. "Human, do you understand me?"

Her mouth dropped open. "I... I do."

"Good. The translator is working."

"There's been a mix-up," she said. "They put the wrong chip in me. I'm not Sabrina. I'm Evelyn. I'm here on a breeding contract, not a nanny contract."

"We know," I said. "Bran realized the error when I brought you home."

Her eyes flickered to Bran, and bright red stained her cheeks. "I'm sorry about last night when you came into my room. I thought you were the king, and I was supposed to breed with you."

"Why were you in her room last night?" Jealousy, all too familiar and unwelcome, seeped through me, which was stupid because I was absolutely not attracted to the female. She was too small for my taste, and her skin was too pale, even for a human female. Of course, her eyes were a fascinating shade of green, her pink lips were plump, and her dark hair...

Krono, I was acting like a fool. Still, it didn't stop me from scowling at Bran and repeating my question. "Why were you in her room?"

"I was checking on Bella, and I heard the human crying. I went into her room to tell her to be quiet so she would not wake Bella."

"What did you do to her?" I asked.

Bran's skin darkened with embarrassment. "I did not do anything to her. She kissed me."

"I thought he was the king, and I was supposed to breed with him," Evelyn said quickly.

"Did you sleep with the human?" Obvious jealousy infused my words.

"Of course not." Bran gave me a look like I had gone mad, but under it lurked a slight hint of guilt. "I pushed her away."

I turned to the human, and I could see her lower lip beginning to tremble and her too-white skin paled even more. "I'm very sorry. I would never have... I mean, if I had known he wasn't the king...."

"King." What she was saying was finally sinking in. "Are you here to breed with King Quillan?"

She nodded, and I turned to Bran. "Krono, she is our future queen."

"The king is taking a human mate?" Bran said.

I nodded. "I'd heard a rumour last moon in the market that he would take a queen soon."

"About time," Bran said. "If he dies without an heir, King Eastolf would take the western province, and then we would all be fu-"

He stopped and glanced at Bella, still staring wide-eyed at the human. Normally, she'd be hollering for her breakfast by now.

"So, um, now that the translators are working, do you think you could get in touch with the palace and let them know about the mix-up," the human said. "Sabrina's translator must not be working yet either."

"It could be," I said as Bran moved away and stirred the faven bubbling in a pot on the stove. "The storm has knocked out all communications."

"Oh." The human bit at her bottom lip in a way that made my dick stir in my pants. "Well, do you think I could trouble you for a ride to the palace?"

"A ride," I said.

I hadn't meant to sound derisive, but embarrassment crossed her face at my tone. "Um, yes, in your land vehicle."

"You think it can drive in the storm?"

"I've never been in a vehicle before," she said defensively. "I didn't know it can't drive in bad weather."

"It is more than bad weather." Bran set a bowl of warm faven in front of Bella. She was still staring at the human, and Bran ran his hand over her dark hair. "Eat, meena."

She didn't move, and Bran sighed, pulled a chair next to her, and sat down. He held a spoon of faven in front of her, and she opened her mouth and ate the bite without taking her gaze from the human.

"No vehicles or ships can be used in this storm, and we have lost all ability to hologram or email with the palace," I said. "Draax storms are not like the storms on your planet. We are cut off from everyone until it ends."

"How long will it last?" the human asked.

"A moon."

"A moon?" She stared at me in shock. "That's a month in human time, right?"

I shrugged. "Give or take a few days."

"I – but what do we do now?" Evelyn was chewing on her bottom lip while she rubbed her side. "I'm supposed to be breeding with the king."

"He will have to wait until the storm ends," I said. "Just like we have to wait for our nanny."

Her gaze flickered to Bella. "So, we're stuck with each other for the entire month?"

"Yes." I moved to the stove and spooned some faven into three bowls as the human smiled tentatively at Bran.

"Okay, well, uh, my name is Evelyn." She glanced briefly at me. "I know his name is Court, but I didn't catch your name."

"Bran." Bran deliberately avoided looking at her as he spooned another mouthful of faven into Bella's mouth.

"It's nice to meet you," Evelyn said.

He just nodded, and I grabbed some spoons from the drawer. Evelyn was sitting on the other side of Bella, and she smiled at her before reaching out to touch her arm. "Hi, honey. What's your -"

She made a strangled sound of fear when Bran's hand dropped onto her wrist. "Do not touch her."

"Bran," I warned as Evelyn stared at him in stark terror. When Bran released her arm, she folded her arms over her torso protectively and leaned back in her chair. She was visibly trembling, and I scowled at Bran.

He didn't notice. He was giving the human a steely-eyed glare, and she licked her lips anxiously as he pulled Bella's chair closer to him. "We will allow you to stay in our home, human, but there are rules you must follow."

"A-all right."

"You are not to touch Bella." Bran studied his daughter before turning back to the human. "Ever. Do you understand me?"

She nodded, and my tail flicked rapidly when Bran said, "I mean it. You are not to go near Bella at all. If I see you touch her, your punishment will be severe."

"For Krono's sake," I said, "she is not -"

"You are free to move around our home, but do not go into my room, Bella's room, or Court's room," Bran continued as if I hadn't spoken. "Do not go outside. You will get lost in the storm and freeze to death, and I am not losing my head just because the king's future queen was not smart enough to stay inside during a storm."

The human flushed and stared at the table as I set the bowl of faven in front of her. "Eat, human."

She picked up the spoon and stirred at the faven as I grabbed the other bowls and set one in front of Bran before lowering myself into the chair next to the human. Bella had finally started to eat on her own, although she was still staring at the human, and Bran began to eat.

"Eat," I said again.

The human tasted the faven a bit tentatively before smiling at me. "It's good. It tastes almost like oatmeal."

"What is oatmeal?" I asked. I had taken human studies in school just like every other Draax, but I didn't remember much.

"It's a grain that we grow on Earth. You can bake it in things like cookies or cook it in water and eat it for breakfast. You can add milk and fruit if you like it sweeter."

"We do not have milk here," I said. I knew my face had a look of disgust on it. "Draax do not drink the bodily fluids of animals."

"I don't need milk," she said immediately. "I'm not picky and will eat whatever you want me to eat. I won't be any trouble, I promise."

I frowned a little. The human's behaviour was bizarre. Dana had been very vocal about her dislikes regarding, well... anything. Her refusal to do anything she didn't want to do was an annoyance that I'd found hard to ignore. I assumed that all human females were the same.

This human was practically cowering in the chair, making me feel weirdly guilty. I looked over at Bran. He steadfastly ignored the human, staring into his bowl of faven and occasionally glancing at Bella as she ate.

When I turned my gaze back to the human, she also stared at her bowl of faven. Her hand was pressed against her side, her formerly pink lips were now the same pale white as her skin, and I could see the sheen of sweat on her forehead.

"Human, are you sick?"

She shook her head. "No, of course not. I'm fine."

"You are not eating," I said. "You need to eat. If you are sick, then you must tell us, so -"

"I'm not sick." She scooped up a big spoonful of the faven and shoved it into her mouth. She swallowed and then took a sip of water. "I just wasn't hungry last night. I'm perfectly healthy."

She was lying. Anger burned in the pit of my stomach. The human may not be vocal about her dislikes, but she lied just like Dana. My unsettling concern for the human disappeared in an instant. What did I care if she was sick? She wasn't even our nanny, and, in a moon or so, we'd be rid of her. Draax did not get human diseases, so there was no fear she would make Bella sick. If the human wanted to suffer, so be it. It wasn't my problem.

"Uda?" Bella's voice made me turn toward her.

"What is it, meena?"

"Girl?" She cocked her head in a questioning way and pointed at the human.

"Yes, she is a girl," I said.

"Girl?" Bella said to Bran. It was clear she didn't believe me.

"Yes," Bran said. "Drink your juice, Bella."

Bella took a swig of her juice, studying the human the entire time she drank. The small town we lived near had a few human females mated to Draax, but I didn't think Bella had ever seen them. Neither Bran nor I were particularly social, and we rarely went to town for anything other than supplies. She studied the human's pale skin before staring down at her own purple skin.

"So, um, what do you do for a living?" Evelyn asked.

"We are farmers," I replied.

"What do you farm?"

"The gallberry plant."

"That's interesting," the human replied. "We can't grow it on Earth."

I gave her a look that suggested I thought she was simple, and she ducked her head in embarrassment and stared into the bowl of faven again. "Sorry, you know that, obviously."

There was silence. The human stirred the bowl of faven before giving Bran and me a quick peek. "So, um, are you two, a couple?"

My mouth dropped open, and Bran made a loud snort. "No, human. We are not mated."

"Bran and I are only friends. We like females," I said.

"Are there any Draax who are gay?" she asked.

"A few," Bran said shortly. "It does not happen often, but some prefer the company of other men."

"Is that, like, a taboo?" Evelyn asked.

"What does taboo mean?" I said.

"Um, like forbidden or frowned on."

"Why would it be taboo?" I said. "There are humans who are gay, are there not?"

"Yes. But many years ago, some humans thought it was wrong or bad, and it was considered taboo."

I rolled my eyes. "A Draax is free to love whomever they want."

"That's good."

"Girl," Bella said again before pointing at Evelyn.

The human started to smile at her before seeming to think better of it and staring at her ceaselessly stirring spoon instead. "What does uda mean?"

"Uncle," I replied.

"So, you're her biological father?" Evelyn said to Bran.

He nodded, scraping the bowl with his spoon to get the last bit of faven out.

I waited for the human to ask about Bella's mother, inwardly preparing to keep my cool over her prying and hoping Bran would do the same.

To my surprise, the human didn't ask. Instead, she said, "What about meena?"

"It is a pet name," I said. "It means little one or small one."

"She is tiny," Evelyn said with a quick look at Bella.

"She is normal size for her age," Bran snapped.

Evelyn recoiled, dropping her spoon into her bowl. "Of course. I didn't mean, that is... she looks very, um, healthy and normal."

I sighed inwardly. If the human was going to be this afraid every time Bran said something sharp to her, it would be a long storm. My best friend was a good man but wasn't known for his caring or patient nature unless it was with Bella.

I was relieved when the human pushed her chair back and stood up. She blanched, her hand holding her side again while the other gripped the table's edge. I could see sweat sliding down her temple, and her smile looked more like a grimace.

"If you'll excuse me, I think I'll have a nap." Her voice was so faint I had to lean forward to hear her. "I, uh, I didn't sleep very well last night. Thank you for breakfast."

She walked quickly out of the kitchen, her body stiff and her hand pressing against her side.

"She's sick," Bran said to me when her footsteps died out.

"Yes."

"We should give her juice."

I shrugged. "She lied to us, Bran. If she does not want to be truthful with us, why give her gallberry juice?"

Bran frowned, but I ignored him and carried my empty bowl and the human's full bowl to the counter. I told myself I didn't feel sorry for the human as I emptied the faven into the garbage. She was a liar, just like the other females of her kind.

CHAPTER 6

Evelyn

My mouth was so dry. Keeping my eyes closed, I unstuck my tongue from the roof of my mouth with difficulty before swiping it across the cracked landscape of my lips. I was getting worse. I could try to deny it, but something bad was going down internally, and if I didn't do something about it, I was going to die.

Drama queen.

I croaked out a sound that was almost a laugh before peeling open my eyelids. I stared blearily at the ceiling of my room and then checked the clock I'd found in the nightstand drawer yesterday. It was almost six in the morning, and every part of my body pulsed with pain.

It was ironic that after all the times I'd been beaten by Alex, I'd never needed a doctor until I was stuck on a completely different planet with no access to medical care. The storm raging outside had only grown worse in the thirty-six hours or so I'd been here, and I understood now what Court meant by the storm being different from Earth storms.

I'd never seen a blizzard like this one. The house was solidly built, but every now and then, it would shudder at a powerful blast of wind, and the snow was falling so hard and thick that I could see less than half a foot when I peered outside my bedroom window.

The house was freezing despite the heat constantly blowing out of the vents and the fireplace in the living room. I didn't have much in the way of winter clothing and didn't have time to pack what little I did have, which meant I was always cold.

If I even ventured out in search of medical help... I shuddered and groaned when it made my side throb with fiery pain. Nothing could survive outside in a storm like this.

I licked my lips a second time. My tongue felt like a fuzzy caterpillar and kept wanting to stick to the roof of my mouth again. I had a fever. I could feel it raging through my body, drying everything out. There wasn't enough moisture in my body to pee anymore.

Considering how much it hurt to pee, that was a good thing.

After yesterday morning's disastrous breakfast, I'd stayed in my room for the day. Neither Draax had tried to coax me out for lunch. I'd dozed fitfully off and on all day, but the pain was growing steadily worse despite how I tried to ignore it. I made an appearance at dinner, afraid that if I didn't, my lie about not being sick would be discovered.

The dinner was awkward and painful to sit through. I had no appetite, but worried they would realize I was lying about being sick, I'd forced myself to eat half of the food on the plate.

Unlike breakfast, where at least Court had shown some interest, neither of the Draax spoke to me at dinner. They barely talked to each other, either. Their attention was mainly on the adorable little girl and ensuring she ate and drank. She'd studied me all through dinner but was as quiet as her father and uncle.

I'd excused myself as soon as dinner was over and returned to my room, vomiting my dinner into the toilet only ten minutes later. It had hurt to barf - a lot, actually - but I couldn't stop. After, I'd stripped out of my clothes and tried to shower.

The bathroom attached to my bedroom had a fantastic shower. The bathroom at my old apartment was small, and the shower produced a tepid trickle of water at best. This shower never seemed to run out of hot water, no matter how long I stood under it, and the showerhead sprayed a steady stream of water the way it was supposed to.

I'd taken three showers yesterday, trying to warm myself and hoping the hot water would ease the pain in my side, back and shoulder. I couldn't wash my hair, my arm wouldn't lift high enough, so I'd only rinsed it instead. But when I'd tried to take a fourth shower after dinner, the pain in my side and from the bruising was so great that the pressure of the water hurt more than helped.

Now, I tried to roll to my side, a whimper escaping when it sent excruciating pain across my lower back. I closed my eyes, breathing through the agony, ignoring my urge to vomit. The pain was like nothing I'd ever felt before. God, maybe I really was dying.

You need gallberry juice.

I stared blearily at the ceiling again. Right, of course. The damn juice. I'd seen the little girl drinking it at breakfast and dinner yesterday. I needed to get my hands on some of it. But

I couldn't ask them for it. They'd know I was sick if I did that. I had to steal it.

Evie, stop. You're delirious from the pain and the infection. You don't have to steal it. These Draax aren't the king, remember? They won't care if you're sick and can't breed. Just ask them for a glass.

But they might tell the king. If they did, I was screwed.

Evie! You're not thinking straight. If they give you the glass of juice, you'll be healed, and you can fuck the king. Just ask them for some juice.

I croaked out a laugh. My inner voice had a death wish. I couldn't just ask them for juice. Maybe the fever was making my inner voice delusional? Probably. Yeah, it was the fever. Just ask them to give me juice... that was crazy talk.

I had to steal it, and I had to do it before they woke up.

Despite the pain that infused my whole body, I pushed myself up into a sitting position. I shoved the covers down and leaned against the headboard. My hand slapped over my mouth to muffle my moans of pain while sweat slid down my forehead and into my eyes.

My entire body was coated in a slick layer of sweat. My tank top was sticking to my chest, and my thin cotton shorts were soaking wet. I was freezing cold and shivering madly but I couldn't stop sweating.

I took a deep breath and lowered my hands. A flash of purple caught my eye, and I turned to see Bella sitting on the bed next to me. I froze, my hands halfway to my lap, as I stared wide-eyed at her.

"Girl," she said before giving me a shy smile. "Hi, girl."

"H-hi," I whispered. I glanced at the door to my room. It was open just enough for a small girl to slip through. "You shouldn't be in here, honey."

"What your name, girl?" She scooted a little closer, and

when her hand reached out and touched my thigh, I made a low moan of dismay.

"Don't do that, honey," I said. "You can't touch me, okay? It'll make your daddy mad."

"What your name?" she said again. Her fingers traced the pale skin of my thigh and she lifted her fingers and studied them intently before retracing my skin.

"Evie," I said.

"I am Bella."

"I know. You need to return to your room now, okay, honey? Before your daddy and uda wake up."

"Uda and Papa," she said gleefully and loudly.

Too loudly.

"Shh." I tossed another nervous glance at the door as her tail flicked out from behind her and brushed against my arm.

"Pretty girl," she said.

I squeaked out another moan of dismay when she climbed into my lap and sat on my thighs. "Hi, Evie girl."

"Hi, Bella." I kept my hands at my sides. "You need to go back to your room now, honey."

She studied the bruise she could see on my shoulder. "Ouchy."

"A little," I said. Shit, I needed to get her out of my room immediately.

"You play with me, Evie girl?" she said hopefully.

"Um, I can't right now," I said. "Can you go back to your room? Please?"

A scowl crossed her face. Her skin, the loveliest shade of purple I'd ever seen, darkened, and her bottom lip pouted out. "Why you not play with me?"

"Honey, I can't, I… oh shit."

The little girl had leaned forward and pulled the neck of my tank top out so she could peer down it. She studied my naked breasts with frank interest before staring up at my face. "What are those, Evie girl?"

"Um…"

The door banged open, and Bran, followed by Court, stormed in. Both wore sleep pants and nothing else, and Court's hair was sticking up in the back again. They stared in shocked silence at us as Bella let go of my shirt and grinned at them. "Hi, Papa. Hi, Uda."

"What are you doing to my child?" Bran's voice was low, but the anger in it made fear flood my entire body.

Adrenaline kicked in, dulling the pain enough for me to scramble out of the bed like a poisonous snake had bitten me. The punishment would be severe, he'd said. In the state I was in, if he punched me now, I was dead. I had to try to explain before he punished me.

"Whee," Bella said as she tumbled off my lap and onto the bed. She sat up, giggling wildly, as I backed away from the two angry Draax.

I held my hands out. The room was spinning out of control, and my ears rang strangely. "Please," I rasped out. "I didn't touch her. I swear I didn't touch her. She came into my room, and I was sleeping and I…"

The Draax were starting to go burry. I blinked rapidly, trying to focus on them, but the room's spinning was worsening, and my legs were folding under me. The adrenaline had faded, leaving the worst pain of my life. I couldn't catch my breath, I couldn't think, I couldn't feel anything but the horrendous burning agony of my side and lower back.

Blackness was edging around me, the Draax were being swallowed by it, and I took a stumbling, staggering step forward.

"Please don't hurt me. Please…"

Darkness descended.

Bran

Court was quicker than me. He shot forward and caught the human, his tail lashing around her waist before she could land face-first on the hard floor. He sank to his butt on the floor, cradling the human in his lap as I crouched beside him.

Heat radiated from her. Her cheeks were bright red, and the skin under her eyes was a dark purple. The rest of her face, including her lips, was as white as a maluken in the cold months.

"Bran, she is burning up," Court said.

I pressed my hand against her forehead, wincing at the heat. It was like pressing my hand against the engine casing of our deocatcraft. I studied the bruise on her shoulder. It was large and a deep, dark purple that hurt me just to look at it.

"What happened to her shoulder?" I asked.

Court shrugged. "How would I know?"

"Ouchy, Papa."

Bella had joined us, and I gave her a distracted nod. "I know, meena. Her shoulder hurts."

"No, Papa. Look."

Bella was pointing at the human's side. Her tank top had risen, and something that felt a little like horror washed over me. "Court, sit her up."

He sat her up. Her head lolled on her neck before falling forward into Court's throat, her body limp against his. I lifted her shirt a little higher as Court craned to see.

"Krono." He sounded as horrified as I felt. "Her side, Bran. How is she even still standing?"

"She is not," I said. "It is not just her side either."

I tugged her shirt higher until it was just below her breasts and studied her lower back. Dark and malignant bruising covered her lower back, and her flesh was swollen.

"What in Krono's name happened to her?" Court said.

I studied the bruise on her side, its shape making anger rise inside me. "Someone did this to her."

"How do you know?" Court said.

I pointed to the footprint-shaped bruise. Court stared at it for a long time before glancing up at me, his skin dark with anger. "She is so fragile. Who would beat her like this?"

"I do not know," I said. "But she needs gallberry juice. She is burning up with fever."

"Papa, what are these?" Bella tugged on my arm with her tail.

I looked down, heat rising in my face, and I heard Court groan softly. Bella had pulled the neckline of the human's tank top out, giving us all a view of her naked and – I didn't want to admit it, but perfect looking – breasts.

"Bella, no." I pulled her hand away from the human's shirt. "Do not do that."

"What are they, Papa?" Bella said again. Her tail poked me in the ribs, and I stood and picked her up.

"Court, put the human in her bed. I will be back with the gallberry juice."

I carried Bella to her room and placed her on the bed. "Meena, you must stay in your room for a little bit. Play with your toys, and then I will get you for breakfast."

"All right, Papa," she said.

I kissed her forehead and stroked her dark hair. "You are a good girl, and I love you very much."

"I love you," she said.

I left her playing on her bed and ran to the kitchen. I

grabbed a glass and the jug of gallberry juice and returned to the human's room. Court had placed her on the bed, and he studied the juice in my hand.

"She is unconscious, Bran. What will we do? Pour it down her throat?"

"We need to wake her up."

"How?" he said.

I poured some juice into the glass and set it on the nightstand before taking Evelyn's arms and pulling her into a sitting position. Her head fell back, and even unconscious, she groaned in pain.

"Prop her up."

Court slid behind her on the bed, letting her head rest on his broad chest as I patted her thigh. "Human, open your eyes."

There was no response, so I squeezed her smooth leg. "Human, wake up now."

"She is not going to wake up that way," Court said.

"Do you have a better idea?" I said.

He didn't reply, and I patted her on the cheek this time. "Human, look at me."

"Her name is Evelyn," Court said.

I cursed under my breath and gave him an exasperated look before patting her cheek again. "Evelyn, wake up."

Her eyes rolled behind her eyelids, giving me some hope. "Evelyn, can you hear me?"

Her eyes continued to roll, and she made a soft moaning sound, her hand grasping weakly at Court's thigh. "Hurts," she mumbled.

"I know," I said. "Open your eyes, Evelyn."

Her eyelids fluttered, and she gave me a hazy look. I immediately pressed the glass of juice to her lips. "Drink, Evelyn."

She didn't move. Her eyes started closing again, and I shook her leg roughly. She cried out, and Court glared at me.

"You are hurting her, Bran!"

"I have no choice," I said. "She must drink. Evelyn, look at me. Now."

She opened her eyes again, her look one of dazed confusion.

"You need to drink," I said. "Open your mouth and drink."

I pressed the glass harder against her lips and tilted it. Some juice spilled down her cheeks, and I breathed a sigh of relief when she opened her mouth and drank a few swallows.

"Good girl," I said. "Drink some more."

She drank more. Her eyes closed, but she continued to drink until the glass was empty. I quickly refilled it as Court wiped the juice from her mouth and chin.

"Open, Evelyn," I said as I pressed the full glass against her lips.

"Cold," she moaned.

"I know you are cold," I said. "Drink this, and then we will warm you."

She drank the juice obediently, falling back against Court with a small groan when she was finished. I set the glass down and held my hand to her forehead. "She still has a fever."

"It does not work that quickly," Court said. "At least not in juice form. She needs a kadana who can administer serum by IV."

"This is the best we can do," I said as the human shivered in Court's arms. "We will wake her up and make her drink the juice every few hours."

Court nodded and slid out from behind her. He eased her onto her back on the bed and climbed off of it before picking her up.

"What are you doing, Court?"

"She is freezing. This is the coldest room in the house."

He carried her out of the room and down the hallway to his room. Like me, he had a fireplace in his bedroom, and he motioned for me to turn it on as he tucked the human into his bed. He pulled the covers to her chin, studying her pale face for a moment before turning around.

He scowled at the look I was giving him. "Do not look at me like that, Bran. We need to heal the human. She is our future queen. What do you think the king will do to us if we let his queen die?"

CHAPTER 7

Court

I studied the human in my bed. The fever had finally broken after dinner, but she was still pale, and the bruising had not lessened. I'd piled two extra blankets onto my bed and kept the fire going all day, but she still shook so hard the bed frame rattled.

Was she cold because she was sick or because she wasn't used to our cold months? Dana had complained bitterly during the cold months, but I couldn't remember if she'd shaken from the cold like this human did.

Probably because I'd done my best to purge every memory, every thought of the wretched female from my head.

The human shifted to her side, and I winced when she cried out in her sleep. I wondered if her shivering made her body hurt worse. Probably. I glanced at the door to my bedroom. Bran was putting Bella to bed, and based on how long he'd been gone, she was fighting her sleep ritual as usual.

The human made another soft groan of pain, and I studied her trembling, shaking, blanket-covered body before making a sudden decision. Who knew what the king would do to Bran and me if the female died. I had to do whatever it took to keep her alive and well.

I stripped off my shirt and pants and slid into the bed beside her. Moving gingerly, I put my arm around her, careful not to touch the bruise on her side, instead resting my arm on her hip. I grunted in surprise when the little female immediately shifted closer, pressing her entire body against mine like a lover, slinging her arm around my waist, and burying her face in my throat.

I knew she was only seeking out my heat, but my cock was already half-hard. I muttered an earth curse, hating how my body reacted to the female. But I couldn't blame it. It'd been over three years since I'd fucked anything but my own hand, and while my head might hate the human females, my cock had no problems with them.

She was still shivering madly despite the added warmth of my body heat, and without thinking, I rubbed her back. Her sharp cry of pain and the way her soft body stiffened against mine made guilt wash over me, and I snatched my hand from her back.

"Krono," I said. "I am sorry, human."

I could feel wetness against my throat, and more guilt covered me. I'd hurt her so much she was crying in her sleep. I rubbed her hip as she shifted against me again, and her dark hair brushed against my chest like strands of pure silk.

"I am sorry, little human," I murmured, even though she wasn't awake. "I did not mean to hurt you."

"What are you doing?"

I twitched guiltily as Bran stood next to the bed. He was

giving me a look of disbelief, and… was there a little jealousy in his gaze?

As much as I hated to admit it, I felt a certain amount of satisfaction. If Bran really was jealous, perhaps now he better understood what I went through with Dana. Now, he was the one standing on the outside looking in and wishing he could have the same love and affection.

What is wrong with you? The human is not in your bed because she wants to be, and she did not ask you to join her and dismiss Bran. You're acting like a froden.

My sense of smugness faded, and I gave Bran a weary look. "The human is still cold. I am trying to warm her."

"Is that right?"

The doubt in Bran's voice made my anger flare.

"Yes, Bran. In case you have forgotten, this woman is our future queen. If she dies -"

"How could I forget? You have been mentioning it all day," Bran said.

"Because our lives depend on keeping her alive," I snapped.

He snorted irritably, and I scowled at him. I didn't want to fight with him, and I hated that even two years after Dana, our friendship was still not how it used to be.

It never will be. You should leave. Leave Bran with his daughter and find your own path.

Like always, that thought sent panic skittering through me. The moons I'd spent on my own had almost driven me mad with loneliness. I would rather live with Bran and be reminded daily of what I'd lost than return to living alone.

"Court, did you hear me?"

I made myself focus on Bran. "What?"

"I said it is not working. The human is still shaking."

Bran was right. The little female was still shivering wildly.

She was hitching in breath in weird, erratic motions, and every few seconds, she made a low moan.

"I just climbed into the bed with her," I said. "She will warm soon."

Bran glanced at the fireplace before stripping off his shirt. I watched in shock as he yanked down his pants and left them on the floor before sliding into the bed behind the human.

"What are you doing?" I asked.

Bran grabbed my tablet from the nightstand and scrolled through the screen. "Setting an alarm so we can feed the human more juice in a few hours."

"No, why are you in the bed?"

He gave me an impatient look before sliding closer to the human. "Helping to warm her."

"If you touch her back, you will hurt her," I said.

"I am aware of that." He left only a sliver of space between his chest and her back. "But it will still help."

I didn't reply, and he closed his eyes and rested his head on the pillow behind the human. I also closed my eyes, only vaguely aware that my hand was still rubbing her hip. To my surprise, her shivering ceased after a few minutes. Her breathing evened out, and the small cries she made in her sleep stopped.

Bran was already asleep. The sound of his rhythmic breathing filled me with both an aching sadness and contentment. It had been years since Bran and I had shared a bed with a woman and the familiarity of it was almost overwhelming.

Krono, I had missed this. If I tried hard enough, I could pretend this was our life again. The way it was before Dana destroyed us.

Evelyn

I BECAME AWARE OF TWO THINGS SIMULTANEOUSLY. I WAS finally warm for the first time since I landed on the Draax planet, and the horrifying, vomit-inducing pain in my side and back was gone. I was still not one hundred percent. My back and my ribs ached, and my shoulder felt tender, but I was no longer in the agony I was.

I could have cried with relief. My body had finally started healing, and my immune system had kicked in and killed the infection. Thank God.

Not your immune system, Evie. You'd be dead now if it weren't for the Draax.

I frowned as hazy memories of the two Draax forcing me to drink something sweet and cold surfaced. I kept my eyes closed and tried to focus. Did they actually give me something, or did I only dream it in a fever-induced delirium?

I thought hard for a few minutes. No, I decided, I hadn't dreamt it. They'd given me juice. They had come into my room when the little girl was sitting on my lap, and I had tried to explain, and then they'd...

I curled into the warm body in front of me, burying my face in hot, hard flesh as I tried to think. The warmth behind me shifted closer, the hand on my breast squeezing and then releasing. My back ached a little from the added pressure, but I didn't try to squirm away. The heat was nice, and it was worth a little back pain.

The hand on my ass cupped me a little more firmly. The thigh between mine rested snugly against my sex as he made a low snort. I pressed a kiss against his skin and stroked his lower back. He gave my ass another squeeze in response before his big body relaxed.

What did the two Draax do when they came into my room and saw me with Bella? Why was it so hard to remember?

They gave you juice, Evie.

They did. They had to have. The way I felt better, the memories of drinking that sweet, strawberry like juice… it had to be real.

My mouth watered at just the thought of the gallberry juice. I'd never had it until yesterday and barely remembered drinking it, but my craving for it was almost painfully intense. I hoped the Draax would give me more. The way I was feeling, I would go mad if they didn't.

Ask them for more.

I couldn't do that. I hadn't opened my eyes yet to check the time, but it felt early. They were most likely still sleeping. Maybe I could sneak to the kitchen and drink some before they woke.

Hey, idiot? There's a Draax in the bed with you.

I scoffed at my inner voice, pushed my face away from the warmth I had buried it against, and opened my eyes.

There was not a Draax in the… holy crap. There was a Draax in the bed with me.

I stared wide-eyed at Court's face. He was sleeping soundly, the little lines around his eyes softened, his firm lips parted just the tiniest bit. My face was only inches from his on the pillow, and feeling a little panicky about what he might do to me if he woke up and found me in the bed beside him, I eased my head back.

I froze immediately when a second face buried into my hair and the hand cupping my breast squeezed tight.

What in the holy hell was happening?

My inner voice made a gleeful giggle when my confused mind finally figured it out.

I was in bed with two large and powerful Draax aliens. I had one hand cupping my breast, one hand cupping my ass, and – oh crap times a *thousand* – one hard cock pressing against my ass and one hard cock pressing against my lower belly.

I tried to sit up, but both Draax immediately tightened their grips, preventing me from moving. Bran slipped his hand under the neckline of my tank top and cupped my bare breast, running his thumb over my nipple until it hardened into a tight bud. Court's hand was busy sliding under the waistband of my shorts and – *shit* – the waistband of my panties. He stroked the curve of one ass cheek and then squeezed my ass possessively.

Heat was rising in my belly, and my pussy was tingling, and please, dear God, tell me I was not getting turned on by this?

Bran moved a little closer, his dick pressing even tighter against my ass. I arched my back, making my ass rub against his dick and giving him more of my breast to squeeze. He made a low moan of approval, and his fingers pinched my nipple.

My soft sound was more need than surprise.

Crap. I was getting turned on by this.

Court

THE LITTLE FEMALE LYING AGAINST ME WAS SOFT AND WARM. The ass cheek in my hand was not as full as I preferred, but – I gave it another hard squeeze – still wonderfully firm.

Still groggy from my dream, I tried to remember when Bran and I had made the trip to Earth. I couldn't even remember seducing the little human. Perhaps I'd had a couple of the ethanol-based liquid drinks the humans so enjoyed drinking. It wasn't to my taste, and I rarely drank the liquid. It made my head hurt, my memory fuzzy, and my tongue feel like it was coated in duthen moss, but sometimes human females became angry if you didn't drink with them.

I could feel Bran's hand moving against my chest, and I knew he was touching her tits. Not surprising. I'd always had a fondness for asses, but Bran loved breasts. He could spend hours sucking and licking our female's nipples until she was moaning and begging for us to make her come.

I bent my head and opened my eyes, staring directly at the human's chest. Bran's hand was inside her shirt – why was she even wearing a shirt? – and I could see his fingers moving against the fabric as he plucked at her nipple.

I leaned back a little, wiggled my free hand out from under the pillow and grasped the neckline of her shirt, pulling the stretchy material down until her breasts were bared to my greedy gaze.

Krono, I could see why Bran was so fond of her breasts. They were beautiful, with pale white skin and perfectly shaped nipples. Her nipples were the colour of the pink roses that grew on Earth, and I watched as Bran pulled at one.

The human gasped, her back arching, and I reached out and played with her other nipple, enjoying the contrast of her pale skin against my green skin. Her hand dug into my back, and she moaned softly when I ran the fingers of my other hand along her ass cheek. I scowled when I felt her panties rubbing against my knuckles. Why in Krono's name was the little human not naked?

More importantly, who was the female we had seduced?

Blinking the sleep from my eyes, denying my impulse to just tear her clothes free and sink my aching dick into her pussy, I glanced up at her.

I stared directly into Evelyn's light green eyes. She was biting her lip, moaning quietly as Bran and I teased her nipples, and her pale skin was flushed pink with need. My hand clutched her ass compulsively as I realized what we were doing. She made a soft sound of pain before I released her and yanked my right hand away from her breast and my left hand out of her panties and shorts.

I pushed back in the bed and stared in silent shock at her.

"I'm so sorry," she said. The sudden look of terror on her face made my stomach twist. "I didn't mean to make you angry. I'm sorry."

My gaze dropped to her tits, where Bran was still plucking and pulling at her nipples.

"Bran!" I grabbed his wrist and yanked his hand away from her. Evelyn pulled her shirt up as I jumped out of the damn bed and stalked around to the other side. Bran was giving me a bleary look of confusion. I threw back the covers, grabbed his arm, and hauled him out of the bed.

"What's wrong?" he asked. "What's…"

He glanced at Evelyn, his body going still before he stared down at his cock. Even through his briefs, his erection was noticeable, as was mine, and I watched the little human's face flush a bright red as she stared at our crotches.

"We are sorry," I said, dragging Bran to the door. I pulled him out into the hallway and shut the door before leaning against it.

"Shit." The human's curse word fell easily from my mouth. "We fucked up, Bran."

When he didn't answer, I glanced over at him. He was still

staring at his damn erection like he'd never seen his own cock before.

"Bran!" I snapped. "Did you hear me? We just attempted to mate with our future queen!"

"I was sleeping... dreaming," Bran said. He finally tore his gaze from his dick.

I glared at him. "As was I. Do you think the king will care when she tells him we touched her without her permission? He will kill us both the moment she tells him what we did."

Bran's skin turned a pale green, and he rubbed compulsively at his throat before staring at Bella's bedroom door. "Bella would be an orphan."

"Yes," I said as my stomach twisted and turned.

"We have to convince her not to say anything. Tell her it was an accident," Bran replied.

"We do. But not now." I glanced at the door to my bedroom. "Bella will be awake soon. You take care of her and I will start breakfast while we give the human time alone. After breakfast, we will speak to the human together."

Bran nodded just as Bella called for him.

"Be right there, meena," he called back. He hurried to his bedroom, and I took a deep breath and walked to the laundry room to grab a spare pair of pants. Everything would be fine. We would explain to the little human that we had only meant to help keep her warm, and she would believe us.

CHAPTER 8

Evelyn

I hadn't intended to go downstairs during breakfast. Nope, I planned to stay in my room for the next oh... month, give or take a couple of days... and not even worry about eating. I could drink water from the bathroom sink, and I had some extra meat on my bones, right? I could probably go for a month without eating. No problem. Who needed food... not me. Not when it meant facing two Draax who were probably pissed off that I had tried to seduce them.

You didn't mean to do it, and besides, they were touching you.

True, but it wasn't like I'd exactly pushed them away. Being in the bed with them had been both oddly comforting and more than a little erotic. The way they'd touched me at the same time...

Fresh pleasure speared into my belly. Maybe Candy was right about the two Draax being better than one. I stopped in the hallway outside my room, tempted for a moment to go back in, lie on the bed and masturbate.

Are you nuts, Evie? They'll hear you!

Shit. They probably would. The house was big, but I still didn't want to risk it. Besides, my urge to masturbate had already disappeared and been replaced by the real reason I was joining them for breakfast.

I hadn't realized my craving for the stupid gallberry juice would grow steadily worse. It was easy enough to ignore as I hurried from the bedroom that was most definitely not mine and down the hallway to my own.

It wasn't as easy to ignore as I brushed my teeth and had a shower. The realization that even though my shoulder was still bruised, I could lift my arm above my head had pushed the craving back for a moment, but it crept back in as I washed my hair.

By the time I'd dried off and gotten dressed – hallelujah, I could put my damn bra on – it was impossible to ignore. My body wanted it and there wasn't enough willpower in the world to resist its demand.

It's not like I would waste it if I asked for more, right? I was still injured. There was no blood in my urine this morning, but my back and side were aching, and the black and purple mottling that had spread across my pale skin was rather gruesome looking. If they refused to give me the juice, I would show them the bruising. That would change their minds.

I walked down the hallway to the kitchen and, taking a deep breath, stepped into the room. Bella was sitting at the table, with a bowl of faven already in front of her and a cup of gallberry juice. She was studying her father and Court, standing at the counter with their backs to us. They were talking in low voices, and I stared again at Bella's juice, my stomach cramping with need. If I moved silently enough, I could take her juice and drink it before they even realized I was in the room.

Evelyn! What is wrong with you?

I slumped against the door jamb, rubbing my fingers across my forehead as the need for the gallberry juice thumped and thudded in my veins. I'd been about to steal juice from a little girl... I was losing my damn mind.

"Hi, girl!"

I smiled at Bella. "Hi, Bella."

Both Draax whipped around, giving me identical shocked looks. It would almost have been amusing to me if I hadn't caught sight of the jug sitting on the counter and forgot entirely about the Draax. The jug was filled with gallberry juice, I knew it was, and my mouth watered with an intensity I'd never experienced.

Another painful cramp of need went through my belly, and I stumbled into the kitchen, almost falling into the chair. I stared wordlessly at the jug of gallberry juice. I needed to apologize, needed to say something, but I couldn't think past the need.

Court grabbed a glass and filled it to the brim with gallberry juice, to my immense relief, before setting it in front of me. I was shaking so much I had to lift the glass to my mouth using both hands.

I drank.

The cold liquid slid down my throat, and a rush of pleasure went through me like a heroin addict getting their first hit of the day. Not caring that I looked ridiculous, I drank the entire glass of juice in noisy, large gulps. I put the glass down and wiped my mouth with the heel of my hand.

Without speaking, Court refilled the glass. I drank it as quickly as the first and could have wept with happiness when Court gave me a third glass.

The craving had subsided enough that I could drink this one almost normally. God, it was so good. I could live off of it. Who needed food when you had gallberry juice? I took another couple of swallows and set the half-full glass down.

Bran and Court stared at me, and my cheeks flushed bright red. Oh shit, why had I come down to breakfast? This was a mistake, but I'd needed the gallberry juice.

Now that my craving was satisfied and I could think normally again, the mortification about my behaviour this morning was overwhelming. What was I thinking? I was about to become queen, and I'd had no problem letting two Draax I didn't even know touch me so intimately. If the king found out...

My face blanched. If the king found out, he'd kill me. I stared wide-eyed at Court and Bran. If they told the king what I did this morning, I was dead or worse... I would be sent back to my stepbrother.

"Human, are you all right?" Court made a motion to the glass in front of me. "Drink more juice."

My hands shaking again – this time from fear – I drank more juice. I needed to ask them not to say anything to the king. Hell, I would get down on my knees and beg them if I had to.

"Girl likes juice," Bella said.

"Yes, meena." Bran was setting bowls of faven on the table. "Eat your breakfast."

Court was refilling my glass even though it wasn't empty, and I gave Bella's cup a guilty look. What if I was taking the juice she needed? I was a terrible person.

"I don't need anymore," I said. "Um, but thank you."

Court frowned at me as Bran sat beside Bella and pushed her bowl of food closer. Bella had faven all over her face, and he wiped it off gently.

"You need more juice," Court said to me. "You are not fully healed."

"I don't want to take your daughter's juice from her," I said. "On Earth, it's hard to get and -"

"This is not Earth," Bran said. He wouldn't look at me, instead studying a spot on the wall just to my left. "There is plenty of gallberry juice. Drink."

I flushed with embarrassment. Of course, there would be plenty. They were gallberry plant farmers, for God's sake.

I drank a bit more and smiled at Court when he pushed a bowl of faven in front of me. "Thank you."

I stirred it as Court sat beside Bran and ate a few bites. I needed to eat, but it would be impossible to swallow any food past the lump of fear in my throat. What if they told the king? What if they told him I was a whore who would make a terrible queen, and it would be best if he sent me back to Earth? Alex would beat me so badly that the pain from this one would feel like kisses.

"Eat, human," Court said.

I had to say something, had to convince them that they couldn't tell the king what happened. I could do this. Staying calm and not freaking out would be the best way to convince them. I just needed to be composed and speak slowly and confidently.

"Human, you must eat." Court gave me an irritable look.

Okay, I could do this.

"Please don't tell the king that I'm a whore," I said. "I'm not a whore, I swear. I didn't mean to do what I did in bed this morning. I was half asleep, and I didn't realize that... I mean, I would never have... please don't tell the king what I did. Please. I'll do anything you ask. I swear. Just don't tell the king I'm a whore."

Nice work, Evie. You sound completely calm and rational.

Bran and Court were staring at me, the looks of shock plastered back on their faces. I made a horrified noise when

Bella banged her spoon on the table and sang, "Whore, whore, whore."

Bran's green skin darkened, and he put his hand on Bella's hand. "Hush, Bella."

His look toward me was tinged with frustration. "Bella will mimic words. You must watch your tongue around her."

"I'm so sorry," I whispered. "I forgot, that is, I haven't been around many children and I… I'm sorry."

"Whore, Papa," Bella said cheerfully.

Bran rubbed the smooth patch of skin between his eyebrows. "Eat your faven, meena." Another dark look of disapproval passed over his face. "Make no reaction when she says it, human. It will only encourage her to keep saying it."

"A-all right," I said.

Bran elbowed Court, who shoved his bowl of faven to the side. "Human, what happened this morning was our fault. Not yours. We," he took a quick sidelong glance at Bran, "did not mean for it to happen. It will never happen again, and we certainly will not share the details with the king. In fact, we would ask you not to tell the king."

His gaze flickered to Bella, and fear crossed his face. "If the king believes we tried to seduce his queen, we would be imprisoned or executed, and Bella would be alone."

I shook my head, horrified at the thought of the little girl growing up without her father like I did. "No, no, I would never tell the king. Ever. I promise."

"Good," Court said. "Then we have an understanding. Now eat."

I ate a spoonful of faven to appease him before drinking more gallberry juice. "Out of curiosity, why were you in the bed with me this morning?"

Now it was Court's turn to look embarrassed. "You were

freezing and shaking the way you did hurt you. We were trying to warm you."

"Oh," I said. "It worked. I was nice and toasty warm this morning when I woke up."

Court frowned. "Toasty warm? Toast is cooked Earth bread, is it not? Why would you compare yourself to toast?"

"It's an expression," I said. "Because toast is warm."

They didn't say anything, and I took another drink of juice, feeling like a world-class idiot. "Thank you for giving me gallberry juice. I feel much better."

"You are not completely healed," Court said. "Who injured you this way?"

I supposed I could have told them the truth. It seemed like they believed that the less the king knew about any of us, the better, but I couldn't bring myself to admit that my stepbrother beat me. It was shameful and humiliating, and I didn't feel like sharing my life story with a couple of aliens I barely knew.

"I was in a vehicle accident right before I came here," I said.

"Were you?" Court said.

I nodded, squirming under the sudden intensity of his gaze.

"Strange, considering that not two days ago, you told us that you'd never been in a vehicle. Is that not right, Bran?"

"Court, do not -"

"Is that not right?" Court repeated slowly.

"Yes," Bran said.

"Were you lying before or lying now?" Court asked me.

I swallowed hard, my hand tightening around my spoon in a fist. The familiar fear was stealing into my chest, making it tighten, and it was hard to breathe and think past the panic.

"Answer me, human."

"Before," I whispered.

I knew immediately that I'd made the wrong choice. Court's eyes flashed copper fire, and his nostrils flared as he dragged in a breath. "Stop lying, human. We saw the bruising on your side. Who hurt you? Tell us immediately."

My hand touched the foot-shaped bruise on my ribs, and when I didn't answer, he slammed his hand down on the table. A whimper of fear escaped my throat, and I pushed my chair back, my arms crossing across my torso and my hands automatically trying to cover my kidneys and liver.

"Uda, mean."

Court froze before turning to stare at Bella. Her little face was drawn down in a scowl, and she pointed her faven-covered spoon at Court. "No be mean to girl, Uda. Bad, Uda. Bad!"

Bran patted her arm. "Uda did not mean to yell, meena."

"Bad, Uda." Bella's scowl grew fiercer, and she puffed her chest out before her long purple tail snaked out from behind her. She made a jabbing motion with it at Court. She certainly wasn't afraid of the angry Draax. "Say sorry to girl, Uda."

Court's tail flicked rapidly in the air behind him, and his chest rose and fell rapidly. He gripped the edge of the table before studying me again. "I am sorry, human."

I nodded. Fear had made my throat dry as a bone, and my heart beat faster than a havoc cruiser hitting hyperdrive. My hand shaking, I picked up my glass of juice and drained it dry before standing. "Please excuse me."

My legs trembling, I walked out of the kitchen.

"No, Evie, you can't go out there," I whispered to my reflection in the bathroom mirror before returning to the bedroom, climbing back into the bed and pulling up the covers. I lay on my uninjured side and closed my eyes. I was freezing again, more from the never-ending chill in my bedroom rather than being injured, and I buried my cold nose under the covers as my back and side ached dully.

It was early afternoon. After the horrible scene at breakfast, my determination to stay in my room was renewed. But that was before the craving for the juice had come back. I groaned, trying to ignore my gallberry juice cravings and how my stomach growled with hunger.

"Hi, girl!"

I screamed thinly and almost fell out of the bed. I rolled over and stared wide-eyed at Bella lying under the bed covers. Her dark brown eyes were full of glee, and she sat up when I did, sitting cross-legged on the bed.

I glanced at the door to my bedroom. It was closed, and I stared at Bella. "How did you get in here?"

"Door," she said and pointed at it. "Girl, napping?"

"Um, yes. Sort of," I said. "Honey, you have to stop coming into my room, okay?"

"Okay," Bella said before touching my hair. She scooted closer. Her tail poked at my face, and I tried to bat it away. She slid into my lap while I was distracted and clung to my sweater when I tried to lift her off my lap.

"No, girl!" she shouted.

"Shh, honey," I said with a nervous look at the door. "Shh, okay?"

"Shh," she said before holding her hand next to mine. She studied my pale skin and traced her fingers along the back of my hand. "Pretty."

"Thank you," I said.

"Bella is pretty?" She cocked her head at me and batted her eyelashes, and I couldn't help but laugh.

"Yes, you're very pretty."

She held up two fingers. "Bella is two. Bella is smart."

"Very smart," I said.

She touched my face with her tiny fingers, tracing my eyebrows and the shape of my lips before staring intently at my eyes.

"Green," she said.

"That's right, my eyes are green," I said.

"Papa and Uda are green. Bella is purple."

Her tail was waving back and forth behind her and when she saw me staring at it, she grabbed it and stroked the tuft of black hair at the end. "Bella's tail."

"It's, um, nice," I said.

"Where girl's tail?"

"Oh, um…"

There was a knock on the door, and Bran's voice drifted through it. "Human, may I come in?"

I froze, my breath escaping in a harsh gasp when Bella shouted. "Come in, Papa."

The door opened. Bran, carrying a tray of food and – my mouth began to water – a glass of gallberry juice, stared at the way Bella sat in my lap.

"Hi, Papa." Bella waved at him.

"I'm sorry," I said, holding my hands next to my head like I was being arrested as panic settled in my belly. "I didn't know she was in my room when I returned from the bathroom. She-she was hiding in the bed, and she climbed into my lap on her own. I swear I didn't touch her. Please don't hurt me."

A grimace crossed his face. "I will not hurt you for touching Bella, human."

I wanted to believe him, but I didn't know him at all, and it was obvious that he and Court were incredibly protective of Bella.

He obviously saw the doubt in my face because he walked forward, set the tray on the bed, and stared intently at me. "No one in this house will hurt you, human. Ever."

I believed him this time. Maybe it was the sincerity in his dark eyes, or maybe it was just because he'd been worried enough about my safety to give me gallberry juice and sleep in a bed with me to keep me warm.

"You are supposed to be napping, Bella," he said as he handed me the glass of juice. "Drink, human."

I took the glass and drank eagerly. It quelled the craving in my belly, and Bran studied me. "Better?"

"Yes, thank you."

"Do you need more?"

I shook my head, and he frowned a little. "If you need more, just say so, human. There is plenty, and there is no point to you being in pain and also suffering with cravings."

"Why do I crave it?" I asked as Bella climbed off my lap and snuck a piece of something yellow and juicy off the tray. She popped it into her mouth and smiled happily.

"Bella, the warracot is for the human," Bran chastised. He glanced at me. "If you are sick, you crave the gallberry juice until healed. Why did you not join us for lunch?"

"I wasn't hungry," I said as my stomach growled loudly.

Bella giggled. "Eat, girl."

Bran picked up the tray and set it closer to me.

"Thank you," I said.

"Come, Bella," Bran said.

Bella pouted at him. "No, I stay with girl."

Her tail wrapped around my forearm like a snake. "I stay with you. Okay, girl?"

I gave Bran a timid look. "It's okay with me if she stays."

"It is her nap time," Bran said. "Bella, do not argue with me."

Her lower lip pouted out, but her tail unwrapped from around my arm, and she slid across the bed to drop onto the floor. She crossed her arms over her chest and shook her head when Bran held out his hand. "No. Papa mean."

Bran ruffled her dark hair. "Perhaps, but you still need your afternoon nap. Come, meena."

He stopped in the doorway. "Court did not mean to scare you earlier."

"He didn't," I said.

He sighed and stroked Bella's dark hair again as she leaned against his legs. "May I give you some advice, human?"

I nodded, and he said, "We will spend the moon together. Stop lying to us. Court does not care for lying, nor do I."

He picked up Bella and left the room, shutting the door behind him.

CHAPTER 9

Bran

I sat on the edge of my bed, staring at my cock. I'd been hard this morning. A woman had made me hard. That hadn't happened since...

Since Dana stopped allowing Court into her bed.

I closed my eyes, scowling a little. There hadn't been an exact moment where I'd stopped getting an erection, but I couldn't deny that the day Dana finally made it clear she no longer wished to have both of us was the catalyst.

The old and familiar guilt crept into me. I rubbed at my forehead, my tail flicking back and forth across the bed. I'd chosen Dana over Court and would never forgive myself for it. Even worse – neither would Court.

I studied my crotch again. In the beginning, when it became clear that I wouldn't get an erection, no matter what she did, Dana was hurt. The hurt quickly turned to anger, like it so often did with her. The woman Court and I loved had a quick temper and sharp tongue.

Did you love her, though?

I had loved her. As did Court. We'd brought her to our planet believing that she was our mate and we would spend the rest of our lives together.

I snorted in disgust. How she kept putting off the mating ritual once she moved in with us should have been our first clue. But my paternal urges had begun, and I was blinded by my love for Dana and the need to have a child. And while Court hadn't yet felt the same desire to be a father, he wanted a mate as much as I did.

She never loved either of you. Nor did she love Bella.

No, she hadn't. While I was over the fact that she'd left me, I would never understand how she could have left her child.

She left because you couldn't satisfy her, and she knew you would never allow her to take Bella with her. It's your fault Bella doesn't have a mother.

More guilt tinged with despair made me feel sick. I pushed all thoughts of Dana out of my head and headed to the kitchen. It was Court's turn to cook, and he was scrolling through recipes on his tablet. He glanced up at me. "What do you think about maluken stew for supper?"

"We need to talk about the human." I sank into the chair beside him.

"What about her?" Court said.

I scowled at him. "What if she tells the king what we did?"

"She will not," Court said.

"You cannot be certain of that."

Court pushed his tablet aside. "I am. Bran, you saw the look on her face this morning at breakfast. She is more terrified of the king discovering what happened than we are."

Court made a good point. The human had looked panicked that we would tell the king. Of course, she looked panicked about everything.

"She is afraid of us," I said. "You need to be nicer to her."

"Me?" Court said. "You were the one who threatened her if she even touched Bella."

"You yelled at her this morning," I said.

Court took a deep breath, running his hand through his hair with short, angry pokes. "Fine, I will be nicer to the human, as will you. But, honestly, I do not think it will make a difference. She startles as easily as a grundleswat."

"She does," I agreed. "Bella is fascinated by her. She was in the human's room again when I took her lunch to her."

Court shrugged. "That is not a bad thing, is it? I am confident that the human will not hurt her. And, when we finally get our actual nanny, perhaps it will make the transition easier for Bella. She will already be used to a human."

"You believe I should allow Bella to spend time with this human?"

"I believe it will be impossible to stop her," Court said with a wry grin. "You know how Bella is."

"I do." My own smile curved up my lips.

"Do you find the human attractive?" Court asked suddenly.

"Why does that matter?"

"She liked what we were doing to her this morning," he said.

"She was terrified, not aroused," I said.

"Only after I realized it was her and she believed I was angry," Court said. "Before that, she was aroused."

"So, what?" I replied. "She was half asleep, just like we were."

"It has been a long time since we shared a woman," Court said.

My mouth gaped open. "You want to share this human? Have you gone mad? She is our queen and not for us, Court."

Court shrugged. "She is not queen yet. If she is willing, why should we not take her to our bed? It will make the time pass faster and perhaps improve your mood."

"You are one to talk," I said. "You have been acting like a moody teenager for moons."

Instead of getting angry, Court nodded. "I know."

I sighed and stared at the table as Court leaned back in his chair. "We could ask her. There is no harm in asking."

"She is terrified of us," I repeated.

Court crossed his arms over his chest, a look of defeat on his face. "You are right. It was a stupid idea. Besides, even if she stopped being so afraid of us, she is undoubtedly innocent. The king would want an innocent for his queen, and if we took her virginity…"

"The female who was supposed to be our nanny, this Sabrina, was an innocent," I said.

Court blinked at me. "How do you know?"

"It was in her application for the nanny job."

"Why does it matter as a nanny if she is an innocent?" Court asked.

"I do not know," I said. "But it is one of the questions they are required to fill out."

"We could ask her," Court said again.

"Ask her what? If she is an innocent or if she would like to fuck us both until the storm ends and she goes to the king?" My voice was sarcastic, but Court shrugged.

"Both."

"We cannot," I said. "What if the human fell in love with us? Then what?"

Anger flashed across Court's face. "Fell in love with us or with you?"

"Stop it," I said. "Dana loved you too."

"Dana never loved me," Court said. "She only used me to get what she really wanted."

"That is not true," I said.

"It is, and we both know it." Court gave me an angry look. "You are right. Not about mating with this Evelyn, but about sharing her. It is not a good idea."

Hurt flooded through me. "You would fuck the human without me?"

I winced even as I was saying it. Why shouldn't Court sleep with a female without me? After all, I'd slept with Dana without him. Besides, in the moons after Court moved out, he would have had plenty of opportunity to go to Earth and fuck a human on his own. It's not like we could only sleep with a human if we were together.

"Do not look at me that way, Bran," Court said. "It is probably best if I am the only one who fucks the human. If she does tell the king, then it will be only me who is imprisoned or killed, and you can find a new mate and raise Bella with her alone. The way you want."

"That is not what I want!" Dark and dangerous anger was curling my hands into fists. "That was never what I wanted and if you truly believe that, then our friendship is damaged irreparably."

We stared at each other, our skin identical shades of dark green, our tails flicking back and forth, our breathing laboured and rough with anger. This was the closest we'd ever come to talking about Dana and what happened, and a part of me wanted to turn and run away with my tail tucked between my legs.

"That is not what I believe," Court finally said.

"Good." My hands uncurled, and I took a deep breath. Now was the perfect time to talk about what happened with

Dana, but I didn't say anything when Court grabbed his tablet and scrolled through it again.

Even after two years, the anger and hurt between us had not lessened.

Maybe it never would.

Evelyn

WHEN I WOKE UP FROM MY AFTERNOON NAP, MY CRAVING FOR the gallberry juice wasn't the only thing that had returned.

I sat up, pushing my hair out of my face and rubbing my shoulder a bit gingerly. "Hello, Bella."

"Hi, girl!" Bella was sitting cross-legged at the end of my bed. "Girl have a nap like Bella?"

"Yes," I said.

She crawled toward me, and I didn't stop her when she sat on my lap again. Her tail brushed back and forth over my arm. I had stripped down to my tank top and sleep shorts to nap, and I was growing cold away from the warm cocoon of the covers.

Bella studied the goosebumps on my arms before pressing one small hand against my breasts. "What these, girl?"

"Honey, my name is Evie. Can you call me Evie?" I said.

"Evie," she said. "Evie girl."

I smiled. "Good enough."

She rubbed her hand across my chest. "What these, Evie girl?"

"They're called breasts," I said.

"Breasts," she mimicked.

"That's right. Girls – women – have breasts. When you grow up, you'll have them too."

"I look," she said. She pulled my neckline out and stared at my naked breasts. I let her look her fill, figuring she'd be constantly trying to peek at them if I didn't. After a few minutes, her curiosity was satisfied, and she let go of my tank top. "Evie girl play with Bella?"

I couldn't resist her sweet and hopeful look. "Sure. Just let me get dressed first."

I slid off the bed, put on my bra and a t-shirt, and layered my sweater over top of that. I'd have to ask Court or Bran where their laundry machines were. I didn't have many clothes, and this sweater was the only one thick enough to keep me somewhat warm in the house.

"You cold?" Bella said. She was studying the goosebumps on my bare legs.

"Yes, it's very cold in here." I studied the t-shirt and pants combo she was wearing. "Are you not cold, honey?"

She just shrugged. I took off my shorts and slipped my yoga pants on. My ribs and back protested, but compared to how they used to be, I could handle the pain. Although – my mouth watered – a glass of gallberry juice would definitely help.

Bella leaned forward on the bed and stared at my ass. "Where your tail?"

"I don't have a tail." I sat down on the bed next to her, smiling a little when she used her tail to tug on the hem of my sweater. "I'm a human, and humans don't have tails."

"Human?" Bella cocked her head at me.

"That's right." I pointed to myself. "I'm a girl human, and you," I pointed to her, "are a girl Draax."

She giggled and took my hand, jumping off the bed and pulling me toward the door. "Play with me, Evie girl."

I followed her down the hallway to her room. Her room was small but stuffed full of toys and books. We sat on the floor, and Bella handed me a purple doll. "Draax girl."

"What's her name?" I said.

"Noola." Bella picked up a toy spaceship and zoomed it around in the air. "Noola go in spaceship."

I handed her the doll, and she stuffed it inside before waving the spaceship in the air. "Noola flying."

I picked up a stuffed animal. It was brown with yellow spots on its hindquarters, a bushy yellow and brown striped tail, and antlers protruding from its head. "This is a grundleswat, right?"

"Yes. Grundleswat." Bella made a snorting noise before giggling.

I'd done some research at the library about the Draax and knew that the grundleswat was very similar to deer on Earth. They were the main meat eaten on the planet Draax, along with...

I frowned, rubbing my side absently as I tried to remember. "Bella, what is the animal that turns white in the winter."

"Winter?" Bella cocked her head at me before setting the spaceship down.

"The cold months," I said. "The animal that turns white... it's small, and you eat it." I made an eating motion, chewing in an exaggerated motion.

Bella jumped up and ran to an overflowing toybox in the corner. She rummaged through it, tossing out books, stuffys, spaceships, and land vehicles of all shapes and sizes before making a triumphant squeal.

She returned with a brown stuffed animal in her hand. "Maluken."

"Right, maluken," I said. "In the winter, they turn white to blend in. Kind of like our rabbits."

Bella grinned at me before pressing a button on the stuffed Maluken's head. I watched in amazement as the stuffed animal's fur turned from brown to white. "Wow. That's very cool."

"Very cool," Bella mimicked.

She dropped the stuffed animal and skipped across the room to yank a plastic sword from the toybox. She turned and swung it in a wide arc before jabbing it at another stuffed animal sitting on the floor.

Was it weird that she had a toy sword? I thought so. "Bella, where did you get that?"

"Papa give me," she said. She jabbed it at the stuffed animal again. "I fight like Papa and Uda fight."

I frowned. Court had said they were farmers. I was sure of it.

Bella had returned, and she plopped her tiny body into my lap. She was holding a children's book and opened it to the middle. "Read, Evie girl."

"Um…" The book was written in Draax. "I can't, Bella."

"No read?" Bella pouted at me.

"She can't read Draax, meena."

I glanced up. Court was standing in the doorway. His lovely copper eyes dipped briefly to my chest, and for some reason, my stomach muscles fluttered, and my nipples hardened. I looked away quickly as Bella jumped out of my lap and ran across the room to Court.

"Uda, I hungry." She grabbed his hands and swung her body back and forth.

"It is supper time, meena. Wash your hands and then go to the kitchen, please," Court said.

Bella ran from the room, and I stood up, acutely aware of how sore my back was from sitting on the floor.

"How do you feel?" Court asked.

"A little sore," I admitted. "Would it be all right if I had more gallberry juice?"

He nodded. "You do not need to ask. Just help yourself to it whenever you want."

"Thank you," I said.

Looking directly into his gaze made me feel a little fuzzy in the head, so I stared at his chest instead. Big mistake. His shirt was tight across it and brought back memories from this morning. I'd been too shocked to take a close look at his naked chest. Was it smooth and hairless like Bran's? Did he have a six-pack?

My gaze wandered down to his stomach and then to his crotch. He'd had an erection this morning. Both he and Bran. *That* I could remember. In fact, the way their dicks had pushed at their briefs seemed to be burned into my brain.

My face was flushing, and the chill I constantly felt disappeared. Now, I was too warm and resisted the urge to fan my face.

"Human?"

I tore my gaze from Court's crotch and stared at his face. There was a look of – was that amusement and lust? – on his face, and I quickly looked away again as a fresh new blush covered my skin. I studied his hands instead. They were big and strong and callused. I knew that because they'd been cupping my ass and playing with my nipple this morning. His hands were rough and hard and –

Evie, stop it!

I took a deep breath as Court cleared his throat. "Will you eat dinner with us or in your room?"

"Oh, um, I'll eat with you if that's okay?" I still couldn't look at him. I was suddenly afraid I might do something inappropriate… like hump his damn leg.

"Yes, we would like it if you joined us."

There was silence, and then Court said. "We will see you in the kitchen?"

I nodded. "Yes, I'll be right down."

I waited until his footsteps had faded before I walked from Bella's room to my own. I checked my reflection in the bathroom mirror, groaning at how red my face was. My thick sweater hid my hard nipples, thank God, but my pussy felt swollen and achy, and my panties were definitely damp.

What the hell was wrong with me?

CHAPTER 10

Court

The human was a mixture of anxiety and arousal. I disliked that she was anxious but couldn't deny that her arousal was intoxicating. I glanced at Bran. His face was a blank mask, but I knew he could smell her arousal as well as I could. And after what happened this morning, there was no way he didn't enjoy her arousal just as I did.

"Eat, human," Bran suddenly said.

I frowned when I realized the little human was stirring the stew in her bowl rather than eating. She did that a lot.

"You must eat more, human," I said. "The gallberry juice will help heal your bruises, but proper nutrition is also vital."

"I know," she said. "Hey, could you try calling me Evelyn or Evie?"

Bran turned a dark green and nodded. "Yes."

I felt my own rush of embarrassment and nodded in agreement. "Sorry, hum – Evie."

She smiled at me, and my embarrassment turned to pleasure. Krono, she was pretty. Her pink lips were the same shade as her pink nipples, and for a moment, I allowed myself to imagine her lips red and swollen and wrapped around my cock.

The front of my pants was now too tight, and I berated myself internally. Not only was Bella sitting at the table with us, but wishing that our future queen would suck my dick was a stupid idea.

Still, I couldn't deny that if I knew the king would never find out, I would have the soft little human on her knees before me. Krono, how beautiful she would look.

"Evie girl, eat." Bella picked up a piece of the warracot off her plate and held it out to the human – no, Evie, her name was Evie. Evie smiled and took it before popping it into her mouth.

"Thank you, Bella."

Bella grinned at her, ate a few more bites of food, and slid out of her chair. Before Bran or I could stop her, she climbed into Evie's lap.

"Why Evie girl no eat?" Bella asked her.

"I'm eating, honey," Evie said.

"Too hot?" Bella leaned over and blew into Evelyn's stew. Evie and I both laughed, and Bran even smiled as Bella handed the spoon to Evie. "Eat, Evie girl."

Evelyn took a few bites of stew. "It's delicious. Is this, um, grundleswat?"

"No," I said. "It's maluken stew."

"I like it. It kind of tastes like chicken," Evie said.

"Those are the feathered creatures that lay eggs?" Bran said.

"Yes. You don't have anything like that here, huh?" she said.

"No," I said. "We have creatures that lay eggs, but they are more like your," I searched for the word, "lizards."

"There is talk in the market of bringing in some of these chickens from Earth," Bran said.

"Market?" Evie asked.

"There is a town not far from us," I said. "We go there for supplies when the weather is good."

"Oh. How big is the town?" Evelyn asked.

"About ten thousand Draax," Bran replied. "It has a few different markets and other businesses, a hospital, and a school."

"I read that you guys have hospitals and doctors, um, they're called…"

"Kadanas," I said.

"Right. I read about that but never really understood why you have hospitals. Doesn't the gallberry juice heal everything?"

"It does," I said. "But the kadanas help guide our elders to the other side when the gallberry juice no longer heals, and they help the humans deliver our babies and administer gallberry serum in intravenous form to the gravely wounded to heal them faster."

"The gallberry plant helps to heal us," Bran said, "but sometimes even it is not enough. If a Draax does not receive it fast enough, they can and will die."

"The king's mother died in childbirth," I said.

"Really?" Evie said.

"Yes. She was giving birth to her third child, a girl, and it was too much for her and the child. They both died even with the gallberry plant."

"That's so sad," Evie said.

Bella, who'd been leaning quietly against Evelyn, suddenly sat up. "Papa?"

"Yes, meena?" Bran scraped the last of his stew from his bowl.

Bella pressed her hands against Evelyn's breasts. "Breasts, Papa. Evie girl's breasts."

Evelyn turned a bright red, and Bran quickly looked at his empty bowl. Bella grinned at me. "Breasts, Uda."

"Uh, I know, meena," I said.

Evelyn cleared her throat. "Sorry, she wanted to know what they were, so I told her. I hope that isn't a problem."

"It is not," Bran said. He was still staring at the bottom of his stew bowl, his tail flicking back and forth behind him.

"So, she's never seen an adult female before?" Evelyn asked.

Bran shook his head. "No. There are only a few human females in town mated to Draax, and Bella has never seen them."

Evelyn pulled on her bottom lip with her teeth, and I had to look away. Krono, my erection would not go away.

"So, um, you guys are farmers, right?"

"We are," Bran said.

Evelyn glanced at Bella. "When I was playing with Bella in her room, she had a toy sword and said that Papa and Uda fight."

"We used to be in the military," I said.

"Almost every Draax male joins the military," Bran says. "It is not required, but it is encouraged. The more of us who know how to protect our world, the better."

"That makes sense," Evelyn said. "It's good that so many of you know how to fight. It's why our world doesn't belong to the Gokmards."

"Gokmards!" Bella made a face and growled before hooking her hands into claws and swiping the air. "Gokmards, rawr!"

I laughed, as did Bran, but Evie gave us a nervous look. "Has she seen a Gokmard before?"

"Only in books or on her tablet," Bran said.

"Have you seen Gokmards?" Evelyn asked.

I glanced at Bran before nodding. "Yes. The war for Earth was over before we were born, but we were a part of the Vokine war."

"Vokine?" Evelyn said.

"Another planet, not far from here. The Gokmards attacked the Vokine planet, and we provided military assistance."

"For the same reason you helped Earth?" Evelyn asked.

"No. The Vokine females are not compatible with us for breeding," Bran said. "They provided us with some of their advanced technology, and we provided them with the gall-berry plant."

"Does the plant grow on their planet?" Evie said.

"Under certain conditions," I replied. "They cannot grow it in a field like we do – their planet has an extremely hot climate - but the atmosphere of their planet does not kill it immediately like Earth's does."

"Do you have lots of planets in your solar system?" Evelyn asked.

"Many," Bran said. "Your Earth knows of some of them but not all."

"Why are the Draax the only ones who come to Earth?" Evelyn said. "I mean, I get why the Gokmards came, but why haven't any of the other worlds? Is it because you protect us?"

I didn't know how to say it without insulting the little human. Bran had no such fears.

"Your planet and its inhabitants are primitive. Your technology is laughable, and your natural resources are nearly depleted," Bran said. "The Gokmards wished to have it only because that is what they do. They seek out other worlds and conquer them. Other planets know there is nothing of worth on Earth."

Evelyn gaped at him, and I scowled. "Bran, enough."

"What?" Bran gave me a genuinely confused look. "It is true, Court. We would never have gone near Earth if their females had not been breeding compatible."

"You hurt the human – Evie's – feelings," I said.

Bran stared at her. "How?"

"You insulted her entire planet," I replied.

Bran studied Evelyn. "That was not my intention," he finally said.

She nodded. "I know, and I suppose you're right. Our technology does improve with every generation, but we are far behind the Draax."

"And we are not even that technically advanced. Compared to the Vokines or even the Scuun, we are almost as primitive as Earth."

"Scuun?" Evelyn said.

"Great yellow beasts," Bran said. "Big brains, many tentacles."

"Scuun!" Bella shouted. She moved her arms in a wavy, ripple-like motion. "Scuun!"

She smiled at Evelyn, and the human gave her a small grin before patting her arms. "Are these your Scuun tentacles, Bella?"

Bella giggled. "Bella not Scuun. Bella Draax."

"That's right," Evie said. "And what am I?"

"Evie girl human."

"That's right!" Evie crinkled her nose at her in a cute little way that made my cock twitch in my pants again.

"Kiss, Evie girl?" Bella puckered her lips, and Evelyn gave Bran a nervous look.

"Kiss Bella!" Bella pulled on Evelyn's arm. "Kiss!"

"It is fine," Bran said.

Evie bent her head and kissed Bella. She giggled and leaned against Evie's chest before smiling at Bran. "I colour now, Papa."

"All right, meena. But make sure you colour only in your colouring book. I do not want to find the walls and all the pictures in your bedroom coloured on like the last moon. Do you understand?"

"Yes, Papa." Bella slid off Evie's lap and skipped out of the kitchen.

"She's very sweet," Evelyn said.

"Yes, she is." Bran drank some water before pointing at the juice in front of Evelyn. "Drink your juice."

She drank a few swallows and ate more stew before smiling tentatively at us. "So, you guys have been friends for a long time?"

"Since we were small boys," I said. "Our families lived beside each other, and our mothers were very good friends."

"That's nice. Were your mothers human?"

Bran shook his head. "No. The breeding program had already started with the humans, but our mothers were some of the last of our female kind. It was a miracle that either of them even bred successfully. They were both very old when they had us. My mother died when I was ten and Court's when he was thirteen."

"I'm very sorry," Evelyn said.

Her tone was genuine, and the look on her face suggested she knew of the same pain that Court and I felt. Before I could ask, she said, "How long do the cold months last on Draax?"

"Only three or four moons," I said.

"Okay, that's good," Evelyn said.

"Are you cold, human?" I asked.

"I'm fine," she said with a nervous look at both of us. "I'm not used to this type of cold, but I'm sure I'll adapt quickly."

"Is that why you did not bring enough warm clothing?" Bran said.

"Um, yes."

Krono, the human was a terrible liar. I felt the familiar annoyance that she was lying and tamped it down. Female humans lied. It was what they did. I should not be surprised that Evelyn was no different. But for some reason it bothered me that she lied to us.

"Our planet is very pretty during the warm months," Bran said. "You will enjoy it. The flora and fauna on Draax are," he paused, searching for the right word, "incredible."

"There is a garden in the palace with artificial light in the cold months," I said. "During the cold months when it is not storming, the king opens the gardens to all in the province who wish to enjoy it. You will have access to it every day.

She set down her spoon and crossed her arms over her torso. "So, do you know much about the king?"

"He has not been king for long. He was the head of the king's guard, and his older brother was king. But his brother was killed in a ship crash before he had any heirs, and Quillan was crowned king."

"Is he," Evelyn hesitated, "a nice king?"

I shrugged. "We do not know him personally."

"He has a reputation for being impatient and short tempered," Bran said.

The human paled, and she rubbed at her side. "He does?"

"A bit." Bran studied the human. "What is wrong?"

"Nothing," she said.

She was lying again. It was evident that what Bran told her had frightened her. I was not surprised that she was scared. She was very timid, and if the king was impatient with her, no doubt it would terrify her.

The thought that our king would frighten her sent a strange wave of possessiveness over me for the little human. I didn't like the idea that she would be at the castle, alone and terrified, with a Draax who did not have a reputation for being patient.

Suddenly eager to ease her fear, I said, "He will be kind to his queen."

She gave me an anxious smile, and I had to stop myself from stroking her soft cheek. Instead, I said, "You are important to him, and he will treat you well."

Even though I didn't know the king, I wasn't lying. Draax loved the little human females. They were special and precious, and if a Draax was lucky enough to have a female for breeding purposes, they did everything they could to convince the female to mate with them permanently.

But would he be patient with her? Many human females were nervous around us. Bran and I had spent enough time at human bars on Earth to know that, but this human's fear went beyond that. Would the king recognize that Evelyn's fear of us was abnormal and do what he could to make her feel safe?

That I didn't know.

"Do you have family?" Bran asked.

"My mom died when I was a baby, so I don't remember her," Evie said. "My father remarried when I was seven to a woman with a son only a few years older than me. But then my dad died in a work accident when I was twelve, and my stepmother died a few years ago. I lived with my stepbrother before I came here."

"What did you do for work?" I asked.

"I worked a few odd jobs at retail stores," Evelyn said. "Alex, my stepbrother, didn't like it when I worked."

"Why?" Bran asked.

She shrugged and stared down at her glass of juice. "I don't know."

"What did your stepbrother do for work?" I asked.

Evelyn looked extremely uncomfortable. "He did different jobs."

"Like what?" I persisted.

She hesitated, her cheeks colouring. "He was in the, um, pharmaceutical business."

"Were you close to him?" Bran asked.

"No," Evelyn said. A look crossed her face, disgust with a hint of fear in it. "I didn't like him very much."

For a moment, I wondered if it was this Alex who had beaten her before I dismissed it. Not only was he her brother, and it was his duty to protect her, but females were precious. A human male would be a fool to injure one in such a manner. The little human would have died from her injuries if not for the gallberry juice.

Someone hurt her, Court. You saw the footprint shaped bruise on her side. Do you believe another female did that to her?

"What illness did you have that made you join the breeding program?" Bran asked.

"Oh, um, I wasn't sick," Evelyn said.

Bran gave her a curious look. "But you said you did not care for your brother."

"Step-brother, and I didn't. He wasn't sick either."

"Then why did you join the breeding program?" I asked.

"My neighbour's child was very sick with a disease called cystic fibrosis."

"That is a curable disease on Earth, is it not?" Bran said.

"Yes, but Candy was a lower like me and couldn't afford

the earth medicine that would cure her son. I joined the breeding program and got the juice for him."

Bran was giving her a shocked look. "You joined the life-time breeding program for a neighbour?"

"Candy is a very good friend, and her child was dying," Evelyn said defensively.

"Still, you can never return to Earth, human," Bran said. "The king will not allow his queen to return even for visits."

"I know," Evelyn said.

There was a moment of silence, and then I said, "What was your real reason for joining the program?"

Evelyn stared at me before swallowing hard. "That is the real reason." She stood and picked up her bowl of half-eaten stew. "I'm not great at cooking, especially with Draaxan food, but I'd still like to help. I'll clean up after meals."

I looked at Bran, who made a slight shrug before standing and carrying his empty bowl to the sink.

I was suddenly determined to discover why the little human had joined the program but now was not the time. I would give her a few more days to relax and realize we would not harm her before I questioned her again.

CHAPTER 11

Evelyn

I sunk to my chin in the bath and breathed a sigh of relief. I'd been in the tub for almost an hour and was warm for the first time all day. Even yesterday, I'd still been too sore to climb into the stand-alone tub in my bathroom, but today, the bruising and the soreness had dissipated enough that getting into the tub wasn't an exercise in torture.

I lifted my foot out of the water and used my toe to push the button on the wall next to the faucet. It sent another stream of sweet-smelling liquid into the steaming water. It turned to bubbles as soon as it hit the water, and I sighed happily and closed my eyes. God, it felt good to relax in a tub. Our apartment didn't have a tub, and it'd been years since I –

"Hi, girl!"

I gasped and jerked in the tub. The water rose to the edge and almost spilled out before receding. I blinked at Bella and then studied the bathroom door that was now partially open. My bedroom and bathroom door didn't have locks, but I hadn't even heard her open the door. It was becoming increasingly obvious that Bella was actually a tiny, purple, silent ninja disguised as a two-year-old.

"You having bath, Evie girl?" Bella said. She was wearing her nightgown, and her long dark hair was hanging down her back.

"I am," I said.

"I have bath too."

Before I could stop her, she'd stripped off her nightgown and climbed into the tub with me. She sat at the other end, smiling happily at me as her tail flicked out and above the water and sprayed drops of water and bubbles everywhere.

"Hey, watch that tail," I said as I wiped my face.

She giggled before cocking her head. "Evie sad with no tail?"

I smiled. "No, it doesn't make me sad that I don't have a tail."

Bella scooted a little closer and used her tail to pick up my shampoo bottle from the side of the tub. "What this?"

"That's shampoo to wash my hair," I said.

"You wash Bella's hair." She slid under the water and popped back up, her hair wet and her face covered in bubbles. She blew them off her mouth and stared at my wet hair. "Wash Bella's hair like girl's?"

"Sure," I said. Bella climbed into my lap, facing me, and I washed her hair, massaging her scalp before washing the long strands.

"You have beautiful hair," I said.

She was touching my upper chest, staring at her purple skin against my pale skin. "Why girl no purple? Evie girl sick?"

"No," I said. "I'm not sick. Humans don't have purple or green skin."

"Ouchy." She poked the healing bruise on my shoulder hard enough to hurt, and I winced.

She gave me a look of remorse. "Bella hurt girl. Sorry, girl."

"That's all right. Tilt your head back, honey."

She tilted her head back, and I used my cupped hand and the bath water to rinse the shampoo from her hair. "There, nice and clean."

She smiled. "Nice and clean."

There was a knock on my bedroom door, and I heard Bran's muffled voice. "Human – Evie, may I come in?"

"Papa!" Bella shouted.

The door opened, and Bran said, "Bella, where are you?"

"In the bath, Papa!" Bella shouted again. "Come here!"

I clamped my arms across my breasts and shouted, "No, don't come in! I'm in the bathtub, too."

When Bran spoke, his voice was just outside the partially opened bathroom door. "You are bathing with Bella?"

"I was already in the tub, and she climbed in with me before I could stop her," I said. "I'm sorry."

"Bella, you must not bother the human when she is in her room," Bran said. "Get out of the tub and come to me, please."

"No," Bella said and grinned at me.

"Bella, out of the tub," Bran repeated.

"I bathing with Evie-girl, Papa." Her tail splashed the water. "You bathe with us too!"

"Meena, do as I say." Bran's voice was stern, and Bella's face fell. Her lower lip pouted out, and her look turned pleading.

"Bella stay with girl. Okay, girl? Please?"

Oh my God, no one could resist that sweet face.

"I'm almost finished," I said. "I don't mind if she stays with me a little longer."

There was silence, and then Bran said, "I do not expect you to be her nanny while you are here, hum – Evelyn."

"I know," I said. "But I don't mind, I swear."

"Girl no mind, Papa!" Bella shouted.

I laughed, and Bella grinned at me. "Bella stay with girl, Papa."

Bran sighed. "All right, meena. But be a good girl."

"I be good," Bella said before sliding off my lap to the other end of the tub.

I waited until I heard Bran's footsteps fade away and the bedroom door close before unclamping my arms from my breasts. "Come on, honey. Let's finish bathing and get out of the tub."

"Sure, Evie girl."

When Bran knocked the second time, I was sitting on my bed, my fingers twined through Bella's hair as she sat before me. I wasn't wearing a bra, but I had my thick sweater on to hide that fact, and my bare legs were tucked under the quilt.

"Come in," Bella shouted.

I laughed, and Bella grinned as Bran opened the door a crack and said, "Human, may I come in?"

"Yes," I said.

Bran walked into the room. Apparently, he'd had his own bath or shower because his dark hair was wet, and his shirt clung damply to his chest. I concentrated on finishing braiding Bella's hair and not staring at his body as Bella yawned hugely.

"Evie girl braiding my hair, Papa."

"I see that, meena." He stood self-consciously at the foot of the bed. "Thank you, Evelyn."

"It's no problem," I said.

He frowned a little. "She should not be bothering you when you are in your room. I will speak with her in the morning when she is not so tired and make her understand that you need your privacy.

"If that's what you want to do, but I'm okay with spending time with her," I said.

I really didn't mind Bella's company. She was a cute kid, and while her ninja skills took some getting used to, I enjoyed getting to know her. Besides, I would have a kid of my own soon, and it would probably be good to get some practice with a toddler, right?

My stomach twisted a little at the thought of sleeping with the king. They'd said he was impatient and short-tempered. What if I couldn't please him in bed? What if he got angry with me when it became apparent that I didn't know what I was doing when it came to sex?

For a moment, I wished that I'd slept with a few more guys once I'd been accepted into the breeding program. Maybe even tried sleeping with a Draax so I would know what it was like.

That's what I should have done. I'd only had a few days between finding out I was accepted to the breeding program and leaving Earth, and it was difficult to slip out of the apartment with Alex and Troy watching me like a hawk, but I could have managed something. God, I was so stupid. I could have been practicing sex with a Draax on Earth, and then I wouldn't have to worry about not pleasing the king. Why hadn't I thought of that before I left Earth?

Hey, Evie? You have a couple of Draax right here that you could practice with.

My face went bright red, and I stared at Bella's dark hair before continuing to braid. I was embarrassed, but maybe I should ask one of them to sleep with me. It was obvious that they found me attractive.

Do they, though? Maybe they were just half-asleep like you were and would have touched any woman in their bed.

Maybe, but I didn't think so. At least not in the case of Court. The way he looked at me sometimes... I might have been a bit naïve about sex, but I knew lust when I saw it. I was pretty sure he wanted me. Bran, on the other hand... I was more of an annoyance to him. I couldn't blame him. I'd be annoyed, too, if I was expecting a nanny for my kid and got someone without experience with children.

I wound the elastic around the end of the braid and smoothed the sides before smiling at Bella. "There you go, honey. All done."

"Bella pretty, Papa?" Bella said.

"Very pretty. Come, meena. It's time for bed," Bran said.

"Evie girl come too." Bella wrapped her arms around my neck and her tail around my arm when Bran tried to lift her from the bed.

"Bella." Bran's tone was slightly exasperated, and I slid off the bed, holding Bella in my arms.

"It's fine. I can carry her to her room."

"You are injured," he said.

"I'm feeling better," I said. "It doesn't hurt to hold her."

I was mainly telling the truth. I did have a dull ache in my kidneys and lower back, but it was manageable.

I was wearing shorts, and he stared at my side where my thick sweater covered the bruising before studying my bare legs. The cold air had made goosebumps break out on them, and Bran frowned. "You need to put on warmer clothes."

"I'm okay," I said. "Come on, Bella, let's get you to bed."

I followed Bran into the hallway, Bella's tail thumping against my hip. "Uda!" she shouted, making me jump a little. "Uda, where are you?"

The door to Court's bedroom opened, and he stepped out. My mouth dried up, and I quickly looked away. He was wearing just a pair of pants, and I didn't know if it was possible, but his chest and stomach seemed even more muscular than Bran's.

No chest hair, just like Bran. Do you think that's a Draax thing, or do they wax?

I ignored my inner voice as Bella made a soft sound of happiness. "Uda, say night night."

"Night, night," Court said.

Bella pointed her tail at him. "Kiss, Uda."

He walked toward us, and I kept my gaze on Bella's braid as Bella puckered her lips.

He kissed her and tickled her belly. She giggled and pushed at his hand. "Bella loves Uda."

"I love you too. Sleep well, meena."

"Sleep well, Uda," she mimicked.

He stepped back, and I walked by him, trying not to flinch when my elbow brushed his bare chest. "Sorry," I murmured without looking at him. God, he was so warm. I could feel the heat even through my thick sweater. Were all Draax that warm? Also, why the hell were my nipples so hard?

I walked into Bella's bedroom and set her down on the bed when Bran pulled the quilt back.

"Kiss, Evie girl."

I pressed my mouth against Bella's and stroked her damp hair. "Good night, Bella."

"Sleep well, Evie girl."

She was so cute. I stepped back as Bran, holding a book in

one hand, sat on the edge of the bed. I was about to slip out when Bella patted the other side of her bed. "Papa read to you too, girl."

I hesitated before sitting next to Bella on the other side. Bran opened the book, and I listened in fascination to his deep voice as he told the story of a little Draax girl named Ulena and her quest for a golden statue. Bella listened silently, her eyelids closing for longer periods until Bran closed the book and tucked the quilt to her chin.

Her eyelids fluttered open, and she gave him a sleepy look. "Bella loves Papa."

"Papa loves Bella," he said before pressing a kiss against her forehead. "Sleep well, meena."

I followed him out into the hallway. He shut off the light to Bella's room and closed the door. Court was no longer in the hallway, and we stood in silent awkwardness for a moment before I said, "She's adorable."

"She is," he said.

He didn't look irritated for the first time since I'd met him. It was apparent how much he loved Bella and how much she loved him. The way he was with her reminded me of my father, and an aching sadness settled in my belly. I missed my father, even after all these years.

"Human, are you all right?"

I nodded, blinking back the tears that were dangerously close to spilling past my lashes. "Yes. Bella loves you very much, it's obvious."

"She is my girl, and I love her," Bran said. "It is still rare for females to be born, even with the humans, and the moment I saw her face…"

He stopped, his throat working, and said, "She is special."

"Did her mother die in childbirth?" Despite Bella's purple skin, I knew she was half-human. It didn't matter if the

Draax babies had human mothers. The males were always green, and the females were always purple. I wasn't sure of the exact reason, although I vaguely remember studying it in biology in high school. Something about the gene that decided skin colouring was dominant in the Draax.

I also knew that while extremely rare, occasionally, a woman would die giving birth to a Draax baby, even with the gallberry plant.

"No," Bran said. "She returned to Earth a moon after Bella was born."

I couldn't contain my look of surprise. What woman would voluntarily leave their child on another planet?

"That's strange," I replied, trying to keep my voice neutral. "I've never heard of a woman leaving the breeding program after having a baby."

"She was not in the breeding program," Bran's voice grew strained. "She joined us as our mate because she wanted to."

"Us?"

Bran studied the wall. "Court and me. We shared the females we slept with."

Hot colour flooded my cheeks. I wasn't surprised. I'd woken up to both of them touching me, but still... it was one thing to suspect they did threesomes and quite another to hear it put so bluntly.

"Oh, right," I said stupidly. "Draax like, um, threesomes."

He didn't reply, and I chewed on my bottom lip. "I didn't realize that two Draax would mate with one woman, though. I thought it was more of a casual thing."

"It is unusual but not unheard of for two Draax to mate with one female," Bran said. "We preferred to share our female, even as a mate."

"Was?" I said.

Bran's mouth tightened into a thin line. "We do not share our women now."

"Why not?" The question was asked before I could stop it.

He glared at me, his anger radiating in thick, slow waves. "That is none of your business, human."

I stumbled back, my hands protecting my kidneys. "You're right. I'm sorry. I shouldn't have been so nosy."

The anger left his face, and he gave me a remorseful look. "I will not hurt you, human."

"No, uh, I know that," I said as I backed down the hallway. "I'm just really tired now and… um, good night, Bran."

"Good night, Evelyn."

CHAPTER 12

Evelyn

I shot into a sitting position, my heart thudding in my chest and my arms raised to protect my head as I peered into the darkness. The last shreds of my nightmare clung to me, and I rubbed my chest and tried to take deep, calming breaths.

I wasn't on Earth now, and Alex would never hurt me again. I dropped my hand to my side and rubbed. I must have been tossing and turning because my sheet and quilt were tangled, and my side was aching. It'd been a terrible nightmare, and I shuddered all over. I'd been back in our dingy apartment, asleep on my mattress. Alex had come into my room and dragged me off of the mattress by my hair and into the living room. Troy stood in the room, and Alex threw me at him before walking away.

I shuddered again. The nightmare had been so real. I could still feel Troy's hot breath on my face, smell the garlic lingering on his breath as he bent over me and grinned.

"Mine, you little bitch. You're all mine now, and you'll never get away."

My pulse was speeding up again, and I pushed back the quilt and the sheet and climbed out of bed. I was already craving some juice and knew I'd never go back to sleep without a glass. Hell, I probably wouldn't sleep anyway – the nightmare was still too fresh – but at least my side wouldn't hurt as much.

I slipped out of my room and padded to the kitchen. By the time I arrived, I was freezing and wishing I'd put my sweater on over my tank top. The house was even colder at night, and my fingers were numb. I grabbed a glass from the cupboard and the jug of juice from the Draax version of a fridge and poured myself a glass.

I gulped it down, relishing its taste as it slid down my throat, but the cold juice only made me colder. My body shaking, I went to rinse the glass, muttering a curse when it slipped out of my numb fingers and fell to the floor. It shattered against the tile, and I winced and quickly looked at the doorway before crouching and picking up the larger pieces.

"Ouch! Shit!" My finger was bleeding, and I stood and eyed the sink and then the pieces of glass on the floor. Blood started to drip, and I used the edge of my tank top to stem the flow. Shit, I would have to go and grab some shoes. If I tried to walk over to the sink, I'd end up with glass in my foot and –

"What is going on?"

The deep voice scared the hell out of me, and I whirled around. The man standing in the dark doorway was not a Draax, but Alex. Alex, with his cruel sneer and hands already balling into fists, ready to hit and hurt and make me beg for mercy.

His big body blocked my only exit, and I skittered away

until my back hit the far wall. I slid down and covered my head with my arms, the hot tears already falling.

"I'm sorry," I said. "I'm so sorry. I'll clean it up right away, Alex. I promise. Please don't hurt me."

"Shh, Evie."

The big body knelt in front of me, and I took in a whooping gasp of air. The man standing in front of me wasn't Alex, but Bran. The light flicked on, and Court hurried over and joined us.

"What happened?"

"I am not sure," Bran said. "Evelyn, are you -"

"She is bleeding." Court's voice was full of alarm. "Little human, where are you hurt?"

My heart was still thudding like an elephant in a stampede, and I couldn't stop crying. Alex wasn't here. He couldn't hurt me, and I knew that, but for some reason, the fear was still eating at my stomach, making my body shake and my breathing shallow.

"She cut her finger, I think," Bran said.

He reached for my hand, and I flinched and ducked my head.

"Shh, little human. I will not hurt you." Bran's voice was oddly gentle.

He stood, and I made a sharp cry of fear when he tugged me to my feet.

"Shh," he said again, lifting me into his arms.

I stared wide-eyed at him as he carried me out of the kitchen. "Court, please grab some bandages and a glass of gallberry juice."

Carrying me easily, Bran strode into the living room and set me on the couch before turning on the fireplace. The flames roared to life, and I didn't object when Bran took the

134

blanket from the back of the couch and dropped it around my shoulders.

"Let me see your hand, Evie," he said.

I held out my hand. Blood still dripped from my finger, and I moaned when it splashed onto the floor. "I'm sorry. I'll clean that up and the broken glass in the kitchen."

"Do not worry about it," Bran said as Court walked in. He sat down on the other side of me, frowning a little when I automatically flinched but held out the bandages as Bran studied my finger.

"Should we rinse it first?" Court asked.

"I think it is all right. The bleeding is already slowing, and I do not see any glass in the cut."

As Bran dabbed the cut with a bandage, Court held out the glass of juice. "Drink, Evelyn."

I drank. The juice was cold, and my teeth chattered when I finished it. I huddled deeper into the blanket, trying not to cry from humiliation, as Bran finished bandaging the cut.

"I will get you another glass of juice," Court said.

I shook my head. "N-no, that's okay. I'm freezing right now, and my finger isn't stinging anymore. I just want to clean up my mess and go to bed, okay?"

Court and Bran stared at each other over my head, and I blinked back the hot tears. "I'm sorry."

I tried to stand, flinching again when both Bran and Court put heavy hands on my arms. I knew in my mind that they wouldn't hurt me, but after years of being punched and kicked, my body couldn't control its reaction.

"Please," I said again, "I want to go to bed."

"Soon," Court said. "But first, you will tell us the truth."

"Court," Bran said. "She is afraid and -"

Court reached out and grasped my chin with gentle fingers,

tilting my head up until I stared straight into his copper coloured eyes. "I know you are afraid, little human, which is why you need to tell us the truth. It will help lessen the fear."

Would it? I honestly didn't know, but something in Court's gaze made me long to tell him everything. I couldn't, though. If they knew how pathetic I was, if they knew that I'd basically been held prisoner by my stepbrother because I was too afraid to leave, they might tell the king I was weak and not fit to be his mate.

Evie, don't be stupid. They won't. You know they won't.

I couldn't take the risk. I just couldn't.

I opened my mouth to plead for them to allow me to return to my room again, but before I could say anything, Court rubbed his thumb across my bottom lip. "Tell us, little human. Tell us so we can keep you safe."

His promise to keep me safe shattered my resolve to keep my secrets. Since my father died, I'd had no one to protect me, no one to care for me, and I was so tired of being afraid.

"Alex," I said. "He was the one who hurt me."

"Your brother?" Bran frowned. "He is supposed to care for you and protect you. It is his duty. Females are precious, but they are weak and require a male to keep them safe, not harm them."

"He's my stepbrother," I said, "and even if he had been my actual brother, it doesn't always work that way on Earth. Human men don't think of women as precious. I mean, some of them do, but not in the way you guys do."

Bran made a low sound of disgust as Court released my chin. "How often did he hurt you?"

"A lot," I admitted. "He started pushing me around and being rough with me before my stepmother died. She didn't like me very much, but she at least didn't let Alex full-on punch me or anything like that. After she died, Alex started beating me up. He didn't really have a job. He sold drugs and did some other illegal things. Anytime I had a job, he would make me quit after a few weeks, so I didn't have enough money to escape him."

I licked my lips, hating how weak I sounded. "I should have run away, but I didn't have anywhere else to go, and I was afraid of him. He told me that it didn't matter where I went. He would find me and kill me."

I stared at my knees. "He would have, too. He was – I mean, he had some mental health issues before he started doing the drugs, but the drugs made it so much worse. He said he was my guardian, and I had to do exactly what he said."

I didn't want to sound completely pathetic, so I said, "I ran away once. I took my last paycheque from a job that he made me quit, and I took a bus to a different city a few hours away. I got a cheap motel room, but Alex found me after only a few days. I don't know how, but he found me. And then he," my throat was dry as dust, and it made a painful sounding click when I swallowed, "he beat me so bad that I couldn't get out of bed for two days. That was the first time I started peeing blood."

Court and Bran didn't say anything. Afraid to look at them, I continued to study my knees. "He didn't hit me in the face very often. He didn't want people to start asking questions. So, he hit and kicked me a lot in the kidneys and the liver."

Court made a low sound in the back of his throat. I glanced up at him and made an anxious squeak at the look of pure fury in his gaze. It made me want to try and protect my kidneys immediately, but I resisted, looking back at my knees instead.

"So, that is why you joined the lifetime breeding program?" Bran said.

"Mostly. Alex had a friend – Troy. He was a drug dealer like Alex and just as mean. He, uh, he liked me." Gallberry flavoured bile rose in my throat, and I swallowed it down. "I was a virgin, and Troy liked that. He said it was hot that I'd never been with a man before and that he was going to be my first."

Another low growl from Court, and I crossed my arms over my torso, my hand resting against my kidneys. "I went to a bar one night, found a random guy, and slept with him. I figured if I weren't a virgin, Troy wouldn't want me anymore. I made sure that some of Alex's other friends were at the bar and that they saw me go home with the guy. Alex was waiting for me the next day when I came home."

I shuddered at the memory of what happened. "He was so mad. He beat me up badly again, but I didn't care because it worked. Troy didn't want me anymore."

I took a deep breath and, this time, glanced at Bran. There was anger on his face but also pity, and fresh shame flooded through me. I should never have told them the truth, but it was too late now.

"Anyway," my voice was dull, "it only worked for a bit. After a few weeks, Troy decided he didn't care that I was used goods, and Alex told me I would marry Troy at the end of this month. I applied for the nanny program months ago but knew I would never get chosen. I didn't have any experience with kids."

I shifted on the couch a little, my thighs pressing against Court's and Bran's. After being hurt by Alex so much, I didn't like people in my personal space. It usually made me anxious and uncomfortable, but I didn't mind this. The heat from their large bodies felt nice.

"The day after they told me I had no choice and that I was marrying Troy, I had the genetic testing done for the breeding program. Three days after I discovered I had the breeding compatible gene, the agency told me they'd found me a mate. Apparently, I'm what they call a guaranteed breeder. They said I'd probably get pregnant on the first try, and because I signed up for the lifetime program, they matched me with the king."

"Did your stepbrother find out you joined the breeding program?" Court asked. "Is that why he beat you again?"

I made a bitter laugh. "No. He had no idea. He was just drunk and high and in a bad mood the night before I was leaving. He came into my room and tried to pick a fight with me about marrying Troy, and when I refused to talk to him, he beat me up. I passed out from the pain, and normally, he stops hitting me when that happens, but I don't think he did that time. I woke up in the morning and was in a lot of pain. I only had about ten minutes before the land vehicle from the agency arrived, so I had to pack quickly without waking up Alex. It's why I don't have many clothes and personal items. I didn't have much to begin with, but I had to leave behind most of it. I had to sneak out because if Alex had seen the agency coming to get me, he would have killed me. I know it."

"He nearly did kill you." Court reached out to touch my side before seeming to think better of it and dropping his hand into his lap.

"I tried to hide my injuries because, at first, I thought you were the king. I didn't want you to send me back to Earth because you thought I was too hurt to have sex with you and bear your children," I said to Bran.

"Once you knew about the mix-up, why did you continue to lie to us?" Court asked.

I didn't reply, and his fingers grasped my chin and tipped my head up again. "Tell us, little human."

I searched his face, instinctively knowing that the worst thing I could do now was lie to him. "I was afraid you would tell the king I was weak and he should send me back. I can't go back to Earth. If I do, I'll have no choice but to go back to Alex, and then he really will kill me or, worse, marry me off to Troy. My mom and dad are dead. I'm a lower with no money and no real job experience. If I'm banned from the breeding program, my only choices back on Earth are to be homeless and starving or be married off to a disgusting, brutal pig of a man."

Court released my chin, and I pressed my lips together before saying, "I loved my dad a lot, and the day he died was the worst day of my life. I miss him every day, and I hate that I'll never get to see him, hug him, or tell him I love him ever again. It's why I'll never tell the king what happened with us in the bed that morning."

I glanced at Court and then at Bran. "I don't want to go back to Earth, but more importantly, I don't want Bella growing up without a dad like I did. She needs you. Both of you."

A small semblance of a smile crossed Bran's face. "We know you will not say anything, little human."

We sat in silence for a few minutes before I stood. "I'm sorry I lied to you, and I'm sorry I woke you up by breaking the glass. I'll clean up the glass and then go to bed."

"We will clean it up," Bran said. "Go to bed."

"No," I said. "It's my mess, and I should clean -"

Court stood and touched my dark hair for a moment. "Go to bed, little human. No more arguing with us."

I chewed on my bottom lip before nodding and, keeping the blanket wrapped around me, trudging out of the living room and back to my bedroom. As I climbed into the bed, there was a part of me that wanted to be ashamed that I'd told my pathetic life story to them.

Instead, there was only an odd sense of relief. Lying to them made me feel sick to my stomach. I closed my eyes and took a few deep breaths. Everything would be fine. Court and Bran would keep my secrets, and, in a few weeks, I would be with the king and starting my new life. I'd never see either Bran or Court again.

That thought sent trepidation through me. Never seeing them again shouldn't bother me, they were practically strangers, after all, but it *did* bother me.

It bothered me a great deal.

CHAPTER 13

Bran

"Bella went to bed easily tonight," Court said when I walked into the living room.

I sank onto the couch and stretched my legs out. "She wanted Evelyn to put her to bed."

Court stared at me over his tablet. "Are you serious?"

I nodded. The storm was particularly fierce this evening, and the house was creaking and shuddering in the wind. I wondered idly if I should give Evie more blankets for her bed. I had already given her an extra two, but I doubted it would be enough to keep her warm.

Dana had experienced one cold season, which had driven her nearly mad with irritation and boredom, but I didn't remember her constantly being cold like Evelyn.

"Bran? Did you hear me?" Court said.

"Sorry, what?"

"I said it is strange that Bella wanted Evelyn for her sleep ritual. She does not even like me to do it."

"I know, but she insisted," I said.

"Does that bother you?"

I stared at the flames in the fireplace and thought about Court's question. Did it bother me? It had only been a week since the little human had confessed about being abused and her real reason for joining the breeding program, but Bella was very taken with her. She followed her around and insisted that Evelyn play with her, bathe her, and be in her room for her bedtime ritual.

To my surprise, Evelyn had indulged her, and I even suspected that the human was growing as fond of Bella as Bella was of her.

"Does it?" Court asked again.

"It does not," I said.

"She is a sweet girl," Court said.

"She is."

Court didn't say anything else, and I raised one eyebrow at him. "Say what is on your mind, Court."

He tossed his tablet on the table next to his chair. "We should not allow Bella and Evelyn to grow so close. Evelyn will be leaving after the storm, remember?"

"I remember," I said, "but I do not see how we can keep Bella from her. She is relentless and very stubborn."

Court smiled a little. "That she is."

He picked up his tablet, and I stared into the flames for nearly half an hour. In the last week, the human had started to relax around us. She assured us that her bruising was gone entirely, but we still insisted that she drink gallberry juice every day, and she did not fight us on it. Her anxiety was much less, but she still flinched if Court or I moved too quickly around her.

My scowl deepened. How a human male could hurt any female, let alone a female as sweet and kind as Evie, I would never understand.

"Why are you scowling?" Court asked.

"Why do the human males treat their females so poorly?" I asked.

Court shrugged. "I do not know. But Evie did say that not all of them are like that."

I made a snorting noise as another blast of wind shook the house. "I do not understand females. We would never hurt them in such a manner, yet they still will not breed with us without getting the juice in return."

"Some do," Court said.

I looked away from his gaze, fresh guilt searing into my guts. Dana had been willing to mate with us. At least she made us believe she was. Perhaps it was better most human females only bred with us in exchange for the juice. At least we knew their intentions from the start. At least we did not believe that they truly loved us the way we loved them.

Court stood up abruptly. "Do you want anything from the kitchen?"

I shook my head. For the first time in moons, there had been a contentment between us, and I had ruined it.

I always ruined it.

Court left the room, and I picked up my tablet and opened the planting schedule program for the warm season. I made a few adjustments to how many seeds we were planting in the west field – last season, the soil showed signs of a rugenroach infestation - and tapped in the new numbers to the east field. We would need to pick up a new part for the deocatcraft. Court had repaired it three times, and it still didn't perform correctly. It was an added expense, but with the excellent crop last season, we could afford it.

The loud hiccup made me look up from my tablet. Evelyn was standing in the room, and she hiccupped again before slapping her hand over her mouth and giggling.

"Oh my gosh, *excuse* me," she said. "That is so – *hiccup* – rude."

"Evelyn? Are you feeling all right?"

She staggered toward me, her cheeks bright red and her curvy body swaying enticingly. She sat beside me, her thigh touching mine, and giggled again. I tried to move over, but the arm of the couch blocked me. Evie never sat this close to either Court or me, and just the feel of her thigh against mine made my cock stir.

I grimaced a little. A moon ago, I would have been thrilled that my dick even noticed a female, but that was before the, not one, but *two,* dreams I'd had about the little human in the last week. I'd woken from both with seed all over my belly and a vague feeling of shame. I hadn't lost control over my own body in such a manner since I was a teen.

"Hi." She smiled at me. The lovely green of her eyes was only a small ring around her weirdly large pupils, and I jerked all over when she rested her soft hand on my thigh. "How are you, Bran?"

"I am fine," I said. "Is Bella asleep?"

"She sure is. She fell asleep after ten – *hiccup* – minutes. She's so sweet. I love spending time with her. Thank you for letting me do that."

"You are welcome. Evelyn, are you ill?"

"I feel great!" She grinned at me. "Can I tell you a secret?"

"Yes." I froze when she moved her hand a little higher on my thigh.

"I think you're cute." She giggled before leaning forward and rubbing the tip of her nose against the side of my arm. "Do you think I'm cute?"

"I – yes," I said.

145

Her grin widened, and she said, "Can I tell you another secret?"

Her fingers were now stroking my inner thigh, and my cock was half-hard and pushing against the front of my pants.

She didn't wait for my reply. "I've never had sex with a Draax before, and I am, like, super worried about banging the king."

I stared at her in silent shock. What was going on with the little human?

"I'm worried that I'll be bad at it, and he'll just, like," she fluttered her free hand in the air, "send me right back to Earth. Oh, *and* I'm worried that he'll want me to bang him and a friend and then what do I do? I have to do it because he's the king, but what if it hurts? What if it hurts so much that I cry, and he and his friend get angry at me? You guys have big dicks, right?"

Before I could answer, she said, "My friend Candy says you have stupidly big dicks and the human guy I was with... I think he was just, like, average. Maybe? I don't even know. But it didn't feel that big to me. It hurt a little when he put it in me, but I think that was because it was my first time. But I didn't come. I pretended to because he kept asking me if I was going to come while we were fucking, and it was getting awkward, so I just faked it."

She sat up, her hand squeezing my leg. "Candy says you guys are awesome at sex and that I'll want to have two of you banging me. She says it'll change my life. She says you're all about making a woman come. Are you, Bran? Do you and Court like making women come during sex?"

"We... enjoy bringing pleasure to a woman, yes." Krono! I sounded like a froden, but I was utterly unnerved by how close she was to me and how she spoke.

"That's good... really good." Evelyn had a pleased look on her face. "Hey, will you and Court have sex with me?"

My brain was buzzing with shock, but my body... well, it was more than willing to give Evelyn exactly what she asked for.

"Evelyn, what..."

My voice died in my throat when the soft little human straddled me. Her pussy rested against my growing erection, and her tiny hands curled into my shirt collar. She pressed her mouth against mine, and I groaned, my hands cupping her hips. She licked my bottom lip, and I opened my mouth to her, groaning again when she slipped her tongue between my lips.

I cupped the back of her delicate skull, threading my fingers through her amazingly soft hair, and angled my mouth over hers. I pushed my tongue into her mouth, kissing her harder and deeper, rocking my pelvis against her when she made a soft moan.

She tasted unbelievably sweet, like gallberries and...

Krono! I pulled my mouth away and cupped her head in a firm grip when she tried to kiss me again.

"Bran, please," she whimpered. "Kiss me." She stuck her hands up my shirt, her fingers tracing my stomach muscles.

I groaned, trying to ignore how good her touch felt against my skin. "Evie, did you -"

"Bran!" Court came running into the living room, holding the bottle of gallberry wine in one hand and a glass in the other. "The human drank some wine!"

"Hi, Court," Evelyn's smile was both shy and seductive at the same time. "Why don't you join us? Bran said you guys would be happy to make me come."

"Krono." Court's mouth dropped open. "She is drunk, Bran."

"Yes," I said, tugging Evie's hands from under my shirt. "I realized that when she kissed me, and I tasted the wine."

"She kissed you?" There was no disguising the jealousy in Court's voice.

"Because she is drunk, Court," I said.

"I'm not drunk," Evie protested as I gently eased her onto the couch beside me.

"You are." Court showed her the wine bottle and the glass before sitting them on the side table. "You drank some wine."

"Well, yeah, but only half a glass. I don't drink that much but I'm no lightweight." She burst into giggles before running her hands over her body. "Definitely not a lightweight. Do you guys think the king will find me too fat?"

"No," I said. "Your body is perfect."

"Thank you." Her pleased smile was back. "I think your body is perfect, too." She eyed Court. "I've been thinking about your perfect bodies a lot this week. Can I see you guys naked? Pretty please?"

Court's face was a dark green, and he gave me a helpless look. "What do we do with her?"

"Put her to bed," I said.

"Yes," Evie giggled before slinging her arm around my shoulders. "Take me to bed, you green studs."

She pealed more laughter as Court raised his eyebrow at me. "Studs?"

I shrugged. I had no idea what she meant either, but it didn't matter. We needed to get her to bed before she passed out.

"You are going to bed to sleep, little human," I said.

Evelyn pouted adorably. "But you said you and Court would fuck me."

Court's gaze turned to me faster than a wicken running through the jungle.

"I did not say that," I said.

"You kind of said that," Evelyn said.

"Bran," Court said.

"I did not," I said. "Court, she is drunk."

"I am not drunk." Evelyn puffed out her chest before giggling. "Hey, do you guys ever use contractions? Like ever?"

"We do not know what…"

"Do not." She grinned at me and pinched my cheek. "Say 'don't', Bran."

"Don't," I repeated.

Her grin widened, and she turned to Court. "Now you."

"Don't," Court said obediently.

She giggled. "So cute."

"Stand up, Evelyn." I stood and took her hands before pulling her to her feet.

She swayed wildly and then leaned against me. "My head is so…" she made a twirling motion next to her head with her finger.

"Because you drank too much wine," I said.

Court joined us as Evelyn frowned. "I only had half a glass."

"Gallberry wine is much more potent than the wine you make on earth," I said. "For someone as little as you, it would only take a few sips for you to feel its effects."

"I'm not little." Her hand traced my chest before she reached out and traced Court's chest. I heard his sharp inhale as she smiled at him. "Although, I suppose compared to you guys, I'm on the smaller side. You're so big, aren't you?"

Court nodded. Evie's hand was still tracing his chest, and I could see his erection tenting his pants.

"I'd like to find out how big you are," Evelyn's voice grew lower, "how big and hard and warm you are."

149

"Krono," Court groaned when her fingers slipped across his stomach and then tugged on the waistband of his pants, "we need to get her to bed, Bran. Right now."

"Yes, please. I want to fuck both of you," Evelyn said.

Court and I groaned in unison, and cursing under my breath, I lifted Evelyn into my arms and carried her toward her bedroom.

"No, your room." Evelyn pounded on my back. "My room is too cold."

I ignored her and carried her into her bedroom. Court pulled back the quilt and the extra blankets, and I put Evelyn on the bed. She was still dressed, but helping her change into her night clothes was dangerous.

As disappointment crossed her face, I pulled up the blankets before she could climb out of bed. "Why won't you guys fuck me?"

"You must go to sleep, Evelyn," I said.

She yawned, disappointment still thick on her face. "I'm not tired. I want to fuck you."

"We cannot," Court said.

"You don't want me," she said.

"We do," Court said.

"Court, be quiet," I said.

He ignored me. "We do want you, little human, but not while you are drunk."

"Tomorrow then?" she said.

Without looking at me, Court nodded. "Yes, if you still want us to fuck you tomorrow, we will."

"Court, enough!"

My voice was raised in anger, and I immediately regretted my tone, knowing it would scare the little human. To my surprise, she reached out and caught my hand without fear. "Don't be angry with him, Bran. Okay? Please?"

"Okay," I said. "Go to sleep, Evie."

Her smile turned sly. "Kiss, Bran."

When I hesitated, she squeezed my hand. "Kiss, Bran."

I leaned over her and pressed my mouth against hers. She pushed her tongue against my mouth, and, unable to resist her, I parted my lips so she could slip her tongue into my mouth. I brushed her tongue with mine and then pulled back before I did something I would regret.

She pouted before smiling at Court. "Kiss, Court."

I stepped back, and Court took my place a little too eagerly. I watched as he bent over the bed and kissed Evelyn. My cock swelled, my pants turning uncomfortably tight, as I watched them kiss with open mouths and questing tongues.

When Evelyn took Court's hand and placed it on her breast, he cupped it and teased her nipple with his thumb. Her back arched, and she moaned. The sound was almost my undoing. Before I lost control completely, I grabbed Court's arm, pulling him away from Evelyn.

He glared at me, and I shook my head. "You cannot."

He ran a hand through his hair before taking a deep breath. "You are right. Evelyn, I am sorry. I should not have done that. Please forgive me."

We both looked at Evelyn. She was already asleep or passed out, and I tugged the covers up to her shoulders, resisting the urge to brush my lips across hers. I followed Court out of her room and shut the door, leaning against it and sighing with relief.

Court studied me. "She wants us to fuck her, Bran."

"She was drunk," I said.

"And when she is sober tomorrow?" Court said.

"She will most likely not remember what happened," I said.

"But if she does?" Court persisted. "If she asks us to fuck her when she is clear of mind?"

"She will not," I said. "But if she does, we have to say no. She is our future queen. Besides, she only wants to sleep with us because she has never slept with a Draax before and is afraid she will be unable to please the king. She worries that he will send her back to Earth if she does not please him in bed and also that he will ask another to join them."

"He probably will," Court said.

"I know." I rubbed at my temples. "She has only slept with one human male, and he did not even make her come."

Court's noise of disgust almost made me grin. "Human males are useless."

"Yes, but we cannot fuck her, Court. If she tells the king…" I glanced at Bella's closed bedroom door.

"She will not," Court said. "You know that, Bran. She does not want Bella to be an orphan like she was."

I knew Court was right, but I said, "Still, we cannot sleep with her. She is our future queen and what if she became pregnant? She said she was highly compatible for breeding, remember?"

"We have plenty of the rubber tubes that humans use to prevent breeding," Court said.

He was right. Shortly after she moved in with us, Dana had begun making Court wear them on the occasional time she would let him fuck her pussy rather than her ass. We hadn't known it then, but her plan to destroy our friendship was already in motion.

"We cannot," I repeated.

Court folded his arms across his chest, that familiar stubborn look stamped all over his face. "If tomorrow, when she is sober, she asks me to fuck her, I will, Bran."

"Court," I said, "do not act like a stubborn froden. The human is not for us."

Court just shook his head before turning and walking toward his bedroom. "I will not deny her what she wants."

Evelyn

I HOVERED OUTSIDE OF THE KITCHEN. I COULD HEAR THE higher pitch of Bella's voice and the low murmurs of Bran and Court responding to her. I rubbed at my aching temples. I just needed to go in there, apologize, and hope they weren't furious with me.

I couldn't exactly remember *everything* that happened last night, but I did remember asking them to fuck me. I groaned, fresh heat blooming in my cheeks as my head ached even more with the extra blood rushing to it. Oh God, what did happen last night? I had some confusing memories of kissing someone... Bran, maybe? Or Court? Hell, it could have been both... I couldn't remember.

All I knew was that I'd made a fool of myself and possibly told them that I was afraid of banging the king and... oh my God, I couldn't go into the kitchen. I just couldn't.

You have to, Evie. You need to apologize. Just be an adult and say you're sorry, and then never, ever, ever drink wine ever again.

I sucked in a breath, walked into the kitchen and sat down in my usual seat.

"Hi, Evie girl!"

Bella's voice was decidedly loud this morning. I tried not to wince as I smiled at her. "Hi, Bella."

"Look, I colour!" Bella showed me the piece of paper sitting next to her bowl of faven. It was a picture of what I was pretty sure was a Skuun. Bella had scribbled yellow and red over the entire piece of paper, not even close to staying in the lines, but I smiled again at her.

"Good job, Bella. Is that a Skuun?"

"Skuun!" Bella hollered before waving her arms and her tail in the air.

She held her spoon in one hand, and faven flew through the air and landed with a splat on my arms.

"Bella," Bran scolded lightly. "No pretending to be a Skuun at the breakfast table. Apologize to Evelyn for getting faven on her."

"Sorry, girl." Bella patted my arm with the end of her tail. "Girl mad at Bella?"

"No, honey, I'm not mad." I took the napkin Court held out to me and wiped the faven from my arms. "Thank you, Court."

"You are welcome, Evelyn."

I glanced up at him, my breath catching in my throat. The way Court was looking at me. Like he was a large jungle cat, and I was his prey was... *shit*... was it turning me on?

I swallowed hard, the napkin pressed against my arm. What the hell happened last night? I hadn't actually slept with them, had I?

Don't be stupid, Evie. You were fully dressed when you woke up. You think you stripped, fucked them, and then got dressed again?

"Here, human."

Bran was holding out a bowl of faven, and I dropped the napkin and took the bowl. He wasn't looking at me like he wanted to lick me all over. In fact, he wasn't looking at me at all, and dismay flooded through me.

I took a deep breath. "I need to apologize for last night. I'm sorry for what I said and did."

"It is fine." Bran was stirring the faven in his bowl, still not looking at me. "You were," he glanced at Bella, "not yourself. We understand."

"I found the wine at the back of the fridge after I put Bella to bed and thought I would have half a glass," I said. "I didn't realize it would affect me the way it did. I'm so sorry."

"We know," Bran said. "You do not need to keep apologizing. Is that not right, Court?"

Court didn't reply, and I risked another look at him. He was still studying me with heat in his gaze, and I squirmed in my chair as my nipples hardened and my pussy tingled. What the hell was happening to me? How could a look affect me like this? There was something wrong with me.

He touched your tits last night, do you remember? He kissed you and felt your tits after you begged him to fuck you.

My face flamed, and I stared unseeingly into my bowl of faven. Oh God. Was it possible for someone to die of embarrassment?

"Court," Bran prompted.

"He is right," Court finally said. His voice was low and rough. I wondered if that's how he would sound after we fucked. After he'd come in me and we were lying in bed, warm and content and –

Evie, stop!

"Okay," I croaked out. "Well, I appreciate how understanding you're being."

I stood up, my embarrassment and my appetite gone completely under a wave of lust so strong it wanted to knock me off my feet.

"Where are you going, human?" Bran asked.

"I'm not very hungry this morning," I said. "Please excuse me."

I hurried out of the kitchen and back to my room. I shut

the door and stared at my bed before walking to the bathroom and turning on the shower. My pussy was throbbing, and I couldn't ever remember being this turned on before.

I shuddered as I stripped off my clothes, stepped into the shower and stood under the hot water spray. Already my hand was inching toward my pussy, and I took a glance at the closed bathroom door before sliding my hand between my thighs. If just Court's voice, if just the way he looked at me, was enough to make me this horny, what would it be like to have him in my bed? Between my thighs? His mouth on my nipples. On my clit.

I moaned and rubbed at my clit, which was already slick with my cream. I braced my other arm on the wet wall of the shower and pressed my mouth against my upper arm to stifle my moans of pleasure as I circled my clit and pretended it was Court's fingers.

No, not just Court. Bran too.

Yes. Definitely. Why be happy with just one when I could have both, right?

Bran in front of me, his dick rubbing against my stomach. Court behind me, his cock nestled between my ass cheeks as the warm water ran down over all three of us.

Bran's hands cupping my tits, his fingers playing with my nipples as Court rubbed my clit and slid his fingers inside of me. Both of them touching me, kissing me, making me crazy with need and...

I cried out into my arm as my climax washed over me. My body trembled, my legs were weak, and my breath came in harsh gasps against my arm as I leaned against the shower wall. I slipped my hand out from between my legs and stared at my fingers.

The orgasm was nice, and it took the edge off, but I needed more. My pussy was still throbbing, and despite the orgasm, I was weirdly unsatisfied. I needed something more than my fingers. I needed...

Dick. Two very large, very green dicks.

I blushed and grabbed the soap before standing under the spray of water again. Sleeping with Court and Bran was something I'd been thinking about all damn week. They both wanted me. Well, I wasn't sure that Bran did, but I knew for a fact that Court wanted me. And right now, I couldn't see what the problem was in sleeping with him.

I needed practice sleeping with a Draax, and I had one willing to let me practice on him. So, what was my hesitation?

Oh, I don't know. Maybe it's because you're supposed to be sleeping with the king, not a farmer! What if the king did find out? What if you got pregnant with Court's baby? The lady at the agency said it would probably only take once. Do you want to be responsible for Court's death?

My stomach curdled, and the remaining lust I felt died instantly. No, I certainly did not. The idea that Court would be killed for sleeping with me... no, that wasn't happening. I needed to stay away from him and hope that I could fake my sex skills enough to keep the king happy.

CHAPTER 14

Evelyn

"**P**retty!" Bella said.

I kissed the top of her head as we stared at the image. "Very pretty."

Bella had been waiting in my bedroom when I got out of the shower, and I'd spent all morning playing with her in her room. Lunch was quiet and awkward, and even Bella's happy chatter couldn't ease the tension between Court, Bran and me.

Over the last few days, during Bella's afternoon nap, Bran and Court had begun to teach me a card game that was popular on Draax. But the idea of sitting with them, trying to concentrate on a stupid game while I pretended I hadn't made a fool of myself in front of them, was unappealing. So, when Bella went for her nap, I hurried to my room like a frightened mouse and stayed there.

Bella had come to my room as soon as she'd woken, carrying a rectangular pink box that, after some fumbling on my part, I'd discovered was a camera.

"Again!" Bella pushed the camera at me, and I held it above our heads, pointing it down at us as Bella rested her cheek against mine.

"Say cheese, Bella."

"Cheese Bella!" Bella hollered, and I laughed and snapped the picture.

Bella stared at the picture on the screen and reached for the camera. "Now Bella take picture."

She pointed the camera at me, her tiny finger poised above the shutter button. "Say cheese Bella."

I laughed again. "Cheese Bella."

She took the picture, and I turned the screen toward me to study it. "Huh, that's not a bad picture, honey."

"Pretty Evie girl."

I kissed her soft cheek. "Thank you, honey."

She stood on my bed and turned around, bending over and wiggling her butt at me as her tail waved back and forth. "Take picture of Bella tail."

"Stop waving it around," I said.

She giggled and flicked it straight. I took the picture and showed it to her.

"Bella tail," she said. "No Evie girl tail."

"That's right," I said. "I don't have a tail to take a picture of."

She studied me for a moment. "Evie girl breasts?"

She tried to stick the camera down my shirt, and I laughed and tugged the camera away from her. "No, honey. We don't take pictures of breasts. Okay?"

"Okay." She grabbed the camera and slid off the bed. "I take picture of Papa. Bye, Evie girl."

"Bye, honey."

She scampered out of the room, slamming the door shut behind her, and I folded my legs under me before opening the nightstand drawer. I pulled out my broken PAR phone and the picture of my father. I studied his face, tracing the line of his jaw as my chest ached with sadness and sudden loneliness. God, I missed him. He'd been the only one who'd ever truly cared for me, and the pain of missing him only seemed worse with each passing year.

There was a knock on my door. Still holding the picture of my dad, I said, "Come in."

The door opened, and heat pooled in my lower belly when Court entered my room. "Hello, Evie."

"Hi, Court." I stared at the quilt as Court walked to the bed and sat down.

"Are you feeling all right?"

I nodded. "I had a bit of a headache this morning, but it's gone now. The gallberry juice at lunch helped."

"Good. Who is that?" He pointed at the picture of my father.

"My dad."

He held out his hand, and I handed the picture over with a slight tinge of trepidation. "It's the only one I have of him. Please be careful."

"I will." He studied the picture and then handed it back. I propped the picture against the lamp on the nightstand. I didn't have to hide the picture anymore. There was no Alex to come along and rip it up just to make me cry.

When I turned back, Court was staring at my breasts. I didn't mind. It made me feel good if I was being honest.

"What is this?' He pointed to my PAR phone.

"It's my phone."

He picked it up, staring at its shattered screen. "I have seen human communication devices, but never one like this."

"It's really old," I said. "Most people have newer versions."

He didn't say anything, and I cleared my throat. "I should

probably just throw it away because it's broken, but I have some pictures on it, and I keep hoping that maybe I'll be able to get them off it somehow."

He stood up. "Come, little human. I might be able to help you retrieve your pictures."

"Seriously?" I slid off the bed and followed him out of my room and down the hall to his.

He nodded and walked to the small desk in the corner of his room. A tablet, a hologram machine, and a large, silver rectangular device I didn't recognize were sitting on the desk. He sat on the chair and studied the bottom of my phone before opening a drawer and rummaging through it. He pulled out a black cord and connected the cord to my phone before plugging the other end into the rectangular device.

"How do you turn on your communication device?" he asked.

I pushed the button until the green light at the top flickered on. "It's on now, but I don't think this will work. The screen stays dark, and even voice commands won't work."

He pushed a button on the rectangular device. It whirred to life, something inside of it making a low humming sound as lights flickered across the edge of it.

"What is that?" I asked.

"It is a hrotti."

"A hrotti," I repeated. "I still have no idea what that is."

Court grinned as a hologram screen appeared in the air above the hrotti. The words were in Draax, and he swiped his finger across the hologram, moving rapidly through several screens. "It is like an earth computer, only better. Much better."

"Oh, okay," I said.

He made a few more swipes, and I squeaked in excitement when my pictures suddenly appeared on the hologram screen. "My pictures!"

Court grunted in satisfaction before pushing a few more buttons. The hrotti's humming noise grew louder, and I watched in fascination as a section of it slid open and a silver square piece of metal was ejected. Court picked it up. It was no bigger than the tip of my finger, and he held it out for me.

"What's this?" I asked.

"I transferred all the pictures and other data on your communication device to this. It is like a," he paused, "storage unit. The king will give you your own tablet when you are at the palace. Ask one of the Draax there to show you how to transfer the information from this to your tablet."

"Really?"

He nodded, and I took the square piece of metal and studied it for a few seconds before slipping it into my pocket. I was stupidly happy, and without thinking about it, I threw my arms around Court's broad shoulders and hugged him hard. "Thank you, Court. Thank you so much. You have no idea how much this means to me."

His arms slipped around my waist, and I twitched when he pulled me into his lap. I tried to stand, and he shook his head, his big hands holding me tight. "No, little human, stay on my lap."

"I'm too heavy to sit on your lap," I said.

He laughed. "Hardly, Evie."

I chewed nervously at my bottom lip, feeling awkward and a little turned on. "Thank you again. I appreciate you saving my pictures like that."

"You are welcome." His gaze dropped to my mouth, and his hands tightened around my hips. "I would like a kiss, Evie."

"I – sorry, what?" His blunt request sent me off kilter.

"A kiss. As a thank you for what I did. One… sweet… kiss."

His voice had gone low and rough again, like in the kitchen, and my lower belly muscles clenched in anticipation. It was madness to kiss him, but that didn't stop me from lowering my mouth to his. I pressed my lips against his, moaning when his tongue immediately flicked across my upper lip.

"Open, Evie," he demanded.

I opened my mouth, and he cupped the back of my skull, holding me steady as he explored my mouth with his tongue. I felt drugged with pleasure almost immediately, the strokes of his tongue, the feel of his hard chest pressing against my breasts, the way he coaxed and teased with gentle brushes of his lips against mine.

Kissing Court was glorious. I wanted it to last forever.

He pulled back, and I whimpered in disappointment before trying to press my mouth against his again.

"Wait," he said.

I took a trembling breath as Court brushed his thumb over my cheekbone. Tight pressure was around my waist, and I looked down to see his tail wrapped around it. He looked a little embarrassed for some reason, and he immediately uncoiled his tail from around my waist.

"I will have sex with you if you'd like."

"Sorry, what?" I stared at him. Did he just say what I thought he said?

"I will have sex with you," Court said. "Bran shared with me what you told him last night."

"What I told him last night…" I sounded like a parrot.

"Yes." Court's other hand rubbed slow circles on my lower back. "That you have never been with a Draax before and are afraid you will not please the king in bed. I will have sex with you and show you what it is like to be with a Draax so you will not worry about pleasing the king."

"Oh, um… that's very generous of you, but we can't," I said.

He scowled, his big body stiffening. "Why not?"

"I'll probably get pregnant," I said.

Court relaxed beneath me. "I have those rubber sheaths."

"Condoms," I said.

He nodded. "Yes, I have plenty of them."

"What about Bran?"

"What about him?" Court tensed again.

"Will he be upset if you sleep with me?"

He shook his head, but I saw the doubt in his eyes. It was my turn to cup his face and make him look at me. "Bran told me you used to share women, but now you don't. Why?"

"It does not matter," he said. "We no longer share our women and are both fine with it."

"Are you?" I studied him a little closer.

"Yes."

"Have you slept with a woman without Bran before?"

He looked away, and I used gentle pressure to turn his face toward me again. "Have you?"

"No," he admitted.

"Then why are you offering to sleep with me?" I asked.

"Because Bran will not sleep with you, and I want you very much."

I hoped he didn't see the disappointment on my face. I was pretty sure Bran didn't want me, but to have it confirmed weirdly upset me.

I wanted to laugh at myself. Not even a month ago, the idea of sex with two Draax at once had terrified me. Now, I was upset that I only had the chance to sleep with one. I was losing my mind.

"Evie?" Court said. "Will you accept my offer to help?"

"You really are okay with sleeping with a woman without Bran?" I said.

"Yes." His voice was sincere enough, but I could see the truth on his face. After years of being terrorized by Alex, I learned to tune in to other people's emotions. Knowing exactly what kind of mood Alex was in, from nothing more than the look on his face or the way he held his body, had saved me from a beating more than once.

Once the gallberry juice had healed me from my beating and I was no longer distracted by the pain, I'd found it easy to read Court's emotions. They washed across his face like water over sand. Bran was difficult to read. I was only sure of his emotional state when he was with Bella. The happiness and love practically radiated from him and couldn't be hidden.

But Court? He might not want to admit it, but his emotional armour was not nearly as thick as Bran's. Even now, I could see the guilt and the anxiety on his face. I could feel it in the stiffness of his body, see it in the way his tail flicked back and forth, the end of it thumping out a steady rhythm against the rungs of the chair.

He wanted to have sex with me, but he would be wracked with guilt afterwards. I couldn't do that to him.

I pressed my forehead against his and took a deep breath. "Thank you for offering, Court, but I don't think it's a good idea."

"It is," he said.

"It isn't. If we sleep together, it'll make you feel guilty and cause tension between you and Bran."

"It will not," he insisted.

I lifted my head, and he cupped the back of my skull

again. "Perhaps there will be some guilt, but just as I am helping you, you can help me."

"What do you mean?" I said.

"Bran does not feel the way that I do. He has slept with a female without me. Eventually, he will look for a mate to help him raise Bella and have more children. We tried to share a mate before, and it," he paused, "ended badly."

"What happened?" I asked.

"I do not wish to talk about it." His tail hit the rungs of the chair so hard I was surprised it didn't crack them. "Just like you must learn how to sleep with a Draax and please the king, I must learn how to sleep with a female on my own. We would be helping each other."

He made a certain kind of sense. Maybe it would be helpful to him. Or was that just my desire to sleep with him convincing me it would? Shit, I had no idea.

"Can I think about it?" I said. "I need a bit more time."

"Yes." He pressed a brief kiss against my mouth. "I want this, little human, but I will not force you to fuck me if you do not wish to. You do not have to be afraid of me."

I gave him a startled look. That thought had never crossed my mind. "I know that, Court. I don't think you'll force me to do anything, and I'm not afraid of you or Bran."

"Are you not?"

"No," I said. "I know that sometimes I flinch or act afraid, but that's an instinct. I hate that I do it and hope I'll eventually stop, but I promise I'm not afraid of you or Bran. You both have been very kind to me and saved my life by giving me the gallberry juice."

He gave me another kiss, but I pulled away before giving in to my urge to deepen it. "I won't make you wait long for my decision. I promise."

Evelyn

NOT MAKING COURT WAIT LONG FOR MY DECISION WAS THE understatement of the year. Our conversation had taken place eight hours ago, and here I was, standing in front of his bedroom door.

I glanced at my body, wishing that I had something a little sexier to wear than my tank top and shorts. Shivering from the cold, I glanced at Bran's closed door. It was late, after midnight, and the entire house was quiet and dark.

I still wasn't one hundred percent certain that I was making the right choice, but my desire to be with Court had overridden the last of my worries.

It would be better if Bran joined us.

I glanced at his bedroom door with my hand raised to knock on Court's. Yes, it would be better with Bran there. In fact, it didn't feel right to me that we were doing this without him despite how little I knew about either of them, but I had no choice.

Bran didn't want me the way I wanted him, and I was afraid the king would send me packing if I weren't good in bed. And Court needed my help learning to be with a woman without Bran.

This was a good thing, I told myself before rapping softly on Court's door. I was helping him, and he was helping me. Soft light spilled out from under his door, so at least I didn't have to worry about waking him.

The door opened, and Court's look of pure delight washed away the rest of my doubt.

"Hello, little human."

"Hello, Court. Can I come in?"

"Yes." He stepped aside, and I walked into his bedroom, my nerves singing at me as I brushed past his half-naked body. He was wearing just a pair of sleep pants, and I stared at him in the flickering light of the fireplace. His room was deliciously warm compared to mine.

He stared at the goosebumps on my arms and legs before his gaze settled on my tits. Warmth ignited in my belly, starting a slow burn of need, and I took a deep breath. "I'm sorry it's so late."

"You do not need to be sorry. I am happy to fuck you any time of the day or night."

A nervous giggle escaped from my lips. "How do you know that's what I'm here for?"

He gave me an adorable grin, pulled me into his arms, and reached down to squeeze my ass cheek. "Is there another reason you are in my room, Evie?"

"No," I admitted.

"I am very happy about your decision." He leaned down and nuzzled my neck, and a bolt of heat went through me when he licked my throat.

"Court," I squeezed his arms, and he lifted his head to look at me. "Are you absolutely certain you want to do this?"

"Yes." He stroked my arms, scowling at the goosebumps he could feel. He pulled the quilt off the bed and spread it out directly before the fireplace before placing a pillow on the floor. He opened the nightstand beside his bed and brought out a condom package that he put on the quilt next to the pillow. "Come here, Evie."

I joined him in the front of the fireplace, and he smiled at me. "You will be warmer here."

"Thank you," I said.

He pulled me into his arms again and traced my collarbone with his fingertips. "You are anxious."

I nodded. "A little."

"There is no need," he said. "I will not hurt you."

"I know," I said. "I'm more nervous about, uh, being naked in front of you and also making sure that you, uh, you know, enjoy yourself as well. I've only slept with one person before this."

He stroked my upper chest with his fingers. "You are beautiful, and I cannot wait to see you naked, spread out underneath me as I taste your sweetness."

"Wait, what do you mean, taste my sweetness?" I said as Court urged me down onto the blanket. The warmth from the fire and Court's body felt incredibly good as I kneeled beside him.

He pulled my tank top over my head and tossed it aside, staring at my naked upper body. I caught my breath when his hands cupped my breasts, and he brushed his thumbs over my nipples. They hardened immediately, and he made an approving sound before bending his head and kissing me.

I clutched at his trim waist, returning his kisses eagerly as he slid one arm around my back and held me tight. Our tongues touched, and I moaned into his mouth. He sucked on my tongue, and when I arched my back, he gave my nipple a light pinch that sent pleasure straight to my pussy.

He pushed me onto my back and laid beside me, one big thigh settling firmly between mine. He stroked my hair back from my face before smiling at me. "You are very beautiful, little human."

"Thank you. So are you," I said.

Tentatively, I ran my fingers over his chest and down his stomach. I could feel his dick pressing against my hip, and it made me a little bold as I slid one finger along the waistband of his sleep pants.

I'd never felt this kind of overwhelming lust before, and I was a little surprised by my strong reaction. Was it normal to be so turned on by a few kisses and touches? I had no idea and no one to ask. I hadn't felt this way with the first guy I'd slept with, but he'd been a stranger, and I hadn't wanted to have sex with him.

Tonight, I wanted sex with Court. Wanted it desperately.

My thumb grazed over one flat nipple, and Court's low groan made me shiver. He pressed a kiss against my neck before kissing his way down my chest. When his mouth closed around one taut nipple, I moaned loudly.

Court lifted his head, and I clutched at his hair, trying to push him back toward my breast. "Court, don't stop!"

"Shh," he said before kissing between my breasts. "You must be quieter, Evelyn. We do not want to wake Bella."

I glanced at his door before giving him a worried look. "I'm sorry."

"It is all right," he kissed between my breasts again, "but you must keep your voice down."

"I will," I said.

"That is my good girl."

I shivered all over when he called me his good girl and arched my back when he sucked on my nipple again. His tongue circled my nipple before he sucked hard, and I clamped my arm over my mouth to stifle my moans.

Holy God, it felt so good. His mouth was so warm, and his tongue... oh fuck, his tongue.

I arched again when he flicked it rapidly against the tip of my nipple before kissing his way to my other breast. His tongue sucked that nipple into an aching hardness, and I gasped when he bit it lightly.

He smiled up at me. His copper eyes were now a stunning reddish-gold, and I couldn't look away. He shifted off of me, and his hands reached for the waistband of my shorts. He tugged, and when I didn't lift my hips, he gave the underside of one breast a sharp nip.

"Lift your hips, human."

The demand in his voice sent fresh wetness to my core, and I raised my hips automatically, allowing him to pull my shorts down my legs. He tossed them aside, and I kept my legs tightly closed as he studied my sex. His fingers traced the small patch of dark brown hair on my mound, and I shivered.

"Court," I whispered. My nerves were returning, and maybe he sensed it because he kissed me again, his hand resting against the top of my pussy but not moving. I ran my hands over his broad back, feeling the muscles flex under my fingertips as he moved closer.

His kisses were beginning to feel like a damn drug to me. I pressed myself against him, my fingers digging into the firm flesh of his upper back as he kissed me repeatedly. When his thigh nudged at mine again, I spread them without hesitation.

His hand slid between my thighs, and his fingers cupped my pussy. I gasped and closed my legs, but his thigh between them blocked me from closing them completely.

"Court," I moaned as his fingers swept across my wet pussy lips.

"Shh, little human. I only wish to see how wet you are for me." A self-satisfied look crossed his face when he raised his hand and showed me his fingers. Before I could say anything, he'd stuck his index finger into his mouth and licked away my cream.

"Delicious," he said.

I flushed with embarrassment, and he smiled before reaching between my legs again. I was squirming beneath him, feeling both awkward and turned on and not sure how to deal with it.

I wanted him to touch me, but the careful way he stared at me as he stroked the lips of my pussy was making me feel naked and exposed in a way I'd never felt before. Was I supposed to –

"Holy fuck!" The expletive came flying out of my mouth before I could stop it.

Court's thumb was brushing against my clit, and his finger was... oh fuck, his finger was sliding into me and...

"Fuck," I moaned again.

"Shh, little human," Court said.

I nodded, my entire body straining toward him as he brushed his thumb over my clit. It was so light, barely a touch, and I grabbed at his wrist. "Harder."

He grinned. "Soon."

"No, now. Please?" I pleaded.

A second finger joined the first, and I clenched around him in surprise. He groaned, his pelvis rocking against mine, and I made another soft pleading sound.

To my relief, he rubbed my clit with firm pressure, and I let my legs fall apart, my nails digging into his wrist as I rubbed my pussy against his hand. It felt amazing. Fucking amazing, actually. The roughness of his thumb against my clit, the way his eyes glittered so hotly as I fucked his fingers, was sending me closer and closer to the edge.

I reached for the pleasure that danced just out of reach, crying out with frustration when Court pulled his hand away from my pussy.

"No!" I smacked him on the chest and glared at him. "Court, no! I was so close."

His teasing grin both irritated me and set me on fire with fresh need. "I want to taste your sweetness, little human."

He kissed his way down my body, this time leaving no doubt in my mind what he meant. I was so worked up, so desperate to come, that I didn't feel any embarrassment about Court tasting my pussy. In fact, I spread my legs wide when he settled his big body between them and pulled on his hair when he kissed the curve of my belly instead of moving lower.

"Not there," I said and pulled his hair again.

He laughed, his breath warm on my skin, and kissed above my navel. "So impatient, little human."

"Do what you said you would do," I said. "Right now."

"Yes, sadora."

I had no idea what sadora meant, but before I could ask, his lips were pressing against my pubic bone, and I stopped caring what it meant. I arched my pelvis, squeezing his shoulders with my legs and pushing on the top of his head.

His low laughter washed over my curls, and then... oh God, then...

The feel of his tongue brushing across my pussy lips made me cry out again. I threw one hand over my mouth and used my other hand to press against the back of his head as he nibbled at my wet lips and then flicked his perfect, beautiful tongue against my throbbing clit.

I jerked and twitched against him, my thighs opening and closing around his shoulders as he licked that swollen, throbbing bundle of nerves until I was nearly frantic with need. His lips closed around it, and he sucked hard as he slipped his finger into my wet opening.

I screamed into my hand and climaxed immediately, the pleasure breaking me wide open and making my body shake wildly. Court licked me clean as I shivered and moaned and tried to drag air into my lungs.

I didn't know why I looked at the door. Was it a flicker of motion? A feeling of being watched?

I didn't know, but my gaze lifted to the door, and my breath caught in my throbbing lungs when I saw Bran standing there. He was leaning against the closed door, his upper half gloriously naked, his lower half covered only by his thin sleep pants.

I was only vaguely aware of Court sitting up and yanking down his pants, of his hand reaching for the condom next to the pillow, of the sound of the foil being ripped open.

I couldn't take my gaze from Bran. Was he really there, or was it just an orgasm-fueled fantasy?

I didn't realize I had closed my thighs until Court pushed on my knees. "Open your legs, Evie."

"Court," I whispered before turning my gaze to him. "Bran is here."

Court stared across the room, and there was no mistaking the happiness that crossed his face. "He enjoyed watching you come on my mouth, little human. We will show him how you look coming on my cock."

He pushed on my knees again. "Open for me."

I let him push my legs apart as I stared at Bran. When my legs were spread wide and my pussy fully exposed, Bran made a low groan. My gaze flickered to his crotch, and I bit my bottom lip. Bran's hand was shoved down his pants, and he was jerking off, the outline of his cock visible against the thin material.

When the head of Court's cock pressed against my opening, I returned my gaze to his in a hurry. He was propped up above me, and he bent his head and pressed a kiss against my mouth. "Relax, sadora."

I rested my hands on his hips and took a deep breath as he pushed forward. I hadn't seen his cock before he pressed it against my hot core, and I was a little grateful for that. If he was as big as I suspected, I might have been tempted to call the whole thing off. I was more nervous than –

"Oh God!" The head of Court's cock sank into me, and I stared up at him as he stopped.

"All right, Evie?"

"Yes, I – yes, I'm good."

He smiled, and feeling nervous, I craned my neck to stare at Bran again. He was still leaning against the door, still stroking his cock, and the slight smile he offered me was oddly comforting. I stared at him as Court pushed forward, forcing my pussy to take inch after inch of his thick cock. Just when I felt stretched and full to the limit, Court stopped and pressed a kiss against my neck.

"Are you all right, little human?"

"Yes," I whispered. I looked back at Court and touched his face with my fingertips. "I… it's a lot."

I blushed at how dumb I sounded, but Court smiled and pressed a kiss against my lips. "Your pussy is so tight, sadora. You have done well to take all of me."

He made a few light thrusts, and I moaned and squeezed my knees around his hips.

"Shh, sadora. Look at Bran," Court said as he hooked one big hand behind my knee and lifted my leg a little. "See how much he enjoys watching you be fucked by me."

I turned my gaze obediently to Bran. Even from across the room, I could see the liquid desire, the heat and the want in his gaze, and Court groaned when my pussy squeezed around him. "Relax your pussy, little human, please."

There was almost a note of begging in his voice, and I

smiled at Bran as a ripple of power went through me. Still holding Bran's gaze, I said, "Fuck me, Court."

Court groaned again, and I clutched at him when he moved in and out. He thrust lightly at first, his hand gripping my knee in a tight hold, but his rhythm soon turned harder and deeper. I clung to his waist, switching my gaze between Court and Bran, listening to their mutual soft groans as Court fucked me with deep strokes and Bran's hand moved harder and faster over his dick.

"Touch yourself, Evie," Court said.

I slipped my hand between my legs and rubbed at my slippery and swollen clit, my breath catching in my throat at the new pleasure.

"You will come for us again," Court said.

"Yes, Court," I said.

I heard Bran groan from across the room, and I looked at him as my fingers rubbed harder and faster.

"Good," Court whispered. "Watch Bran as you come, Evie. Show him how beautiful you are."

I moaned and circled my clit as the pleasure turned into a burning fire of need. I couldn't look away from Bran's face as Court's groans grew louder above me. I pulled on my clit and then climaxed, my pussy squeezing Court's cock, soft little cries spilling from my mouth as the exquisite pleasure infused my body.

Bran moaned harshly at my cries. His entire body stiffened, and his gaze burned into mine as he came, his big body twitching as the front of his sleep pants darkened with his release.

"Evie!" Court's hoarse cry snapped my gaze from Bran.

I stared up at him, holding him tightly as he drove deep into my body before coming with another hoarse cry. His tail flicked back and forth, and his body shook above me as the cords stood out in his thick neck.

He collapsed against me, his hot breath blowing against my neck and sending shivers down my spine. I stroked his back and kissed his shoulder. "You okay?"

"Hmm," he mumbled.

Court rolled off of me, lying on the quilt next to me, one leg thrown over mine and one big hand cupping my breast. I looked toward the door, Bran's name on my lips. I wanted – *needed* - him to join us, and disappointment flooded through me.

He was gone.

CHAPTER 15

Court

"No, Papa!"

When I walked into the kitchen, Bella was sitting in her chair, a bowl of faven in front of her, and her tiny hands balled into fists. Her face was a dark purple, and she was scowling at Bran.

I winced, mentally preparing myself for a very long day. Bella was usually an easy and happy child and was not prone to fits of temper or acts of rebellion. But when she was in a bad mood, she was a real groden, and nothing soothed her or made her happy.

After waking up on the floor of my room alone, I wasn't in that good of a mood myself. I had planned to fuck Evie again this morning before breakfast, and I had no idea how she'd snuck out of my room without me waking.

I'd showered and dressed, trying not to be disappointed, but my mood was dark. I should have been happy. Bran had joined us – sort of – and the lingering feelings of unease and guilt had disappeared when he appeared in my room last night.

I was pleased he'd joined us, but I was worried about the little human. Did she regret what we did? Was that why she left without waking me?

"Bella, eat your faven," Bran said. He looked tired and tapped the table next to Bella's bowl of faven.

Bella glared at him before her tail lashed out to whack him across the arm. "Bella no hungry!"

"No hitting," Bran said in a sharp tone. "Do you want to spend the day in your room alone?"

I blinked in surprise, and Bella immediately burst into tears. Bran wasn't the most patient Draax, but his patience for Bella was usually limitless.

Bran sighed and reached for Bella. "Meena, I am sorry. I did not mean -"

"No!" Bella sobbed and pushed his hands away. "Papa no touch Bella!"

"Meena," I leaned forward and held out my arms, "come to Uda."

"No!" She sobbed harder, her tail lashing back and forth like an angry wicken's. "Uda no touch Bella."

Bran rubbed at his temple as Bella's sobs grew louder. He knew as well as I did that nothing could be done once it got to this point. Bella would refuse soothing from either of us until she cried herself out. I hated it, and so did Bran. Watching Bella cry without being allowed to comfort her was terrible, but we had no choice. If either of us picked her up and tried to soothe her, it would only make it much worse.

"What's wrong?" Evie had to raise her voice to be heard over Bella's sobs as she hurried into the kitchen.

Her hair was wet, and she smelled fresh and clean. My

chest tightened in a weird way that I didn't understand or like. Why would it be so hard to breathe just because she was in the room?

"Bella is having a bad day," Bran said. "She is tired and -"

"Girl!" Bella lifted her head from the table and, still sobbing, held out her arms. "Girl hold Bella."

Bran's jaw dropped, and I knew I had an identical expression of shock. Evie immediately scooped Bella up from her chair. Bella wrapped her arms around Evie's neck and her tail around her forearm, clinging to her as she sobbed loudly.

"Shh, sweetie, shh." Evie swayed back and forth, rubbing Bella's back and kissing the top of her head. "It's all right, sweetie."

She walked back and forth in the kitchen, rubbing and patting Bella's back and murmuring soft words of comfort until Bella's sobs slowed to watery hiccups. Evie eased into a chair and kissed Bella's head again. Bella sat back and stared miserably at her, keeping her tail wrapped tightly around Evie's forearm.

"Oh, honey." Evie kissed her forehead. "Are you having a bad day?"

Bella stared up at her. "Bella no like day."

Evie smoothed Bella's hair back from her face. Without speaking, Bran wet a cloth and handed it to her. Evie wiped the tears from Bella's cheeks. Her face was still a dark purple, and her eyes were swollen from crying. Evie cleaned under Bella's nose and then returned the cloth to Bran.

"There, does that feel better?" she said as she studied Bella's face.

Bella nodded, but another tear dripped down her cheek. "I sad, girl."

"Why are you sad, honey?" Evie wiped the tear away with her thumb.

Bella glanced at Bran, another tear sliding down her cheek. "Bella hit Papa. Bella bad girl."

Bran's face twisted, and Evelyn immediately gathered Bella close before kissing her head again. "Well, it's never nice to hit someone, but I bet you'll feel much better if you say sorry to your papa for hitting him."

Bella leaned against Evie's chest and made a shuddering sigh before staring at Bran. "I sorry, Papa."

"I know, meena," Bran said. "You are not a bad girl."

"Papa love Bella?" Her little voice was pitched high with worry.

Bran leaned over and rested his forehead against Bella's. "Papa loves Bella. Always."

"Kiss, Papa," Bella said.

Bran kissed her before straightening, and Bella turned to me, her tear-streaked face solemn. "Kiss, Uda."

I kissed her, breathing in her scent and Evie's good, clean scent and resisting the urge to kiss her, too.

I settled back in my chair as Bran put a bowl of faven before Evelyn. She smiled, but her cheeks were pink, and she wouldn't quite meet his gaze or mine. "Thank you."

She ate a spoonful of faven, dipped the spoon into the bowl and scooped out more. "Here, Bella. You and I will share my faven this morning."

Bella ate the spoonful of faven without arguing and another wave of surprise went through me. Getting Bella to do anything when she was in a bad mood was incredibly difficult. I caught Bran's gaze, and he shrugged before returning to the sink. I ate my breakfast and watched Evelyn and Bella share their bowl of faven.

"BRAN, ARE WE GOING TO SPEAK ABOUT WHAT HAPPENED LAST night?"

I stood in the living room doorway, blocking Bran's exit. He had done a remarkable job of avoiding me all day, just like the little human, but I was determined to speak with him.

"What is there to talk about?" Bran refused to look at me, staring moodily into the fire instead. "You wanted to fuck the human, and you did."

"Keep your voice down," I said with a glance behind me.

"She is with Bella for her sleep ritual," Bran said. "She will not hear me."

Probably not, but I checked behind me again anyway. Today had been awkward and tense, and my stomach was twisted into a knot so tight I'd had no appetite for dinner.

Bella's bad mood had lasted all day, and the only thing that seemed to soothe her was being with Evelyn. Evie had spent all of her time with Bella. She'd even brought Bella to her room and allowed her to sleep in her bed with her for her afternoon nap.

Bran tried to give Evelyn a break from Bella just after supper, but the little girl threw another tantrum, clinging to Evelyn and refusing to let go. Evie took Bella back to her room and cuddled and played with her until it was Bella's bedtime.

I wanted to blame the tenseness on Bella's mood, but I was fooling myself. The three of us had been walking around on eggshells all day, and I was tired of it.

"You joined us," I said.

He shrugged, refusing to look at me. "I heard the human moaning, and I merely wanted to tell you to be quiet before you woke Bella. When you fuck her tonight, tell her to be quieter."

"Stop it," I growled. "Do not act like you did not enjoy last night as much as I did. You stayed, Bran. You stayed and watched me fuck the human."

Bran's face was dark green, and his tail flicked agitatedly back and forth. "What do you want me to say, Court?"

"I want you to admit that you want to fuck the little human. That you enjoyed last night. That you," my voice caught in my throat, "miss what we used to have."

He didn't reply, and my tail drooped with frustration and sorrow. "She wants us both, Bran."

His body tensed. "How do you know that?"

"She told me. Will you help me give her what she wants?"

"What if she tells the king?"

"You know she will not," I said. "Do not use that as an excuse. I want you to join us, and so does she."

"The last time we fucked a woman together, it did not end well."

I swallowed my frustration and kept my voice even. "Evelyn is not like Dana."

"We do not know that," Bran said. "We barely know her."

"She is not like Dana," I repeated.

He finally turned his gaze to mine. "Dana was sweet in the beginning. Have you forgotten that, Court?"

"No, I have not," I said. "But we cannot judge all females by how Dana was."

He laughed bitterly. "Are you serious? You, of all Draax, are telling me not to judge females?"

My face grew hot. "I am just saying that -"

There was a noise behind me, and I turned to see Evelyn standing in the doorway. She gave us both an anxious look and crossed her arms over her torso. "Bella is asleep."

"Thank you, human," Bran said as he stared into the fire. "I am sorry you had to care for her for the day."

"It's fine," she said. "I didn't mind."

Bran grunted, his tail thumping against the sofa. Evelyn pressed her lips together before taking a deep breath. "Is everything all right with you two?"

"Just fine," Bran said, the sarcasm heavy in his voice. "Why would it not be?"

"Stop it, Bran," I replied.

No reply but the thumping of his tail.

Evelyn's face was bright red, and she looked on the verge of tears. "It's been a long day," she said, "I think I'll go to bed early."

"Human, wait," I said as she backed out of the room.

She turned and disappeared down the hall, and I scowled at Bran. "Krono, you can be a real," I searched my memory for an appropriate earth insult, "asshole when you want to be, Bran."

I left the room before he could reply. I caught up to Evelyn as she reached her room, and I took her by the arm. "Little human, wait."

"I'm sorry," she said as she stared at her closed door. "I'm so sorry. I didn't mean to ruin your friendship with Bran."

"You have not," I said. "Bran and I are still friends."

"You're angry with him." She turned and searched my face.

"Because he is being a froden," I said.

She paused. "What's a froden?"

I tried to think of a similar earth word. "Idiot."

She sighed. "He isn't. He's just upset about last night."

"Are you upset about last night?" I wanted to pull her into my arms, wrap my tail around her waist, and kiss her.

"No," she said. "I enjoyed it very much."

"I enjoyed it as well, little human." I gave in to my desire and pulled her close, snapping my tail around her waist and bending to kiss her.

She pressed her tiny hands against my chest. "Wait."

"What is wrong?" I asked.

"Bran is upset with us. Is he – I mean, does he regret coming in last night?"

"A little." I hated telling her that, but I couldn't lie to her.

She sagged against me, resting her forehead against my chest. "Maybe I should apologize."

I kissed the top of her head. "No, you have nothing to apologize for. It was his choice to come into my room last night, his choice to touch himself as he watched you being fucked."

She glanced up at me, her cheeks red as she licked her lips and studied my mouth. "I really did enjoy last night, Court."

"Does that mean you will join me in my room again tonight?"

She chewed on her bottom lip. "Yes, if you want me to join you."

"I do," I said before nuzzling her neck. "I have thought of nothing all day but fucking your warm, wet pussy."

Her flush deepened, and I grinned before reaching down to grip her ass. "Come to my room, Evie."

She kissed my chest through my shirt. "I just want to have a quick shower first. Give me fifteen minutes."

"You can shower in my bathroom," I said before sucking on her earlobe. "I could help you."

She moaned, her curvy body shuddering against mine. "Thank you, that's very nice of you to offer, but I'm not sure I'm ready for you to see all this," she waved her hand up and down her body, "in the harsh light of the bathroom."

I had no idea what she meant, but I nodded and dropped

my arms. "All right. Come to my room when you are finished."

"I will." She stayed where she was, and I raised my eyebrow at her.

"What are you waiting for, little human?"

Her gaze dropped to her waist, and my skin grew hot again when I realized my tail was still wrapped around her waist. I released her and cleared my throat. "Sorry."

She smiled and slipped into her room. I hesitated in the hallway. I had told Evelyn that I needed her help in learning to fuck a woman without Bran, and that was true, but I couldn't deny if there were even a chance that I could persuade him to join us, I would do it.

I returned to the living room where Bran still sat. "The human is having a shower and then coming to my room. You are welcome to join us again."

Thump, thump, thump.

I played my final hand, feeling a little guilty, but Krono, I had missed sharing a woman with my best friend. "Evelyn has been very sweet and patient with Bella. A simple thank you does not seem enough. Helping to ease her fear about sleeping with two Draax before the king asks her to do so would be a way to repay her kindness."

Thump, thump, thump.

"Just consider it, Bran. That is all I ask."

I returned to my room and quickly showered before turning on the fireplace. The storm was just as brutal tonight and I wanted my room to be warm for Evelyn. I hated that we could not even keep her warm enough. She was our female, and it was our duty to provide for her, keep her warm, protect her and –

She is not your female. She belongs to the king.

I cringed, my hands pausing in turning down the quilt on

186

my bed. There was a knock on the door, and I hurried over and opened it, smiling at Evelyn. "Come in, little human."

She followed me in, and I shut the door before staring down at her. Her soft, dark hair was piled on top of her hair, and I could smell the scent of her soap. She was wearing a t-shirt and a pair of shorts, and she pulled self-consciously at the hem of her shirt.

"I don't have any, um, sexy lingerie to wear," she said.

Lingerie was one human concept that neither Bran nor I – or any other Draax we knew – really understood. We had been with females who wrapped their bodies in silk or that scratchy material they called lace, and while it was pretty enough, I took no real notice of what a female wore when we were about to have sex. What did it matter? I wanted them naked, wanted every inch of their lovely, soft, pale skin revealed to me, and the sometimes difficult to remove clothing they wore only frustrated me.

Evelyn's easy-to-remove shirt and shorts were much preferable, and just knowing that she was naked beneath them made my cock hard.

"I like what you wear," I said to her. "It is easy to remove. There are no strange hooks or fasteners that are too small for my fingers."

She laughed – Krono, I loved her laugh – and said, "Well, I guess that's one argument for not wearing sexy underwear."

"You are sexy without it," I said. "I would prefer for you to be naked all the time."

Another sweet laugh. "I can't walk around naked in front of Bella, and besides, I would freeze to death."

I pulled her close, reaching down to cup her ass. "I would keep you warm, Evie."

"That's very nice of you," she said. I was wearing just my sleep pants, and her hands traced my biceps. "And you are very warm, but I can't spend my entire day glued to your hot body."

I grinned. "Why not?"

"Um… you know, I actually can't think of a reason why not," she said with a small smile.

I slipped my hands inside of her shorts and kneaded her firm ass. "When you slept with the human, did he fuck you in the ass?"

She turned bright red and shook her head. "Uh, no. No, we only had, um, regular sex."

I studied her red face, my fingers tracing the bottom curves of her ass cheeks. "Would you like to be fucked in the ass, human?"

"I'm not sure," she said. "I mean, it isn't something I ever thought of. Do you – is that something you like?"

I nodded. "Yes, very much. But if you do not want it, we will not do it."

"Well, I mean, it's probably something I should try. If the king wants me to sleep with him and a friend, that means the old DP, right?"

"DP?" I asked.

"Double penetration." She fanned her face. "God, this is embarrassing."

I didn't see what was embarrassing about our conversation, but I kissed her forehead and gave her a reassuring smile. "If you wish to practice anal sex with me, I am more than happy to help you."

Her giggle was full of nerves. "Thank you, I think. I just – I've heard it can hurt, so I'm nervous."

She squealed loudly when I slipped my finger between her ass cheeks and traced it along her anus.

"Shh," I said with a glance at a door.

"Sorry," she said, "but warn a girl before you try to stick your finger up her ass."

I laughed and squeezed her ass. "I was not trying to penetrate your ass, Evelyn. I just wanted you to get used to what if felt like to be touched there."

"Weird," she said immediately. "Very weird. I don't think anal sex is for me. Maybe the king won't like anal sex. Or I can convince him we don't need a third person."

"Maybe," I said. I did not want to scare her, but I was sure the king would want to share Evelyn, at least occasionally. Of course, if she said no, he would not force her, but I wasn't certain Evelyn would be brave enough to turn down our king's request. Her timid nature meant she might do something she was not comfortable with.

My tail lashed around her waist, squeezing tight, and she grunted softly. "Ouch, your tail is…"

"Sorry." I relaxed my tail and cupped her face. I needed to show Evelyn that anal sex could be pleasurable before she went to the king. "Having a cock in your ass can bring you pleasure, human. I want to show you how pleasing it can feel."

She swallowed, her cheeks still a bright red. "I – maybe. Can I think about it?"

I nodded, and she squeaked again when I picked her up and carried her toward my bed. I set her down beside it and quickly stripped her of her t-shirt and shorts before pulling my sleep pants down and stepping out of them. I was already half-hard, and she studied my cock with trepidation on her face.

"What is wrong?" I asked.

"Nothing. I just – I didn't see your penis last night, and it's uh… big," she said.

"All Draax have large cocks," I said.

"Right."

I slipped my arm around her waist and pulled her close before kissing her. Her mouth parted, and I cupped her breast, teasing her nipple with my forefinger and thumb as I tasted the minty sweetness of her mouth.

"You are a good kisser," I said when we broke apart.

She giggled. "Thank you, so are you."

I pulled on her nipple, smiling when she gasped. "Have you sucked a cock before?"

She shook her head, her gaze dropping to where my now completely hard cock brushed against her abdomen. "No, I haven't. But I want to learn."

I pressed on her shoulders. "Sit on the bed, Evelyn."

I would have preferred her on her knees in front of me, but I wanted her to be as comfortable as possible the first time she tasted my cock. She sat, spreading her legs so I could step between them. I gave her pussy a hungry look, my desire to have her suck my cock almost overridden by my desire to taste her again.

Krono, had I ever tasted a pussy as sweet as hers? I didn't think so.

"Court?" Her voice was hesitant.

I dragged my gaze from her pussy. "Perhaps I should eat your pussy again instead, little human."

I loved the way her pale skin flushed.

"Stop distracting me," she said with a small smile. "I need to learn how to give oral sex, remember?"

I touched her hair before pulling out the metal pins that kept her long locks on top of her head. I set them on the nightstand before smiling at how her hair flowed down her back. "You are so pretty, human."

"Thank you," she whispered. She was staring at my cock,

and I gripped the base of it and stroked it a few times as she watched.

She traced the length of it with the tips of her fingers, and I moaned, my grip tightening on the base.

"The skin is so soft," she said with wonderment in her voice.

A bead of precum escaped the tip, and I swiped my thumb through it before holding it out. "Taste, little human."

Tentatively, she licked the cum from my thumb. Her eyes widened, and she stared up at me. "It tastes like gallberries."

I smiled at her and cupped the back of her head, urging her mouth forward. "Open, Evie."

She opened her mouth and licked the head of my cock. I groaned, my hand fisting in her hair, and tried not to thrust my hips forward when she licked around the ridge. Her small hand held my cock just above my hand.

I let go, and she took a firmer grip, leaning forward and sliding her mouth around my cock. Her pretty pink lips tightened around my cock, and I groaned her name. It had been years since I had a mouth on my dick, and the feel of her wet, hot mouth was incredible.

She took more, her soft tongue licking my shaft as her hand squeezed and released.

"Take more," I urged, pushing lightly on her head.

She did what I asked, taking more in until my cock rested against the back of her throat. She pulled away, coughing a little, and gave me an apologetic look. "I'm sorry."

"You are doing very well." I rubbed my thumb across her swollen bottom lip. "Continue, sweet Evie."

She sucked on my cock again, already less timid, and I made a few light thrusts into her mouth. She sucked harder in response, and I groaned, rocking my hips back and forth as she sucked.

She reached between her legs, her fingers rubbing at her pussy, and my balls tightened when she made soft and muffled cries around my cock. Her fingers rubbed harder, her nostrils flaring as she sucked my dick.

My control was disappearing, and as much as I wished to come in my little human's mouth, my desire to fuck her was stronger. I pulled out of her with a soft pop, holding her hair firmly when she tried to lunge forward and take me into her mouth again.

"No, little human," I said as I used my free hand to pull her fingers away from her pussy.

"Please!" She pouted adorably at me. "I want to practice."

I leaned down and kissed her hard on the mouth, enjoying my taste that lingered on her tongue. "You will have plenty of time to practice sucking my cock. On your hands and knees on the bed."

She stared at me, and when she didn't move, I took her upper arm and lifted her into a standing position before turning her around and pushing on her back. "Hands and knees, little human."

"Court, I've never, um…"

"I know," I said. "Be my good girl and do as I say."

Her curvy body shuddered all over before she climbed onto the bed on all fours, and I smiled a little. I was not nearly as dominant as Bran, and for a moment, I enjoyed imagining how she would react to Bran's demands in bed.

My gaze flickered to the doorway, and, as if my thoughts had called to him, the door opened, and Bran slipped into the room. I stared steadily at him as he closed the door with a soft click and leaned against it.

His gaze turned to Evie, his eyes burning with the same lust that coursed through my body. The little human had reached between her legs and was rubbing her pussy again, her body rocking against her hand as she tried to bring herself relief. She hadn't noticed Bran, and I crowded closer to the bed and pushed her hand away.

"Stop, human."

She looked over her shoulder pleadingly. "Please, Court, it aches."

"I know, sweet sadora," I said. "Spread your legs for me."

She spread them only a little, and I pressed one hand on her upper back until her head was lowered to the bed and her cheek was pressed against the quilt. I used my other hand to push at her thighs until she was spread so wide I could see all of her pussy.

I smiled when Bran joined me. He stared at our little female's pussy, at how wet it was, at the swollen bud of her clit peeking out between her pink pussy lips inviting us to lick and suck.

Evelyn squirmed on the bed, and I stroked her inner thigh. "Shh, sadora."

"Court," she lifted her head and turned it to look at me again, "are you going to fuck me? I can't wait any... oh my God!"

Her little squeal of surprise was almost funny. But the way she tried to close her legs had both me and Bran reaching out automatically. He curved his hand around her left thigh, and I curved my hand around her right, keeping her legs wide open as we placed our other hands on her lower back and pinned her to the bed.

She squirmed again, and I squeezed her thigh. "Be still, sadora. Let Bran have a good look at your sweet pussy."

"Oh my God," she whispered, her gaze on Bran's face.

Bran raised a trembling hand and brushed his fingers over her swollen bud. She moaned, and her back arched, and more cream dripped out of her opening.

"Do you see how responsive she is?" I said to Bran as he swiped his thumb through her cream and tasted it.

"She tastes so sweet." His voice was hoarse, and he massaged her clit with his thumb as I stepped away. The little human kept her legs spread wide even when my hands left her, and Bran rubbed her clit in approval.

"Good, little human. Keep your legs open for us."

"Bran," she gasped as I tore open a condom package and rolled it over my dick, "please. Rub harder."

Bran gave her clit a little pinch that made her cry out with pleasure. He squeezed her hip. "Quiet, little human."

"I want to come," she said.

He caressed her ass. "You have to wait."

"I don't want to." The human's pout made me grin, but Bran gave her a stern look.

"You will do as I say, little human. You are not allowed to come until I say so."

"Court, please." Evelyn turned her gaze to me, and I shook my head.

"No, sadora. You will do as Bran says."

She made an angry little huff, and my grin widened as Bran laughed. I rubbed my dick against her wet pussy lips, and her angry sounds stopped immediately. She arched her back even more, presenting her sweet pussy to me like a gift. A gift I couldn't wait to play with.

"Good girl," Bran said, and the little human gave him a flushed and pleased look.

"She is so tight, Bran," I said as I pressed the head of my cock against her opening. "But she takes my cock very well."

We both watched her swollen lips spread around the head of my cock as I pushed forward. Bran groaned when I made a harder thrust, and Evelyn's pussy swallowed the head of my cock.

She made a moaning little cry, her body tensing a bit, and we both reached out to caress and rub our female's lower back and hips soothingly.

When she'd settled, I pushed forward again. Her pussy swallowed inch after inch of my dick. I stopped again when she tried to wiggle forward, her hands clenching in the sheets.

"Too much," she moaned. "I can't, please... too much."

"Shh," Bran leaned over and kissed her lower back before reaching under and rubbing her clit. "Shh, sadora. Relax your pussy."

She moaned and wriggled against Bran's finger as I pushed forward again. She made a low cry as she took the last of my cock, and both Bran and I rubbed her thighs and ass as I waited for her to adjust to my size. She was as tight as I remembered, and her tiny pussy clung to me as she panted and moaned.

"Pull her up," Bran demanded. He was stripping off his clothes, and I leaned forward, gritting my teeth when our female's pussy tightened around me, and grasped Evelyn's upper arms. I drew her up onto her knees, adjusting my stance a bit so that I stayed snug in her pussy.

Her hair was hanging in her face, and I used one hand to smooth it back before taking hold of her arm again. Her back was arched, her pussy was tight around my cock, and I kissed her shoulder as a naked Bran circled the bed and knelt on it in front of Evelyn.

She gave him a dazed look of need as he traced one finger between her full breasts up to the hollow of her throat and up the smooth column of her throat.

"Bran," she moaned.

He kissed her hard, and I made a few shallow thrusts as I watched him angle his mouth over hers and slide his tongue deep into her mouth. She took his kisses with eager enthusiasm, her body trembling as I made a deeper thrust.

Bran's hands cupped her tits, his fingers tugging on her nipples until they were a deep rose colour and hard. He bent his head, and Evelyn cried out when he sucked on her right nipple. He worked her nipple with his mouth and tongue as I rocked lightly behind her. Her head fell back to rest on my shoulder, and her mouth dropped open as she dragged in air.

I draped her arms behind my head, offering more of her tits to Bran. He accepted the gift eagerly, his teeth and lips marking her soft flesh as I gripped her hips and fucked her a little harder.

Bran, a small smile on his face, reached between her legs and rubbed her clit. Evelyn bucked her hips at him, and I drove deeper, relishing the feel of her wet, hot heat wrapped around my dick.

"Oh, oh, oh…"

Her soft cries were growing steadily louder. Bran glanced at the door before covering her mouth with his. He swallowed her cries as she rocked harder and faster, and I had to bury my face into her damp neck to muffle my loud groan when her pussy squeezed me tight as she climaxed.

Her body shook, and Bran continued to tease her clit until she tore her mouth away from his. "Please, stop," she gasped. "Too much."

He dropped his hand and bent his head to lick her nipples as she shuddered against me. I was barely holding it together, and Bran was fisting his cock with hard and rapid strokes as he sucked on Evelyn's nipple.

Her head fell onto my shoulder again, and I nuzzled her neck. "Sadora, open your eyes."

She mumbled something I didn't hear, and Bran gave her nipple a little pinch. "Look at us, sadora."

She squinted at us. "What?"

Bran glanced at me, and I nodded before kissing her cheek. "It's time to be our good girl again."

She shivered all over. Bran rubbed his hand over the gentle curve of her stomach before moving until he was kneeling closer to the edge of the bed.

"I want your mouth," Bran said to her. "You will be our good girl and suck my cock while Court fucks you. Do you understand?"

"Yes, Bran," she said.

Bran made a harsh groan, his hand tightening around his cock before he gave me a glittering hot look. "Put her back on her hands and knees."

I tugged on her arms until she lowered them and then pressed on her lower back. "Brace yourself on your hands, sadora."

She did as I asked, and I gathered her hair into a loose ponytail and used it to pull her head up. My tail wrapped around her waist, and I rested my other hand on her hip as Bran rubbed his thumb over her mouth.

"Open your mouth, sadora."

She opened, and I watched as Bran brushed the head of his cock against her lower lip before sliding it into her mouth. He groaned, his hands moving to take my place in holding her hair back.

"Look at me, Evelyn," Bran demanded as I made two hard thrusts.

She cried out around his cock, trying to turn her head to look at me, but Bran shook his head, his hands tightening around her hair. "No. Look at me when my cock is in your mouth."

She stared up at him, moaning softly when he reached

under her to cup one breast. "You are so beautiful, Evelyn. Suck, pretty human."

She sucked hard as Bran rocked back and forth. I was already increasing my pace but was trying to keep some control so that I didn't make our little female choke on Bran's cock. Krono, it wasn't easy. I wanted to fuck her hard and rough, wanted Bran to make her take all of his cock, but I restrained myself. She had never been with two Draax before, and I didn't want to traumatize her.

I could tell Bran was holding back as well, and, as our eyes met over our female, he made a low groan and stroked the base of his cock as Evelyn sucked noisily at the head.

"Good, sadora," he praised, his hand tightening in her hair as he thrust a little faster.

"Bran, I am close," I gasped out, my hips keeping that same steady rhythm that was pushing me closer.

"Make her come again," Bran demanded.

I reached under her and rubbed at her clit, praying to Krono that the little female came quickly. To my relief, she immediately made the little sounds I was already associating with her climax, and when Bran pinched her nipple, her body stiffened, and fresh wetness flooded my cock.

Her pussy squeezed exquisitely around my cock, and I made a low curse before thrusting back and forth. I thrust again, my balls tightening, then came in pulsing waves of pleasure that made my legs shake.

"Swallow, sadora," I heard Bran say. "Good girl. Keep swallowing."

I pulled out of Evelyn, ripped the condom off, and jerked my hand back and forth over my dick. It spurted another stream of seed across Evelyn's lower back as I watched her swallow Bran's release.

I stared at the pale green liquid before reaching out and

rubbing it into the skin of her lower back and the top of her ass. In front of me, Bran was pulling out of Evelyn's mouth, and he tugged her head back before stroking his dick and letting the last of his cum land on her tits.

"Good, sadora," he said as he rubbed his cum into her breasts until they gleamed with his seed.

Satisfied that our female was well marked, I stepped back and helped Evelyn ease onto her side before sliding into the bed behind her. She was panting and moaning softly, her body trembling, but her hand shot out and latched around Bran's wrist when he turned away.

"Stay," she demanded.

He glanced at me, and I nodded in agreement. He climbed into bed, and Evelyn rested her face against his broad chest as he cupped her breast. Her other hand draped along my hip, and I kissed the back of her shoulder.

"Are you all right, sadora?"

"Hmm," she said. "Sleepy."

I kissed her shoulder again, and Bran and I shifted closer. I pulled up the sheet and quilt, and Bran helped me tuck it around our female before we both relaxed. Her soft body was cocooned between ours, and she made another soft moan.

"So warm," she said happily before her breathing evened out.

I glanced at Bran, but he'd already closed his eyes. I sank my head into the pillow and closed my eyes as I breathed in the sweet scent of our female.

CHAPTER 16

Bran

I studied Evelyn's face in the dim light. Although the storm still raged outside, and there was no light to indicate it was morning, I knew it was close to dawn. The little human was sleeping on her side facing me, Court's arm draped around her waist. I may have felt a twinge of jealousy if not for Evie's smooth thigh flung over my hip and her hand resting against my chest.

I smoothed a lock of her satin soft hair back from her face. She was a beautiful little female, and while she might not realize it, I owed her a lot. She had returned my ability to please a woman – something I thought was gone forever. Just lying next to her was making my cock rise. I wanted her badly. I had enjoyed watching her come on my fingers last night, had enjoyed watching her swallow my seed as she sucked me off, but I wanted more.

I wanted to feel her tight pussy on my cock.

I eased back the quilt, not worried our female would be cold. Both Court and I ran hot, and our body heat would keep her warm enough. I stared at her perfect breasts, my fingers itching to caress her nipples into tight peaks.

I cupped one full breast, my thumb rubbing lightly across her nipple. It hardened as her eyelids fluttered open. She stared at me momentarily before a smile broke across her face. My chest tightened, and I immediately bent my head and pressed a kiss against her mouth.

"Hi," she said.

"Hello, Evie." I continued to stroke her nipple as she stretched.

Court made a low grunt and turned away from us to his other side. He snored softly, and Evie glanced over her shoulder before giggling. "It's kind of adorable that he snores."

I kissed her again, touching my tongue against hers, but she pulled away before I could deepen it.

"Trust me, you do not want to kiss me until I've brushed my teeth."

I gave her nipple a light pinch, enjoying the way she gasped and arched her back. I pulled her a little closer until my cock brushed against her abdomen. Her pale cheeks turned pink, and she stared at my cock before turning her gaze to my face.

"I had a really good time last night," she said in a low voice.

"As did I, little human." I bent and pressed a kiss against her upper chest before licking around her erect nipple. "You were a very good girl for us."

She moaned, her hands clutching in my hair. "Bran, that's... oh God, that's nice."

I traced the intoxicating curve of her belly before reaching between her thighs. Her leg was still draped over my hip, and her heel dug into my ass as I cupped her pussy.

I rubbed her pussy leisurely, exploring her warm folds as they grew steadily wetter for me. I brushed a fingertip across her clit, smiling at the way it made her jerk against me, and kissed her neck before giving her throat a little nip.

She cried out, and I lifted my head to smile at her. "You must lower your voice, sadora."

"I'm sorry," she moaned. "I'm trying to... oh my God!"

Her back arched as Court's hand slipped between us, and he cupped her tit. He played with her nipple as I rubbed her clit again.

"Good morning, Court," I said.

"Morning, Bran." Court's voice was muffled as he placed a kiss against Evie's back. "It seems that our little female is enjoying her morning pussy play."

"She is," I agreed as I rubbed her clit firmly. "She is growing very wet."

"Let me see." Court slid his hand between Evelyn's thighs and lifted the top one. She fell back against him, moaning quietly as her entire pussy was displayed to both of us. Krono, she had the prettiest pussy I'd ever seen, and I told that to Court, who nodded his head in agreement.

"Yes, she does."

I slid one finger into her pussy, groaning softly at the way it tightened around me.

"Bran," she whimpered, "please."

I rubbed her clit again. "Do you wish to be fucked this morning, Evie?"

"Yes," she said as Court tugged on her nipples.

"You must ask me nicely, little human," I teased.

She pouted at me, and I flicked her clit with my thumb. "Ask me nicely, sadora."

"Please fuck me, Bran," she gasped out.

"Good girl," I said.

Court turned away for a moment to rummage in the nightstand, and I took the human's contraceptive sheath from him with a nod of thanks. As his fingers replaced mine against Evie's clit, I rolled the rubber down my cock before shifting to my back.

Evelyn was rocking her pussy against Court's hand, her eyes closed and her beautiful tits jiggling. Court moved his hand away, and Evie moaned in dismay, her eyelids fluttering open.

"Court, please," she said.

"Straddle Bran, sadora," Court said.

It barely registered that both Court and I were referring to Evelyn as sadora. We hadn't known her long enough to bestow that particular pet name on her, but it felt natural to refer to her as our sadora, just as it did to refer to her as our female.

I patted my abdomen. "Come here, Evie."

She straddled me, and I groaned when her wet pussy rubbed against the head of my dick. It had been so long since I'd felt a pussy on my dick that I was almost frantic with the desire to slide into her.

But Evelyn was nervous. I could see it in the way she stared at my cock. I gripped the base of it and rubbed her smooth thigh. "Do not be afraid, sadora. I will not hurt you."

"Can we go slow at first?" she said.

"You will control the pace," I said. "Go as slow as you need."

It was only sheer willpower on my part that prevented me from slamming my cock deep inside of her when she pressed the head against the opening of her wet pussy, and it slipped inside.

"Oh," she muttered as she kept one hand braced on my chest, and her knees braced on the bed.

Court was lying on his side next to us, one hand lazily stroking his dick as he stared at Evelyn. "Take more, sadora," he encouraged.

I gritted my teeth, keeping my hands loose on her hips as she moved her body up and down, taking my cock little by little into her warm body.

"She is tight, is she not, Bran?" Court said with a small grin.

"Yes," I gritted out, my hands clamping down on Evie's hips when she made one last push, and her hot pussy took every last inch of my dick.

"Fuck," she breathed, "this might be too much."

"It is not," I said as she started to rise off of me.

"It's going to hurt when we start moving," she said.

"It will not." I held her hips and snaked my tail around her waist, holding her firmly and refusing to let her take my dick out of her pussy. "You are doing very well."

"Says the guy who doesn't have a foot-long dick up his cooch," she muttered.

Court laughed so hard that the bed shook. Evelyn glared at him. "Why don't you try sticking it in your butt? Then we'll see who's laughing."

Court laughed again before reaching out and cupping her breast. He tugged on her hard nipple. "We told you, little human, we are only into females."

Her little pussy tightened around me when Court teased her nipple. I groaned, sweat breaking out on my forehead. "Krono, Court, do not do that. She is going to make me come."

"Isn't that the idea?" Evelyn said before making a couple of experimental thrusts.

I moaned loudly, my hips rising to meet her light thrusts, my tail squeezing her waist.

She gasped and braced her hands against my chest. "Okay, I might have been wrong about it hurting. That feels good… really good."

Court rubbed his dick again as he watched Evelyn's hips rise up and down. "Lean over Bran. Let him suck on your pretty nipples."

Her face flushed, but she did what Court said, leaning over and resting her hands on either side of my head. I kissed her right nipple before sucking hard on it. I loved our little female's perfect breasts, and I sucked and licked, teasing her nipples into swollen hard buds as she moaned and panted above me.

Her hips rose and fell in a languid motion that set me on fire with need. I slid my arms around her hips, pressing the length of her body against mine and thrust into her, over and over, with hard strokes that made both of us shudder with pleasure.

She held onto my shoulders, her head thrown back and her breasts pressed delightfully against my chest. Court was moving closer, and when he glanced at me, unspoken communication passed between us.

I slid my hands down Evie's hips and gripped an ass cheek in each hand as Court dipped his hand between her thighs. She made a little squeal of happiness and lifted her lower body eagerly, giving Court room to slip his hand between my body and Evelyn's and rub her pussy.

She moaned and gasped, her body losing its rhythm against mine as Court teased her clit. When he removed his hand, his fingers were coated in her cream, and she whined.

"Court, no, keep doing that. I was close."

"Shh, sadora," he said as he glanced at me again.

I spread Evelyn's ass cheeks, exposing her tight hole to Court. He pressed one slick finger against her opening, and

Evelyn froze above me. She gave me a startled look before she tried to wiggle away.

"Be still, sadora," I said and tightened my hold on her ass. She reared up, her thighs squeezing my hips as her hands gripped my shoulders, but with my arms and tail around her, she wasn't going anywhere.

"Court, I'm not ready for that," she said.

"You are." Court kept his voice low and calm as he worked one slick finger inside of her.

Her hands squeezed my shoulders, her pussy squeezed my cock, and I bit back my moan as I pressed a kiss against her throat.

"Bran, please," she said.

"Shh, sadora. Be our good girl and relax for Court."

She took a deep breath, and I gave her ass cheeks a soft squeeze when I felt her body relax against mine. "Good, sweet sadora."

She cried out when Court pushed past her tight ring of muscle. "How does that feel, sadora?"

"Strange," she said. "I'm not sure that I... oh!"

Her back arched, her ass taking more of Court's finger. I had let go of one ass cheek, slid my hand between our bodies and rubbed her clit.

She moaned again, rubbing her pussy against my fingers as I began a steady rhythm of thrusting.

"Oh, oh, that's so good," she moaned, clinging to my shoulders and burying her face in my neck. Her soft cries and whimpers were muffled against my skin as Court added a second finger to her ass.

Her pussy tightened around me. I groaned into her ear before rubbing her clit as I fucked her. I stared over her shoulder at the way Court's fingers moved in and out of her ass and nearly came immediately.

Court wiggled his fingers, and Evie squealed into my shoulder, her pussy going exquisitely tight around me as she raised her head.

"Oh fuck," she moaned. "Oh fuck, that kind of feels good.'

Court grinned at me, and I rubbed her clit again as he wiggled his fingers back and forth, his free hand rubbing his dick with hard and furious strokes. Evie's curvy body stiffened, and she buried her face in my shoulder just in time to muffle her scream of pleasure as she came all over my cock.

I grabbed her hips again and thrust wildly in and out before letting the pleasure overtake me. Her pussy milked me hard as I came, and I heard Court's low moan of pleasure as he climaxed as well.

I collapsed under Evie, panting hard as she trembled above me. Court rubbed his seed into her hip, and I waited until he finished before easing Evelyn onto the bed beside me. She sprawled on her back, her pussy soaking wet and her nipples hard as glass. Her chest and cheeks were flushed with colour, and her dark hair stuck to her face.

I brushed it back before removing the condom and tossing it into the garbage can beside the night table. Court was relaxing on his side next to Evie, and I lay on her other side, my hand rubbing her hip as her breathing slowed.

"Oh my God," she said in a trembling voice. "Oh my God, that was... I mean... I've never come so hard in my life."

"You are welcome," Court said.

Evie giggled and reached for both our hands. "You guys are fantastic at this."

I kissed her shoulder. "We like pleasing our ma – our female."

My stomach clenched, and I glanced at Court. He hadn't seemed to notice my slip-up, nor had Evie, but when Bella called for me a few minutes later, I sat up with relief.

As I dressed, Court kissed Evelyn. "Go and shower, Evie. I will start breakfast while Bran gets Bella up."

Evelyn

"AGAIN, UDA! AGAIN!" BELLA SQUEALED HAPPILY WHEN COURT tossed her up into the air.

My stomach muscles tensed, but Court caught her easily, and Bella shrieked excitedly. "Again, Uda!"

Court tossed her again, and the little girl's head nearly brushed the ceiling. I grabbed onto the arm of the couch as Bran patted my thigh.

"Do not worry, Evie. Court would never drop her."

"I know," I said.

Bran rubbed the top of my thigh as Court took Bella's hands and twirled her in a circle until her legs left the ground. "How are you feeling? Are you sore? Do you need more gallberry juice?"

Bran and Court had been unbelievably sweet since I came downstairs from my shower. My thighs and pussy were a little sore, but the two glasses of gallberry juice they made me drink at breakfast had quickly taken care of any lingering pain.

Bella's bad mood from yesterday had dissipated, and she was back to her usual happy self. After breakfast, I played with her in the living room while Court and Bran worked on something related to farming on Bran's tablet. At least, I thought that's what they were doing. There'd been lots of talk about west fields and east fields and – I shuddered – something called a rugenroach. I had no idea what a rugenroach was, but it didn't sound pleasant.

"I feel fine," I said. "The juice at breakfast helped, and if it hadn't, the two glasses you made me drink at lunch would have done the trick."

"What trick?" Bran gave me a puzzled look, and I laughed.

"It's an earth saying. Just means it would have done the job or helped. You know?"

He shrugged, his hand continuing to make lazy circles on my thigh. It shouldn't have turned me on, I'd had a lot of orgasms in the last twenty-four hours, but I was pretty sure my pussy was wet.

I was turning into a sex maniac.

The king will like that.

My burgeoning lust died in an instant. I studied Bran's long fingers, the lovely shade of green that was suddenly my favourite colour. I'd almost forgotten my reasons for sleeping with Court and Bran.

Stupid girl.

Yes, I was a stupid girl. As enjoyable as sleeping with Bran and Court was, as much as I was starting to care about them, I needed to remember that this was a temporary arrangement. As soon as the storm ended, I would never see them or –my chest squeezed tight – Bella again.

"What is wrong, Evie?" Bran asked.

He was sensitive, maybe not as sensitive as Court, and the way both of them could pick up on my moods was a little eerie. I was used to being the one who could read people, not the other way around.

"I'm good." I made my voice cheerful and light. There was no point in being moody about what couldn't be changed. I would enjoy my time with them, learn as much as possible, and then start the life I was meant to live – as the king's mate.

Bella was skipping toward us, her tiny body a little

wobbly and her tail carrying one of her picture books from the bookshelf. She climbed into my lap and leaned against me. "I dizzy, Evie girl."

Court sat down on my other side and stroked Bella's long hair. "I told you it would make you dizzy, meena."

Bella dropped the book on my lap. "Evie girl, read?"

"I can't, honey," I said. "I can't read Draax, remember?"

Bella used her tail to push the book onto Bran's lap. "Papa read book to Bella."

"All right, meena," Bran picked up the book, "but then it is nap time."

Bella rested her head against my chest and wrapped her tail around my forearm before reaching out and grabbing Court's tail with her right hand and Bran's tail with her left. She held them loosely in her lap and smiled at her father. "Read, Papa."

Court and Bran stood in the hallway when I stepped out of my bedroom. They gave me identical looks of desire, and my pulse skittered into hyperdrive.

"Hello, little human," Bran said.

"H-hi." My throat was suddenly dry, and I swallowed with difficulty. "Is Bella down for her nap?"

"Yes," Court said. "She fell asleep quickly."

"Th-that's good." Why was I nervous? I shouldn't be nervous. Both Draax had seen me completely naked. I'd sucked both their cocks, fucked both of them... there was no need for nerves.

Still, I couldn't help trembling when they flanked me in the hallway. The heat of their big bodies made me want to pull them even closer. Court dragged one finger across my collarbone, studying the goosebumps on my skin.

"Are you cold, Evie?" he asked.

"A little," I whispered.

"Would you like us to warm you?" Bran pressed a kiss against my neck.

"Yes," I replied, blushing at how eager I sounded.

Bran took my hand, tugging me along when I automatically stopped in front of Court's bedroom door. He opened the door to his bedroom, and I followed him inside.

I stared at the bed as Court shut the door, stepped in close behind me and cupped my breasts. He pressed his cock against my ass, his fingers already plucking at my nipples through my t-shirt and bra, as Bran walked to the bed.

"Holy smokes," I said. "That's a big bed."

It wasn't just a big bed - it was a *giant* bed. The widest bed I'd ever seen in my life. Three people could easily sleep in it, with plenty of room for each. My stomach dropped as I realized why he had such a big bed. The woman that lived here before me – Dana. They had started off sharing her. It made sense they'd want a bed big enough for the three of them.

Unexpected jealousy made my skin itch. What had she been like? Was she smarter than me? Prettier than me? Not such a scared little mouse?

Bran was pulling the quilt down, and when he caught sight of my face, concern etched into his. "Evie? Are you all right?"

Court was kneading my breasts, and his hands stilled. I leaned back against him, forcing myself to smile at Bran. "I'm fine."

Thinking about Dana and what she'd been like was stupid and pointless. I had no right to be jealous of someone they were no longer with. Hell, I had no right to be jealous, period. I wasn't theirs, and they weren't mine. What was happening between us was fleeting.

"Are you certain?" Bran asked.

"Positive," I said. I lifted my arms when Court grasped the hem of my shirt. He tugged it over my head and tossed it on the floor before reaching for the clasps of my bra. He had me naked and was leading me toward the bed in less than two minutes. Bran was stripping off his clothes, and he stared hungrily at me as Court urged me to lie in the middle of the bed.

As Court removed his clothes, I stared with sudden apprehension at the nightstand. Sitting on top of it were the usual packets of condoms, but there was also a bottle of lube and – my stomach made a nervous flutter – a butt plug. It was probably on the smaller side – although it looked giant to me – and while the plug part was silver in colour, the other end was a pretty pink coloured jewel.

Bran stretched out beside me, blocking my view of the plug. Court was moving to my other side, and I gave Bran an anxious smile as he cupped my breast. "I'm kind of, uh, nervous about the butt plug."

"I know, sweet sadora, but if you want to learn how to take two Draax at once, you must be stretched with plugs first," Bran said.

"And we will stop if you ask us to stop," Court said. "Do not be afraid, sadora."

"What does sadora mean?" I asked.

Both Court and Bran's faces turned dark green with embarrassment, and they stared at each other over my head.

"What?" I said. "What does it mean?"

Court cleared his throat, his tail waving back and forth behind him. "It is just a... pet name."

"Nickname," Bran said hurriedly. "Just a nickname."

"What does it mean?"

Again, that almost guilty look at each other over my head. "Hey?" I grasped both of their arms and squeezed. "Tell me what it means."

"It is like the human's version of," Bran paused, "sweetheart or honey."

"Oh, okay." Warmth rushed through me. I liked that they gave me a little pet name even though I knew it meant nothing. Still, it was very sweet. Although I wondered why they still looked so embarrassed before I could ask, both Draax bent their heads and sucked on my nipples.

I cried out and cupped their heads, feeling the short, smooth hairs on Bran's skull and Court's longer, rougher curls. They teased and nipped and licked at my nipples, their skilled mouths turning me into a frenzy of heat and need almost immediately.

Bran kissed across my stomach, circling my navel with his tongue before pressing a kiss against the top of my pussy. I spread my legs immediately, more heat flooding through me when Bran said, "Good girl," and stretched out between my thighs.

Court lifted his head from my breast and kissed me, his tongue sliding in to muffle my cry of ecstasy when Bran's tongue slicked over my clit. My body arched, one hand digging into Court's back and the other clenching around the sheets.

"Oh God," I moaned when Court released my mouth and returned to my breast.

He licked at my nipple, his hand toying with my other one before grinning at Bran. "Our female tastes sweet, does she not?"

Bran lifted his head just long enough to mutter, "Very sweet," before diving back into my pussy. I clamped my thighs around his head when his tongue invaded my hot core. He pried my legs apart, holding them open as he licked and tasted.

I was on the verge of coming already. The hot suction of Court's mouth against my nipple and the soft wetness of Bran's tongue against my clit made me frantic with need. I wanted to prolong the pleasure, but Bran's tongue demanded my climax.

I threw my arm over my mouth, muffling my scream as I came all over Bran's face. He sucked on my clit, and my feet drummed on the bed. I tried to push his head away, and he made a low growl, the sound vibrating against my wet pussy lips, before capturing my wrist in one hard hand.

"Court, her arms," Bran said.

"Court, no," I gasped when he took both my hands and held them over my head with one hand around my wrists. "I can't come again, not yet. Please don't do… oh God!"

Court ignored me, bending his head to suck hard on my nipple. Bran pushed my legs wide, holding them open easily as he studied my pussy. Cool air washed over it, and I clenched my teeth together to hold back my cries of pleasure when Bran licked my pussy again.

"You will come again for me, little human."

"No," I panted. "No, Bran, I can't."

"You can." He rubbed my clit with his fingers before sliding two of them deep inside of me and fucking me roughly with them.

I was soaking wet, and I squirmed when Bran used some of that wetness on my ass before sliding one finger into my tight hole.

"Oh God," I moaned as he wiggled his finger in my ass, slid his thumb into my pussy, and licked up my slit to my throbbing clit. "Oh fuck, oh fuck that feels…"

Bran sucked on my clit again just as Court gently bit my nipple. My body arched, and Court's hand clamped down over my mouth just as I screamed my second release. My climax went on and on in endless waves that made me shake uncontrollably.

I was barely aware of Bran moving up to lie beside me, of Court releasing my arms and bringing them down to rub gently at my wrists. I shuddered between them as they rubbed up and down my body with gentle hands.

When I finally opened my eyes, Bran was leaning over me and smiling with satisfaction. "You are a good girl, sadora."

"Thank you," I gasped out. Court was rubbing his dick against my thigh, and when he turned onto his back, Bran took my arm and sat me up.

"Come, sadora. It is time for you to fuck Court."

He helped me straddle Court's thighs before handing the condom to him. Court rolled it onto his dick, and the two of them lifted me a little until Court's dick pressed against my entrance. He slid in with barely any resistance, and he moaned with pleasure as my pussy took all of him.

"She's so wet, Bran," he groaned.

Bran made another satisfied grin before pressing on my back. "Lean over Court, sadora."

I did what he asked, pressing my breasts against Court and kissing him as he gripped my hips and pumped into me. It felt delicious, and I buried my face in the curve of his neck, kissing his warm skin and letting him fuck me with long, slow strokes as I held onto his broad shoulders.

When Bran's fingers parted my ass, I didn't protest. I felt weak as a kitten, and the touch of Bran's fingers felt nice. Cool liquid dripped onto my anus, but before I could whine in protest, Bran's strong fingers were rubbing it in, warming it up and massaging it into my tight hole. It felt a little strange, but I'd had Court's fingers there before and –

My head shot up, my ass automatically clenching around the warm blunt object Bran was pressing against my ass. Court's arms wrapped around my waist, and he held me tight as I craned my head to stare at Bran and the plug he was pressing against me.

"Bran, I'm not sure I'm ready."

"You are," he said. "Relax, sadora."

I tried to relax my muscles. Court's thick cock sliding in and out of my pussy was a welcome distraction, and when he wiggled one hand between our bodies and lightly circled my clit, I concentrated on that instead of the increasing pressure against my ass.

"Push back against the plug, Evie," Bran said.

"No way," I said. "I can't do that."

"You can." Bran squeezed one ass cheek. "Push back."

"Court?" I stared at him desperately, and he pressed a kiss against my jaw.

"Do as Bran says, little human."

I made a sulky little whine but pressed back against the plug. My fingers dug into Court's shoulders, and I gasped when there was a brief pop of pain that quickly subsided.

"Good, Evie," Bran praised.

I stared at him over my shoulder, watching in fascination as he pushed the plug in fully. Court made a low groan, but I barely noticed. I couldn't stop staring at the jewel between my ass cheeks. There was no pain, just a feeling of pressure and being full. It actually felt kind of good.

"Krono," Court moaned under me. "She is even tighter with the plug."

"Fuck her," Bran suddenly demanded.

Court's hands tightened around my hips. I made a little

yelp of surprise when he fucked me harder and rougher than he usually did. I braced my hands on his chest, watching his face in fascination as he moved beneath me. His tail lashed out and wrapped around my waist, squeezing tight as he groaned, and his breath came out in harsh pants.

"Kiss me, sadora," he moaned.

I kissed him, teasing his tongue with my own as his thrusts turned short and furious. His big body stiffened beneath me, and he came hard, thrusting into me and groaning into my mouth as his tail tightened even more around my waist.

"Good?" I smiled at him as he shuddered beneath me.

Before he could answer, Bran's hands were grabbing my hips and lifting me off of Court's dick. "Court, move. For Krono's sake, move."

Court released his tail from my waist and slid out from under me. He threw an arm over his head, his body relaxing against the bed, and his tail flicking lazily back and forth as a satisfied smile played at his lips.

I was still on my hands and knees on the bed. I spread my legs when Bran pushed at them with his knee. "Open, Evie."

He pushed on my upper back as his tail slid around my waist. I rested my cheek against the bed, staring at Court as Bran's cock pressed against my pussy. With a low groan, he pushed into me. I made a soft cry of pleasure that mixed with Bran's moan.

"Krono, so tight," Bran said.

A slight grin played on Court's lips. "Told you," he said without opening his eyes.

Without another word, Bran started fucking me. His tail and his hands on my hips kept my lower body completely still for his thrusts. I dug my hands into the sheets, biting my lip as familiar heat invaded my lower body. I couldn't have a third orgasm, could I?

Bran shifted me, and I arched my back, clawing at the sheets when the head of his dick brushed against a spot that – holy fuck!

I tried to wiggle away from the intense pleasure, but Bran was holding me firmly, and I couldn't get away from him.

"Bran," I moaned, "it feels… it feels…"

He made another thrust, and I clawed into the sheets again, my head falling back as he rammed his cock in and out of my willing pussy, the head brushing against that spot with every thrust. When he wiggled the plug in my ass, my orgasm hit me with an intensity I'd never experienced before.

I buried my mouth into my arm to silence my wailing cry of pleasure, my body shaking against Bran's and my pussy clamping down around his cock. He made his own harsh cry of pleasure, thrusting forward, his cock going impossibly deep as he moaned my name repeatedly.

I collapsed onto my face as Court sat up and caught Bran before the big Draax could crash down on me. He helped Bran roll to his side next to me before lying on his side and brushing my hair away from my sweaty face.

Bran's tail was still wrapped around my waist, and Court gave it a short tug. "Bran, release her."

He relaxed his tail, and I took a deep breath, staring at Court as he scowled and rubbed along my ribs. "She has red marks from our tails. We need to be gentler."

"Yes," Bran gasped out. He was lying on his back, staring blearily at the ceiling as his body twitched.

"Are you all right?" I asked.

He nodded before removing the condom and tossing it into the trash. Court turned me on my side and spooned me, his hand cupping my breast and his thighs pressing against the plug in my ass.

"Take it out," I said with a weak wave in the direction of my ass.

"Shh, sadora," Court said before pressing a kiss against my throat.

"Will you take it out? Please, Court?"

"Not yet," he said soothingly. "You should wear it for a little longer."

I pouted at Court. Bran still stared at the ceiling but smiled and said, "No pouting, sadora, or we will make you wear it during dinner as well."

"You guys are the worst, and I don't like either of you," I said.

Court and Bran laughed, and Bran rolled to his side to face me. "The way your little pussy clamped around my cock suggests you do not dislike me nearly as much as you say."

I giggled and relaxed in Court's embrace. "Thank you, both of you. That was incredible."

Court nuzzled his face into my hair as Bran rubbed my hip. "For us as well, little human."

There was a moment of comfortable silence before Bran said, "We want you to sleep in the bed with us from now on. Will you, Evie?"

Warm and sleepy in Court's tight embrace, I didn't even think to refuse. "Yes, I'd like that."

CHAPTER 17

Bran

"Evelyn?" I ducked my head into her bedroom. She hadn't been sleeping in this room for weeks, which was why it was the last place I'd looked for her.

She turned from the window and smiled, but there was no denying the sadness in her face. Worry seized me, and I hurried across the room, putting my arms around her and hugging her tight.

"What is wrong, little human?"

"Nothing's wrong." She leaned against me, and we both stared at the falling snow. "I'm just a little tired of the snow and the cold."

"It will end soon," I said. "Another few days or so, and the snow will stop."

"Yes," she said. A tear dripped down her cheek, and I wrapped my tail around her waist, squeezing reassuringly.

"Do not cry, Evie."

"I'm just sad," she said. "I know what it means when the snow ends."

I kissed her cheek, feeling anxious and angry and a little helpless.

She turned in my arms to face me, draping her arms around my shoulders and smiling at me. "I'm going to miss you and Court and," her breath caught in her throat, "Bella so much. Maybe we can keep in touch after I leave?"

"As queen, you will be busy, and I doubt the king will allow his mate to talk to other males. Besides, once you are in the king's bed, you will forget all about me and Court." I said.

Not used to seeing anger on her face, I didn't realize that's what it was until she shoved me in the chest, pushing away from me and yanking on my tail until I dropped it from her waist. "That's a really mean thing to say, Bran. I will never forget any of you, and for you to think I would..."

Her voice wavered, and my shame grew. "I am sorry, sadora. I did not mean -"

"I won't forget you!" She poked me hard in the chest, and I stepped back in surprise.

Her shoulders slumped, and the anger faded from her face as quickly as it appeared. "I'm sorry. I shouldn't have lost my temper like that. I know that the sex between us doesn't mean anything."

I quickly gathered her back into my arms, dropping a kiss against her forehead. "I like that you trust me enough to be angry with me."

She made a laugh that was half-sob, half-hiccup, and I kissed her again. "And you are wrong, sadora. It does mean something – for both Court and me."

I tipped her chin up, my tail circling her waist again, and kissed her. She returned my kiss, her mouth soft against mine. I breathed in her scent, my hands rubbing warm circles on her back. I would miss our sweet sadora more than

I could even admit to myself, and I didn't think it was a coincidence that Court was becoming more and more sullen with every day that passed.

I deepened the kiss, our tongues tangling together. As Evelyn began to make those soft and intoxicating sounds of need, I considered urging her toward the bed. Bella would be waking soon from her nap, but there was enough time for me to eat her sweet pussy.

"Am I interrupting something?"

Evelyn and I broke apart at the sound of Court's voice. Evelyn smiled at him and held out her hand. "Of course not, join us."

"It seems you are enjoying yourselves just fine without me," Court said.

Evelyn frowned, giving me a quick look of confusion. My temper flared, but I held my tongue. I knew why Court was upset. I'd been cautious to ensure that I was rarely alone with Evie, and most times, I didn't kiss or touch her if Court wasn't in the room with us. I also knew that he didn't want Evelyn to leave, just like I didn't, and that his emotions were starting to get the best of him.

"What's wrong?" Evelyn broke away from me and crossed the room to Court, putting her arms around his waist. "Why are you upset?"

"I am not," Court said.

"You are." Evelyn pressed a kiss against his chest. "Tell me why?"

"I am not upset," Court repeated.

Before Evie could reply, Bella appeared in the doorway. Her hair was sticking up, and she was holding her favourite doll. "Hi, Papa."

"Hello, meena. Do you feel better after your nap?"

"Yes. I want juice, please."

"All right, meena," I said.

I walked toward her, smiling when she gave me her sweet smile and held out her hand toward Evelyn and Court. "Uda and Evie girl come too."

Evelyn

"Court?" I leaned against the doorjamb in the kitchen.

Court was staring out the kitchen window and didn't turn around. "I thought you were joining Bella in her sleep ritual."

"I just finished," I said.

"Where is Bran?"

"He's having a quick shower."

He didn't reply. I joined him by the window and rested my hand on his back. The poffin bread he'd made earlier sat on the counter, and I said, "The poffin bread was delicious. Maybe I'll get you to show me how to make it tomorrow?"

"There is no point. As the queen, you will always have someone else cooking for you."

Court's voice was sullen, and I rubbed his back. "Look at me, honey."

He turned, and I studied his face, my heart aching at the anger and sadness etched into it. "Tell me what's wrong."

"There is nothing wrong."

"Court, you shouldn't bottle up your feelings. It isn't healthy to – oh!"

Court had picked me up, and I didn't say anything as he carried me down the hallway to his bedroom. He set me down next to the bed, cupped my face, and kissed me hard on the mouth. I returned his kiss but caught his hand when he tried to unbutton my shirt.

"Court, wait."

"I want you, Evie," he said.

"I want you too, but Bran is still showering."

In the last two and a half weeks, I'd never had sex with one Draax without the other being present. There'd been more than once when Bran or Court had woken me in the middle of the night or early in the morning, and we'd had sex, but the other was in bed with us, even if they didn't wake up. It was always the three of us together. Truthfully, that was how I liked it. I didn't want to sleep with one without the other with us.

Court's face turned dark green, and his tail thumped angrily against the floor. "Earlier today, you were more than happy to have sex with Bran without me."

"We weren't going to have sex without you," I said. "You're overreacting because you're upset and -"

"The last two times we have been together, you have fucked Bran but only sucked me off." His tail thumped against the floor again.

"Stop, honey. You're reading too much into it."

"I am not!" Court's anger was radiating from him in thick, slow waves. Three weeks ago, I would have been terrified and backing away while trying to protect my kidneys.

Now? Now, I knew without a doubt that Court and Bran would never hurt me, and I didn't feel a lick of fear. Instead, I wrapped my arms around his waist and kissed his chest.

"Honey, it's okay," I said. "I want you as much as I want Bran and -"

"Do you?" he snapped.

"Yes," I said. "I do."

"Why should I believe you." He pushed away and glared at me as his tail whacked the floor.

"What is going on?" Bran walked into the room, staring at Court's body's stiff posture before stepping in front of me protectively. "Stop it, Court, you are frightening her."

"He isn't." I touched Bran's back. "I'm not afraid."

"Why did you bring Evie into your room?" Bran said to Court.

Court's nostrils flared. "Why do you think?"

"You would act so childish as to have sex with our female without me?" Bran said.

"You had no problem fucking Dana without me around," Court snarled.

"You have fucked females without me as well," Bran snarled back. "What is your problem?"

"I have never fucked a female without you!" Court's voice was low but thick with fury. "You may have been fine throwing away our friendship for a female, but I was not."

"What are you talking about?" Bran said. "Neither Dana nor I asked you to leave. You made that decision."

"I left because I knew Dana did not love me and did not want me in the house." Court stalked back and forth, his tail whipping like an angry snake. "My presence upset her, and when we discovered she was with child, I did not want her to lose the baby because of her emotional state."

He stopped, his gaze briefly flickering to mine before turning back to Bran. "You always wanted Dana just for yourself anyway, and now you want Evelyn for you and only you. You cannot have her, Bran! I will not give her up just because you want her."

"You are being ridiculous," Bran said calmly. "Evelyn is neither mine nor yours and never will be. She belongs to the king, and you must control your emotions."

Court's hands clenched into fists, and I stepped around Bran, ready to move between them.

"Perhaps," Court said, "if you had shown more emotion, Dana would not have left, and Bella would not be without a mother."

I gasped and grabbed Bran's arm when he staggered back a step. His face had gone a pale green, and he looked like he'd taken a punch to the kidneys. Without speaking to either of us, he pulled away from my grip and stumbled out of Court's room.

I faced Court. His body slumped, and his tail drooped at the look on my face. "Evelyn, I did not mean -"

"No," I said. "Don't say anything else. I need to talk to Bran to make sure he's okay, and then we'll talk about what you just said."

I turned to leave, and Court said, "Evie, please."

The sorrow and regret in his voice made me return to him. Hating how upset and defeated he looked, I put my arms around him and hugged him hard. He buried his face in my neck, and I kissed his broad shoulder.

"I am sorry." His voice was muffled against my skin.

"I know, honey." I kissed his shoulder again. "I need to check on Bran. I'll come back in a bit, okay?"

He nodded, and when he let go of me, I cupped his face and tugged his head down to press a kiss against his mouth. "It'll be okay, honey. We'll fix this, all right?"

He nodded again, and I gave him a final kiss before leaving his room and heading to Bran's. He was sitting on the side of the bed, and I sat next to him, putting my arm around his waist and kissing his upper arm. "Are you all right, Bran?"

"He is wrong," Bran said. "I did not want Dana for myself. I hated that she did not love Court."

He took a shuddering breath and checked the empty

doorway before saying, "I would never tell Court this, but Dana told me once, right before she left, that she had never loved Court. She only agreed to be with him because she knew it was the only way to be with me."

"I'm so sorry, honey," I said. "That was a terrible thing for her to do and say."

"She turned cold toward him only a few moons after she moved in with us. She stopped letting him into her pussy and would only let him fuck her ass. She said it was because we had decided that I would father our first child, and she did not want to risk the condom breaking. But only a moon or so after that, she would no longer allow him to touch her at all. Court tried to be patient with her, and he tried everything he could to make our mate want him again, but she refused to let him join us in the bed."

"That must have been so difficult for both of you," I said. "I'm sorry you went through that."

"She kept putting off the mating ritual and said that we would do it later, but she did not mean it," Bran said. "After Court left, she wanted to go ahead with the ritual to mate us, but I," he paused, his throat working hard to swallow, "I could not do it. It made her angry. By then, she was already pregnant with Bella, but I could not force myself to do the ritual."

I kissed his arm again and made a soft, soothing sound under my breath. "It isn't your fault, Bran."

"It is," he said. "It is my fault. Dana left because of me."

"I doubt that," I said. "Court was just angry and didn't mean -"

"She left because I could no longer please her in bed," Bran blurted out.

"What do you mean?" I honestly couldn't even picture a

woman not having an orgasm when Bran was in bed with her. He had to mean something else.

"A few weeks after Court moved out, I could no longer," he stared at his crotch, "maintain an erection when I was with Dana. Eventually, I could not grow hard at all, even when Dana used her mouth and hands. She was angry and upset with me, but I did not know why it was happening."

He gave me an embarrassed look. "Dana thought it was because she was growing larger with Bella. I let her believe it, even though it had nothing to do with that. She was even more beautiful with my child growing inside of her. But after she gave birth, I still could not get an erection. A moon after Bella was born, Dana returned to Earth. I begged her not to go, told her that Bella needed her, and I needed her too, but she said that she could not live with a man who could not fuck her."

My mouth dropped open, and I stared in silent shock at Bran. He stared at the floor, his fingers drumming out a nervous beat on one thick thigh. "Dana left because I could not please her in bed. Court is right. It is my fault that Bella has grown up without a mother."

I cupped his face and made him look at me. "No. That isn't true, Bran."

"It is," he said miserably.

"It isn't." My voice was firm. "Bran, no woman who wanted to be a mother would leave her child because her mate couldn't have sex with her. Do you hear me?"

"She said that was the reason."

"She was lying to you. Look, I don't know this Dana woman at all, but she sounds like a real asshole. I'm not surprised you couldn't get an erection after all the ways she screwed you over. You stopped being attracted to her because she was horrible to you and Court. You and Court made it clear to her that you guys were a package deal, right? That you wanted to share a mate?"

Bran nodded. "Yes. Court and I used to go to Earth to…"

I smiled at him. "It's fine. I won't judge you for coming to Earth to get laid."

"We met Dana at one of your bars and spent the night with her. Over the next few moons, we returned often to spend time with her. We were honest with her about sharing a female and wished to have one mate between us. She said she was fine with that."

"But she lied," I said.

He nodded, and I squeezed his arm. "It sounds like she lied about a lot of things, honey. If she truly wanted a child, she would never have left Bella, even if you and she never had sex again."

Bran studied my face. "Do you mean that?"

"Yes," I said. "I know I don't have children yet, but I couldn't imagine leaving them for anything. Dana was a selfish liar who didn't care who she hurt. What happened was entirely her fault. Not yours or Court's. She should have been honest with you from the beginning, but she wasn't. That isn't your fault."

He was still staring at me like he didn't believe me. I cupped his face and pressed a kiss against his mouth. "She was a fool, Bran. If I belonged to you and Court, I would love you both equally. You are both amazing, and I would be happy to carry yours and Court's children."

I kissed him again, staring into his dark brown eyes. "It wasn't your fault."

"Evie is right."

I made a startled gasp, and Bran's tail thumped against the mattress. Court was standing in the doorway, and Bran said, "How much did you hear?"

Court stepped into the room, looking a little uncertain. "Why did you not tell me any of this before?"

"Because I chose Dana over you, and I could not expect you to understand or sympathize with me," Bran said.

I held out my hand, and Court joined us, easing onto the bed beside me. I took both their hands and held them in my lap as Bran sighed. "I should never have chosen Dana over you, and I will never forgive myself for doing so."

"You should have chosen her," Court said. "She is Bella's mother, and you were right to try to make her happy."

"I failed," Bran said. "Our friendship is destroyed for nothing."

Court shook his head. "Our friendship is not destroyed, Bran. Would I have moved back in after Dana left if it was?"

Bran finally looked at him. "You moved back in because you knew I needed help. Knew that I could not look after Bella and work at the same time."

"I moved back in because I missed my friend," Court said.

I blinked back the tears as Bran said, "I am sorry, Court. I am sorry that I believed Dana's lies, sorry that I did not object when she no longer allowed you in our bed, sorry that I chose her over you."

Court took a deep breath. "I know, my friend. I am sorry, too. I know that you did not desire Dana for yourself and did not want me to leave. I left because Dana told me that she had never loved me and she would never mate with me or bear my children. She said that because she was pregnant with your baby, I needed to do the right thing and leave the two of you alone to raise your children."

Bran made a low sound of anger. "Why did you not tell me she said that?"

Court sighed. "You were about to be a father, and I knew you loved Dana. If I told you that she had lied, you would have been angry with her. I did not want to ruin your chance at happiness with her. So, I left."

"I am sorry," Bran said.

"I was jealous," Court said abruptly. "I was jealous and angry that Dana loved you but did not love me, and I have been taking that out on you since I moved back. I am sorry. I should not have done that. It is not your fault that Dana did not love me."

"She did not love either of us or even her child," Bran said. "She was a selfish human who only cared about herself."

They squeezed my hands so tight that my fingers started to ache, but I didn't say anything as Court stared at Bran. "I want our friendship to be the way it was before. Can it?"

"Yes," Bran said.

They smiled at each other, and I waited a beat before saying, "That's it? You're not going to hug it out or something?"

"Hug it out?" Court said.

"When people are angry with each other and then make up, they hug each other," I said. "It's a gesture of goodwill and apology, and the hug takes away any lingering anger or frustration."

Bran cocked his head at me. "I have apologized, and so has Court. We are no longer angry with each other. What need is there to hug?"

I laughed and shook my head. "There isn't. Forget I said anything."

We sat in silence for a few minutes before Court said. "Did you mean what you said earlier, Evie? That you would be happy to carry mine and Bran's children?"

"Yes," I said. "You guys are incredible, and you will make *one* lucky woman very happy someday. I promise you."

Thinking of them with another woman brought on a

wave of sadness and jealousy that was so painful I couldn't breathe. I wanted to be that woman, wanted it desperately. I loved them both, and the thought of them being with another woman...

Shit. Girl, you fell in love with them. What is wrong with you?

I choked back my bitter laughter. I was a fool. I was in love with Bran and Court, and in about a week, I'd never see them again.

No, you won't. So, will you spend that week moping around, or will you spend it with the two men you love and make every moment count?

I straightened my back and swallowed down the lump forming in my throat. I would make the most of every damn moment.

I squeezed their hands and smiled at them. "I want you both tonight."

Court glanced at Bran. "Are you certain, Evie?"

"Yes. I'm ready."

"We can use the plugs for a few more nights, and then -"

"No," I said, cutting off Bran. "I want to make love to both of you together. Right now."

Bran pressed a kiss to my temple. "Sadora, do not feel like you have to do this. If taking two Draax at once is something you do not want, the king will not force you to do it. I promise you."

I smiled at him and traced my fingers over his jawline before doing the same to Court. "I'm doing this because I want you both inside of me, together. No other reason."

Court rested one big hand on his thigh. "We want that as well, sadora."

"Good," I said. "Shut the door, and let's get naked."

I FELL BACK AGAINST THE BED, MY BLOOD WHOOSHING through my ears and my pulse beating out a frantic rhythm. The last aftershocks of my orgasm were still radiating through my body, and I smiled weakly when Bran lifted his head from my dripping pussy and grinned at Court.

"She is wet enough now."

"Good." Court was kneeling beside me, his cock still shiny from my saliva. I had wanted to finish him with my mouth, his cum tasted delicious, but he'd pulled away just as Bran made me come all over his face.

Court stretched out beside me, his hand lazily stroking his dick as he stared at my heaving tits. Bran was rolling on a condom, but Court didn't bother. My stomach made a funny little lurch. He didn't need a condom because he was about to fuck me in the ass.

I waited for the nerves to hit me, but apparently, the two orgasms Bran had just given me were cancelling out any anxiety I might have felt.

Bran handed Court the bottle of lube before lying on his side next to me. He urged me to face him, and I turned to my side, smiling happily when he pressed his big, warm body against mine. I kissed his chest as he lifted my leg and draped it over his hip. He bent his head and kissed me as he stroked my thigh with his hand.

Court pressed the length of his body against my back, his hand slipping around to cup my left breast. He toyed with the nipple as Bran sucked on my right. Fresh lust flowed through me, and I ground my ass against Court's dick as I clutched Bran's head in my hands.

I turned my head, kissing Court frantically as the two men teased and tormented my nipples. When I was panting harshly and making little sounds of need, Bran raised his head and smiled at me.

"Are you ready for both of us, sadora?"

"Yes, God, yes," I gasped out.

He moved his body down a bit, and I moaned happily when the head of his dick slipped into my pussy. He pushed forward, his hand wrapped around my thigh to hold me steady as he made a few gentle thrusts.

"That feels so good," I whispered.

Court kissed the back of my shoulder. I squeaked, my pussy clamping around Bran's dick when the cold liquid dripped over my back entrance, but Court's fingers soon warmed it up. As he pushed two fingers into me and stretched me lightly, Bran distracted me with a few more thrusts. He kissed between my breasts and licked around my nipple as I clung to his shoulders.

Court spread my ass cheeks, and I tensed when I felt the blunt head of his dick against my ass.

"Relax, sadora," he said. "Relax and push back against me."

I took a deep breath as Bran lifted his head and smiled encouragingly. He cupped my breast, rubbing my nipple gently with his thumb as I stared into his dark eyes. "You can do this, sadora. Will you be our good girl?"

I nodded immediately. God, I loved it when Bran called me his good girl. It never failed to make me drip with need.

Bran slipped his hand between us and rubbed my clit with slow and lazy circles as I released my breath and pushed back against Court. I'd been gradually using bigger plugs, but there was still an eye-watering pop of pain when Court pushed the head of his cock past my tight ring of muscle.

I groaned under my breath, and he stopped immediately. Both men soothed me with their hands and with light kisses.

"You are being so good for us," Bran said, pressing kisses across my collarbone. "Good girl, sweet sadora. Very good girl."

His words made my pussy tighten around his cock with pleasure, and he made his own harsh groan as Court pushed a little more.

"You are so tight," Court groaned into my ear. "Can you relax a little more for me?"

I concentrated on how good Bran's fingers felt against my clit, how right it felt to have his cock deep inside my pussy, as I took a few deep breaths and relaxed my muscles.

"Better," Court whispered into my ear. He thrust back and forth, gentle ones that helped stretch me as I tried to accommodate his size. "Good girl, sadora. Good girl."

"Oh God," I moaned when I finally felt Court's pelvis rest against my ass. "It's too much."

"Shh, it is not," Bran said. His hand tightened on my thigh when I tried to move it off his hip. "Stay still for a moment."

"I am trying," Court gritted out.

A small smile crossed Bran's face. "I meant our sweet sadora."

I ignored him and made another little wiggle. Both men groaned, and I gasped as Bran's fingers pinched my clit. I felt full and a little trapped, and… damn if I wasn't loving every single minute of it. I was impaled on two huge Draax dicks, and it felt fucking amazing.

I tightened my ass and my pussy, smiling happily when Bran and Court both made loud moans of pleasure. Without speaking, both of them began to thrust in and out. As one pushed in, the other pulled back, and I gripped Bran's shoulders, the back of my head resting against Court's chest as they fucked me with a slow and experienced rhythm.

It was apparent they knew what they were doing, obvious that this was how it was meant to be with us. Both men inside me, both men finding their pleasure in my body as I found mine with theirs.

Court made another low groan as their rhythm increased, his hot breath stirring my hair. "Bran, I will not last long."

"Nor I," Bran gritted out. "Evie, can you come again for us?"

"Yes, I – I think so," I gasped. "If you rub my clit."

Bran immediately reached down and rubbed my clit again. I squirmed between them, my nipples hard as glass and my pussy and ass stuffed full. Bran tugged on my clit, and I made a sharp cry before burying my face in his neck to muffle my sounds of pleasure.

Both men were moving jerkily now, their rhythm losing that steady pace, their groans growing progressively louder. Court was the first to lose control. His hand clamped down on my hip, his tail curled around my thigh, and he made a hard thrust that pushed me up against Bran. Hot warmth flooded my ass, and I cried out into Bran's warm flesh, my orgasm triggered by Court's and the touch of Bran's fingers against my clit.

I shook against Bran while Court's big body thrust hard into me. Bran's arm wrapped around me, and he surged forward, his cock sliding deep into my pussy as he climaxed with a low groan that sent goosebumps to my skin.

Both men pressed up against me, sandwiching me tight between them as the last of their orgasms shuddered through them. I kissed Bran's chest and reached behind me to squeeze Court's hip, reveling in the feeling and sensation of being with both of my loves.

Too soon, they eased out of me. Bran brushed my hair away from my sweaty face as Court stroked the line of my spine. All three of us were sweaty and trembling, but I smiled at Bran when he pressed a kiss against my forehead. "Are you all right, sadora?"

"Hmm," I said before resting my cheek on Bran's chest. "That was amazing."

Court rubbed my hip. "It was. Thank you, Evie."

"No problem," I mumbled. "Happy to help."

Bran's low chuckle reverberated in my ear, and I smiled as both Draax snuggled me. This was what I wanted, what I needed. I could happily spend the rest of my life tucked between them.

CHAPTER 18

Bran

"Bella? Where are you, meena? It is time for lunch." I stuck my head in Bella's room. She wasn't sitting where I'd left her on her bed, but I could see her colouring book and some crayons on the quilt.

"Court, have you seen Bella?" I asked when Court walked past the door.

He paused and shook his head. "No, but she is probably in Evie's room again."

I put the crayons and the book on the small desk in the corner of her room before heading down the hallway. Evie's door was open, and I saw the end of Court's tail disappear as he walked into her room.

"Meena, your papa is looking for you. It is lunchtime and… meena! What have you done?"

I hurried into Evie's room just in time to see Court pull a photo from Bella's hand. "Meena, no!"

Bella's eyes widened, and I could already see the tears

forming. Court never raised his voice toward her. I took his arm. "Court, what is wrong?"

He showed me the picture in his hand. It was of an Earth male, although Bella had scribbled so much crayon across it that it was almost impossible to tell that. "Meena, why would you do this?"

"I colourin', Uda," Bella whispered as she dropped her crayon, slid off the bed, and inched toward me. "No be mad at Bella."

Court brandished the photo at me as his tail whipped back and forth. "This is the only picture that Evie has of her father. She loved him very much, and it was very special to her. Bella has ruined it."

My stomach dropped, and I stared down at Bella. "Bella, why would you do that?"

"I colourin', Papa," Bella said. She lifted her arms to me, but I refused to pick her up.

"You know that you are only supposed to colour in your colouring books, is that not right, Bella?"

She ducked her head, staring at her feet, and even the big fat tears dropping from her eyes were not enough to quell my growing anger. "Answer me, Bella."

"Yes, Papa," she sobbed.

"You have ruined a picture that was special to Evelyn."

"I sorry, Papa," she cried. "Bella sorry, no be mad. Please, Papa."

She burst into tears, and I ignored my urge to pick her up and soothe her. "Bella, you cannot -"

"What's wrong?" Evelyn was hurrying into the room, and she gave Bella a worried look. "Honey, why are you crying?"

"No be mad at Bella, girl!" Bella sobbed. "Bella sorry, girl. Please."

Evelyn scooped up Bella and kissed her cheek before allowing Bella to bury her face in her neck. She hugged her tight and rocked her back and forth. "Shh, baby. Don't cry. Shh."

"Girl mad at Bella," Bella wailed against her throat.

"I'm not, honey. I'm not mad at you." Evelyn gave me a confused look, and feeling sick to my stomach, I held out the picture of her father.

His face a pale green, Court said, "Bella coloured on the picture of your father, Evie."

"I am sorry," I said as she took the picture from me. "I should have been watching Bella closer. I am so sorry, sadora."

She stared at the picture in her hand as Bella sobbed harder. "Bella sorry, girl. Bella sorry!"

Court's grunt of surprise matched mine when Evelyn dropped the picture on the bed and rubbed Bella's back. "Shh, honey. Shh, it's okay. Stop crying, baby."

She sat on the bed, holding Bella on her lap, and rocked her back and forth until Bella's sobs slowed. She pushed Bella back gently and kissed her forehead. She wiped the tears from her cheeks and smiled at her. "Don't cry, baby."

Bella stared at her and then at the picture on the bed beside them. Her lower lip trembled, and she glanced at me as fresh tears spilled down her cheeks. "Bella break picture?"

"Yes," I said, but my voice was gentle. "You destroyed a very important picture to Evelyn, meena."

Bella stared up at Evie as Evelyn wiped away the new tears. "I sorry, Evie-girl."

Evelyn kissed her forehead again. "I know you are, baby. Thank you for saying you're sorry."

"Evie girl mad at Bella?" Bella stared at her in sorrow.

Evelyn shook her head immediately. "No, baby. I'm not mad at you."

"Evie girl love Bella?" Bella made a wavering little sigh as she stared up at Evelyn.

"Yes," Evie said. "Evie loves Bella."

"Bella loves Evie," Bella said, throwing her arms around Evelyn as she started to cry again. "Bella loves Evie."

"I love you too, honey," Evelyn said.

She scooted back on the bed and laid on her side, holding Bella against her and pressing kisses against her head as Bella's tail wrapped tight around her forearm. I stared silently at them until Court touched my arm.

I glanced at him and followed him out of the room, shutting the bedroom door behind me.

* * *

Court

BRAN WAS SILENT WHEN I LED HIM INTO THE LIVING ROOM. He stared at the fire as I stood near the window. We had been calling Evelyn our sadora for weeks and wrapping our tails around her waist. The pet name and the gesture were both something Draax only did with their mates, but neither of us would admit our love for her.

I would no longer deny it. I couldn't deny it. "I love Evelyn."

I waited for him to call me a fool, to remind me again that she belonged to the king, but his shoulders slumped, and I felt the weight of his sigh from across the room. "I love her too."

"I will not give her up to the king," I said.

"We have no choice." Bran continued to stare into the fire.

"When the storm ends, I could take Evelyn and leave. We could stay hidden. You can tell the king that we fell in love and that you tried to stop me, but we would not listen. Once the king gives up on finding Evelyn and brings in another human female for his queen, we will return to you and Bella."

Bran turned to face me. "It is not possible, Court. Even if the king finds a new queen, you and Evelyn would still be punished for what you did. You would likely lose your head, and Evelyn would go to the Earth prisons for breaking her contract. You would never be able to return home, and you would always be on the run."

"It is better than living without her," I said as panic ran rampant through my veins.

"We cannot do that to Bella or Evelyn. Bella would miss you terribly, and Evelyn…"

He took another deep breath. "Our sadora's life has been one of pain and hardship, and I will not do that to her again. She deserves to be queen, Court. She deserves to be cherished and spoiled and live a life free of fear."

"Even if that means being apart from us?" I said.

"Yes," Bran's voice was low but firm. "We must give her up, no matter how much we love her."

"You love me?"

We both turned at the sound of Evelyn's soft voice. She stood in the doorway, and Bran gave her a guilty look. "Where is Bella?"

"In the kitchen eating lunch." She crossed her arms over her torso. "Do you both love me?"

Bran didn't reply, but I could not deny my sadora anything she asked. "Yes," I said. "We love you, Evelyn."

"I love you too," she whispered before starting to cry.

Bran and I reached her at the same time. We crowded around her, hugging her between us and taking turns pressing kisses against her soft mouth.

"I love you, Court," she said.

"I love you, sadora," I replied.

She kissed me and turned to Bran. "I love you, Bran."

"I love you, Evie," he said.

She kissed him, but she was crying, and we rubbed the tears away from her cheeks.

"Do not cry, sadora, please," Bran pleaded.

"We can't be together," Evelyn said. "I love you, and I'll never see you again in a few days."

I glanced at Bran and he shook his head, but I forged ahead anyway. "Evie, you and I could leave when the storm ends. We could hide and -"

"No," Evelyn said. "You and Bran and Bella are a family, and I won't break you up like that or do anything that would put any of you in danger."

"You are a part of our family, too," I said. "Is that not true, Bran?"

"Yes," Bran said. "You are our family now, Evelyn."

Her smile wavered as she put an arm around each of us. "I love you for saying that, and trust me, I want to be a part of this family more than anything, but a person doesn't always get what they want. I'm not meant for you."

It was getting hard to breathe again, and there was a strange growing lump in my throat that I could not swallow past.

Evelyn stared at Bran and then at me. "Promise me that you'll move on and find someone else after I leave with the king."

"No," Bran snapped.

"We will not," I said.

"You have to," she insisted. "Find a nice woman to be a good mom to Bella and a good wife to the two of you. Okay?"

"No," I said.

"Never," Bran said.

Her tears gave way to frustration, but neither Bran nor I would budge. She glanced out the window. "You said the storm will end in another few days?"

"Most likely," Bran said.

She took a deep breath and kissed both of us again. "Then we're going to make the most of the time we have left. No tears or anger. Just love. All right?"

Bran nodded, and I rested my forehead against hers. "Just love, sadora."

Bran

I STARED AT THE CEILING, LISTENING TO EVELYN'S SOFT breathing and Court's snoring. My stomach was in knots, and I had a headache.

The storm was over.

It had ended around three this morning. The sudden quietness had woken me, and I'd lain in the dark, foolishly hoping that the wind and the snow would begin again. The weight I'd carried since Dana had torn apart our family had finally disappeared after Court, and I forgave each other, but it had been replaced with an infinitely heavier one.

A weight I could barely carry day in and day out.

Evelyn had asked for only happiness and love this past week, and Court and I had done our best to give her that. But every day, the weight of losing her grew until I'd woken to the quiet.

Now, that weight threatened to pin me to the ground, to destroy every last shred of happiness within me. They would come for our Evelyn, and we would never see her again. We would never touch her soft skin, hear her voice, or smell her sweet scent. She would mate with the king and bear his children, and Court and I would spend the rest of our days in love with a woman we could never have.

I sat up and slid out of bed without looking at Evie or Court. No matter how much I wished I could, I could not change what would happen.

The storm was over.

I dressed quietly and left the bedroom. When I stuck my head into Bella's room, she was awake and sitting in bed, staring at a picture book.

"Hi, Papa!"

"Hello, meena."

She climbed out of bed and skipped over to me. I picked her up and kissed her soft cheek before taking her to the bathroom. Once she was finished, we went to the kitchen, and Bella made a little squeal of delight when she saw the light pouring in through the window.

"Papa, light!"

"Yes, meena," I said as I set her in her chair at the table.

She lifted her hand to the beams of light, her smile widening. "Pretty."

"Yes," I said.

She stared at me, her little eyebrows drawing down. "Papa sad?"

I didn't reply, but she reached out and took my hand. "Papa no sad, okay?"

"Okay, meena," I said.

My tablet was on the table, buzzing with a new message as Court entered the kitchen. He bent and pressed a kiss against Bella's cheek. "Hi, Bella."

"Hi, Uda. Look – light!" Bella grabbed his hand and put it in the beam of light.

Court smiled at her. "Yes, light."

Her brow furrowed again, and she stared at Court and then at me. "Uda sad too?"

Court touched the top of her head. "No, meena. We are not sad."

I grabbed my tablet and read the message. My stomach churned, and I glanced up at Court, who took one look at my face and said, "The king?"

I nodded. "Yes. They are coming for her this afternoon."

Court's face twisted, and his hands turned to fists. I waited for him to bring up his plan to leave again. My panic and dismay made me think it might actually be a good plan, but he only said, "You need to reply to them."

I shut off my tablet. "Not now."

"Bran, you can't -"

"Not now," I repeated. "They are coming whether I reply or not."

"Hi, Evie girl!"

Court and I turned to see Evelyn standing in the door-way. She crossed the kitchen and bent and kissed Bella's cheek. "Hello, baby."

She smiled at us, pressed a kiss against both of our cheeks and then walked to the window to stare out of it. She lifted her face to keo and basked in its warmth before turning to us. "They messaged, didn't they? That's what you were talking about when I came in."

"Yes," I said. "They will be here this afternoon."

Her lips pressed together, and for a moment, it looked like she would cry. She took a deep breath, pinched the bridge of her nose, and pasted a smile on her face. "All right."

She crossed to Bella and picked her up, resting her on her hip and smiling. "I love you, Bella."

Bella grinned at her. "Bella loves Evie girl."

"Do you think we could go outside for a bit after break-fast? If I borrow some warmer clothes from you or Court? I would love to get some fresh air," Evelyn said.

I nodded. "Yes. It is still freezing out, but we could go outside for a while."

"Good." She kissed Bella's cheek. "Are you hungry, sweet girl?"

"Yes! Bella wants poffin bread and juice!" Bella shouted.

"Then you'll have poffin bread and juice," Evelyn said with a small smile.

"BRAN, SOMETHING MUST HAVE GONE WRONG. IT IS ALMOST TEN." Court paced the living room. "Check your tablet again."

"I just checked. There has been no further communication," I said.

"Do you think the king has changed his mind?" Court asked.

"Doubtful," I said.

Evelyn walked into the living room, nervously rubbing her hands over her thighs. "Bella is asleep. Any word?"

"Nothing," Court said.

"This is weird, right?" she said. "Maybe they couldn't get out of the castle? I mean, there's been a lot of snow. If they don't have those automatic digger machines that you and Court used this morning to clear the snow from the front door and yard, then…"

She sighed and shook her head. "I'm being stupid. Of course, he would have those. He's the freaking king. But something had to happen. Why haven't they messaged us to say they're running late? God, it's so rude not to let us know they're running late. What kind of king is he? He has no manners whatsoever and… oh my God, I can't stand this."

Court crossed the room to pull her into her arms, kissing her as the tears streamed down her cheeks. "Shh, sadora. It is all right."

"I hate this," she said. "I hate this stupid waiting around. It's awful and -"

My tablet buzzed, and the three of us stared at it like it was a poisonous wracken. It buzzed again, and I reached for it. I scanned the message, relief washing over me as Court said, "What does it say?"

"They are not coming today," I said. "Tomorrow. They will be here tomorrow afternoon."

Court exhaled loudly and hugged Evie against him as I tossed my tablet on the couch and stood. I joined them, and Evie put her arm around me, leaning her head against my chest as I stared at Court.

The relief on his face matched mine, but he knew as well as I did that this would be our last night with our sadora.

Evelyn raised her head, the shine of tears still on her cheeks. "Take me to bed," she whispered. "Take me to bed right now and make me yours."

I rested my forehead against hers, my tail joining Court's around her waist. "Yes, sadora."

CHAPTER 19

Evelyn

"Why you sad, girl?" Bella patted my cheek with her hand.

I cuddled her a little closer. "I love you, Bella."

She giggled and pushed away from me to slide off my lap and sit on the floor of her room. "Come play with me, Evie girl."

I stood up from her bed and joined her on the floor, holding the doll she gave me as she sang a tuneless song under her breath. I wanted to recheck the time but didn't. What did it matter? We had no real idea when they would be here, only in the afternoon.

I studied Bella's dark hair, gleaming in the light from keo. I had braided it this morning, and it hung down her back. Her purple skin glowed in the light, and more tears threatened. I blinked them back savagely. I would miss Bella as much as I missed Court and Bran. The thought of never seeing her again made me feel sick to my stomach. I took a deep breath. I was going to be freaking queen. I would demand that the king allow me to at least hologram with Court, Bran, and Bella. If he didn't, I would... I don't know... withhold sex until he did.

My stomach turned lazily, and I swallowed down the bile. By tonight, I would be in the king's bed, and he would be touching me. More bile rose in my throat, and my esophagus burned as I struggled not to throw up. The idea of sleeping with the king, no matter how kind he was, made me want to run screaming.

Bella suddenly stood with her little head cocked to the side. "What that sound, girl?"

My heart lurched in my chest, and my mouth went dry when I heard the vehicles. The sound cut out, and I climbed to my feet.

Court stuck his head into the room, his copper coloured eyes wide and filled with a mixture of panic and anger that made me nervous. "Court?"

"Stay here," he said.

"I can't," I said.

"Stay in the house," Court said. "Bran and I will speak with the king first."

"You're going to get yourself kil -" I glanced at Bella, "hurt. Don't do anything foolish, Court."

"Stay here," he said and shut the door.

I paced the room as Bella studied me. "What wrong, girl?"

"Nothing, honey. Nothing's wrong."

"We go outside?" she said.

I hesitated before crossing the room to Bella's closet. I pulled out her cloak and a warm pair of boots. "Yes. Come here, baby."

She let me wrap her snugly in the cloak and boots, and I carried her to the front door. I could hear voices as I grabbed Bran's extra cloak and threw it on before stuffing my feet into Court's boots. I picked up Bella and set her on my hip. Then, I opened the front door and stepped out into the light.

The cold took my breath away, and I checked to make sure Bella's cloak was secure around her. She was staring at the Draax standing in front of her father and her uncle, and my stomach dropped. There were so many of them, and all of them carried swords.

Sabrina stood beside the biggest one and – weirdly - holding his hand.

"Where is the human named Evelyn?" the biggest Draax said.

Neither Bran nor Court replied, and a Draax with bright blue eyes scowled at them. "Your king has asked you a question."

They remained silent, and the Draax stepped forward, raising his sword. "Answer your king, or -"

"Here, I'm right here." I pushed my way past Court and Bran. Bella clung to my neck, staring wide-eyed at the Draax before us. I licked my lips nervously and took another step forward before being pulled to an abrupt stop by Bran and Court's tails around my waist.

I held Bella closer as Bran and Court moved until they were flanking us. I stared up at Bran and then at Court, my gaze wavering from the tears. I had to leave. I had to leave them, and it would destroy me.

Faintly, I could hear the soft murmur of Sabrina's voice and the deeper pitch of the Draax beside her. I paid no attention, staring at my two Draax as they glanced at each other over my head.

Before I could tell them not to do anything stupid, Sabrina ran forward and grabbed my arm.

Bran immediately reached to push her hand away, and all of the Draax drew their swords. A voice rang out over the ringing sound of the swords. "Touch my queen, and I will remove your hand, farmer."

Bran's hand paused over Sabrina's, and the three of us stared at her. She rolled her eyes and turned to glare at the Draax. "Quill, stop. It's fine. Just give me a minute."

She turned back to me and studied Bran and then Court before giving me a large smile. "You love them, don't you?"

"Yes," I said. I didn't care that the king was standing right there. I would not deny my love for them.

To my surprise, Sabrina let out a whoop and threw her arms around me and Bella. Bella made a small squeak of surprise and then giggled as Sabrina hugged me tight and kissed my cheek with a loud smacking noise.

"I don't understand what's happening," I said.

Sabrina grinned again. "Girl, you're about to be as happy as I am. Come on, let's get out of the cold, and I'll explain everything."

I STARED NUMBLY AT BELLA. SHE WAS SITTING ON THE KING'S lap in our small living room. Her colouring book was propped up on her knees, and she held a fistful of crayons. As I watched, she grinned up at the king. "Quill, hold crayons."

The king held out his big hand obligingly, and she dropped the crayons into his left hand before putting one in his right hand. "Quill colour with Bella?"

She gave him her most charming smile, and the king grinned before beginning to colour.

"No, Quill!" Bella nudged his hand to another part of the picture. "You colour this part. Bella colour trees."

"Evelyn?" Sabrina touched my hand, but I turned to stare

at Court and Bran, standing by the fireplace with identical looks of shock on their faces.

Most of the other Draax had stayed in the land vehicles, but two had joined us. The one with blue eyes stood next to Quill's chair, and the other stood beside Sabrina, sitting beside me on the couch. Both had sheathed their swords but kept their hands clasped loosely around the handles.

"Galan? Can you stand back a bit?" Sabrina said. "Give Evelyn and me a little breathing room."

Galan hesitated and glanced at the king, who nodded. The Draax moved back, and Sabrina smiled at me. "You okay?"

She'd just spent the last half hour explaining everything to me, Bran, and Court, but I felt a little shell-shocked. I glommed on to one of the last things she'd said. "So, you're pregnant with the king's baby, even though you're not breeding compatible?"

Sabrina nodded and patiently repeated how it had happened. "Yes. So, the test looks for a certain gene, right? I have that gene, but it's a different genetic variant. The test looks for the actual gene sequence, and because I have a variant, the normal test didn't pick up on it. Sigan, he's the king's doctor, adjusted the test and rechecked for the gene and bada-bing, bada-boom, there it was. And that's why Quill could knock me up."

She pressed her hand against her stomach before smiling at me. "Listen, I would apologize for sleeping with your guy, but," she glanced at Court and Bran, "I'm guessing you're not bothered by it."

My giggle was only a little hysterical. "No, not at all." I chewed on my bottom lip. "So, we can just switch places? Won't we get in trouble with the agency?"

Quill looked up. "I am king, and my rule will be obeyed.

Sabrina is my mate. I will kill anyone – human or otherwise – who tries to take her from me."

His voice was low and powerful, and Bella frowned up at him before gently pressing her fingers against his mouth. "Quill, no talk. Quill colour with Bella, please."

Bran turned pale green and took a step forward. "Bella, leave the king and come to me."

She scowled at him, her tail flicking into the air to point at him. "Papa, hush. Bella colourin' with Quill."

Bran closed his eyes for a moment. "I apologize, my king. She is a strong-willed child."

Quill laughed and glanced at Sabrina. "I do not mind." He tickled Bella lightly. "Come, meena. We will finish colouring our picture while my queen and your nanny talk."

She giggled and kicked her feet as Sabrina made a soft sigh. "Oh my God, I didn't think I could love him any more than I already did, but I was wrong."

She took my hand and squeezed it. "Look, I know this is weird and strange, but things worked out for both of us, right?"

I nodded, and Sabrina lowered her voice. "You really are happy with them? You're okay with not being, uh, queen?"

"Yes." I stared at Court and Bran. "I love them both, and I want to be their mate. I couldn't give a rat's ass about being queen."

Sabrina's look of delight made me smile. She hugged me tight. "It worked out for both of us then."

I hugged her back. "Yes, it did."

"My mate, we must return home now," Quill said. "You need to rest."

Sabrina shook her head but gave me a little smile. "I swear, since the moment we found out I was pregnant, he hasn't stopped hovering. It's all kinds of adorable, though."

She stood, and I stood as well. She gave me another hug. "Hey, feel free to say no thanks, but do you think you could visit me at the palace occasionally? Maybe we could even hologram?"

"Yes," I said. "I would like that."

"Good." She squeezed my hand. "Thanks, Evelyn. I know you'll be as happy as I am."

"I will be," I said as I watched Quill kiss Bella's cheek before handing her to Bran. The king held out his hand to Sabrina, and she took it. He kissed her knuckles, and Bran and Court bowed when Quill turned toward them.

"Both of you are welcome at the palace with your mate and child anytime you wish."

"Thank you, my king," Bran said.

Sabrina squeezed my hand before she and the three Draax headed toward the front door. "We'll talk soon, Evelyn."

"Okay," I said.

Bella squirmed out of Bran's arms as the front door slammed shut. The land vehicles started up, and as the low rumble of their engines faded into the distance, I stared silently at Court and Bran.

Bella was singing and dancing around the room, and I stepped toward my two mates as she danced by me.

"Did that just happen?" Court said.

"Are you really ours?" Bran said.

"Yes. Always," I said. "I love you."

Identical grins broke out on their faces, and Bran glanced at Court before turning to me. "We love you too, sadora."

Keep reading for an excerpt from "Rebel," Book Three in the Draax Series.

REBEL EXCERPT

(DRAAX SERIES BOOK THREE)

Galan

Krey flipped the switch to autopilot and sat back in the seat. "Another couple of hours, and we will be home."

I stared at the black nothingness, my stomach still churning from our trip through the jumpgate. Space travel always made me sick, and I stared at the blinking lights on the ship's dashboard as I shifted in the co-pilot's seat. "Did you put in the correct coordinates for home?"

Krey laughed before grabbing the apple he'd bought from the market on the way back to the ship. I did not care for the taste of most Earth food, but Krey loved it. He bit into the red fruit and wiped away the juice from his chin.

"Yes, Galan. I will return you home safely. Besides, we are in our solar system. There is no fear of getting lost."

I rubbed at my roiling stomach. "The Idalia system is one of the biggest in the galaxy. It would be easy to lose our way."

I indicated to the lights on the ship. "For all I know, we could be in a completely different solar system altogether."

Krey took another bite of his apple, chewing noisily before swallowing. "The ship's navigation system has not failed, Galan. We are in Idalia and," he tapped a light on the dashboard, "headed straight for Draax. I promise."

I closed my eyes, waiting for the nausea to settle as Krey said, "If you traveled more by ship, the space sickness would not be so bad."

"I do not like traveling by ship," I said.

Although I couldn't see it, I knew Krey was grinning when he said, "You have never enjoyed space travel, not even as a small boy. I thought the mandatory pilot lessons we took when we joined the king's guard might have cured you of your fear, but I believe it made it worse."

"The simulated crashes that Oren made us endure every single day could be the reason for that."

Krey laughed. "They were occasionally… terrifying."

I cracked open one eye and stared at Krey. He had finished his apple and had his feet up on the ship's dashboard, his fingers interlaced over his flat stomach. "You took to flying right away. Why did you not join the Draax Space Division instead of staying in the King's Guard? You know that Oren would have put in a good word for you. You were always his favourite student."

"I always thought you were his favourite," Krey said.

I grinned. "Truthfully, it was probably Quill."

Krey nodded. "You are probably right."

"Why did you not join?" I asked again.

"I love piloting a ship," Krey said, "it is why I volunteer for as many of the trips to Earth as I can, but I love fighting more."

I laughed as Krey patted the handle of the sword around

his waist. "Besides, I am a mediocre pilot at best but an excellent fighter."

"Calling yourself mediocre does not inspire confidence that we will arrive safely home."

"Relax, Galan," Krey said. "You must learn to have faith in me. You do not hear Sigan complaining, do you?"

I glanced at the door that separated us from the rest of the ship. "Only because Sigan rarely speaks unless necessary."

"It is true. Our kadana is a quiet Draax. But excellent at healing our sick."

Krey sat up, dropping his feet from the dashboard. "Why did you come on this trip, Galan?"

"Because our king asked me to," I said.

Krey cocked his head. "You have turned down Quill's requests to go to Earth on many other occasions."

I didn't reply, and Krey said, "At first, I assumed it was because you wished to lie with a female. How long has it been? Six moons?"

"Longer," I admitted grudgingly.

Krey shook his head. "Which is why I was so shocked when you disappeared from the Earth bar last evening."

I rubbed at the back of my neck. "I am sorry for abandoning you and Sigan like that, Krey. I should have said something before I left."

Krey waved his hand at me. "Do not trouble yourself about it. Besides, I handled both the little females after you left." He grabbed his crotch and tugged at it. "They were equally sated this morning when I left their bed."

"Did Sigan find a female to bed?" I asked.

"I never asked," Krey said. "Why did you leave?"

I just shrugged. Truthfully, I didn't know why I'd left. For the first time in my life, none of the soft and beautiful human females appealed to me. There were plenty to choose from last night, and while I, Krey and Sigan refused to offer a bit of gallberry juice as an incentive for them to sleep with us, I still would have had my pick of females. Plenty of human females were breeding incompatible with us but still enjoyed taking us to their bed for an evening or two.

"If it was not to fuck, why did you come on this trip?" Krey asked.

"I am head of the king's guard," I said. "With Quill's mate so close to giving birth, he did not want to leave her. It is my duty to take his place at the meeting with Earth's officials."

"True, but Teo is happy to go more often than not."

When I didn't reply, Krey said, "Do you think this new system with the humans will work?"

"I believe it will," I said. "Look how many females have already agreed to work at -"

"Galan?"

Sigan's voice came over the intercom. I pushed the button on the panel next to my head. "What is it, Sigan?"

"We have a problem. There is some gallberry juice missing."

"What do you mean? Did we not deliver all of it to Earth?"

"I brought a few extra, just in case," Sigan said. "I was reviewing inventory, and the case has two bottles missing."

I glanced at Krey, who shrugged. "I did not take it."

I stood up, stretching my spine and ignoring the nausea in my stomach. Maybe I would grab some gallberry juice from the extra case. "I am on my way."

I frowned when Krey stood as well. "Where are you going?"

"Relax, Galan." Krey clapped me on the back. "Autopilot, remember?"

I grimaced but didn't say anything as Krey followed me to

the back of the ship. Sigan was standing beside a grey shipping container. I peered inside, studying the empty spots where the bottles should have been.

"Maybe the case was not filled completely," Krey said.

"I checked them myself before we left Draax," Sigan said.

"Well, they did not simply grow feet and walk away," Krey said. "They must -"

"Quiet." My voice was low, but Krey stopped talking immediately, his hand dropping to his sword.

I had heard something, the slightest scrape of metal against metal, and I stared at the door of a small storage space to my right. I withdrew my sword, and Krey did the same. I stepped in front of the door, holding my sword in my right hand as I nodded to him.

Moving quietly, he approached the door and eased his tail around the handle. He jerked it open at my nod, and a young human male fell out of the narrow space and onto the floor at my feet.

Before he could scramble to his feet, I held my sword at his throat. "Slowly, human."

He stood up slowly. He was wearing rough pants, which humans called jeans, and a sweater that was too big. It zipped up at the front to his chin, and he had the hood up and pulled shut so that only his face was visible.

His clear blue eyes were clouded over with pain, and sweat poured down his face. His features were delicate, almost feminine-like, and he made a low groan of pain, biting down on his full bottom lip as he pressed one hand to the side of his head.

"Who are you?" My voice was cold, and I pressed against his chest with the tip of my sword. "Why are you on our ship?"

The male was wearing a backpack, and as he shifted on

his feet, his hand still pressed against his head, I heard the distinct clink of bottles.

"I guess we found our thief," Krey said. He studied the man as Sigan moved closer to get a better look. "Do you know what we do with gallberry juice thieves, boy?"

The human opened his mouth, and I stepped back as he vomited onto the floor.

"Krono!" Krey skittered back and stared at his own feet in disgust. "Ugh, there is vomit on my boots now. What is wrong with you, human?"

"He does not understand you," Sigan said. "Not without a translator."

The male wiped his mouth with a shaking hand, and I grunted in surprise when he made a high-pitched scream and grabbed at his head. His eyes rolled back in his head, and he crumpled to the ground.

"Sigan, stay back," I said when the kadana knelt beside the earth male.

Sigan ignored me, peeling back the human's eyelid and studying his pupil. "There is something very wrong with this human."

"There is vomit on my boots," Krey repeated.

Sigan gave him an impatient look as he stood and crossed the room to a metal cabinet. "Galan, put the human on the table."

I sheathed my sword and crouched, sitting the human up. I took the backpack off of him, leaving it on the ship's floor, before sliding one hand around his back and another under his thighs. I lifted him, frowning at how light he was, and carried him to the table. The ship was too small to have an infirmary, but the cabinet Sigan was rifling through was stocked with a few basic medical supplies and bags of gall-berry serum in intravenous form.

I laid the unconscious human on the table as Sigan joined me. He had a pleirdox in his hand and ran the small silver box over the human's body and past his head. He stared at the screen and frowned. "The human is burning up from fever. He will die if we do not get him cooled down."

He pushed another button on the screen. "He has an infection, but I do not know what. The pleirdox does not recognize it, and nothing is coming up from my database of Earth infections. Krey, bring me a needle and a bag of serum."

"Will the serum help?" I asked.

"It should," Sigan said. "I do not know this type of infection, but the gallberry plant cures everything in humans."

"Why are we wasting gallberry serum on a thief?" Krey asked.

I frowned at him, and he held his hands up. "Just a question."

"Bring Sigan his supplies, Krey."

Krey walked toward the cabinet as Sigan pushed a button on the pleirdox. A screen popped up in mid-air, and Sigan read the information printed on it. "Perhaps it is an infection that only Earth males can get. I mostly have studied the female humans."

He glanced at the human. "Galan, remove his outerwear, please. We must get him cooled down as quickly as possible."

As Sigan scrolled through the screens of the pleirdox, I untied the laces holding the hood tight and pulled down the zipper. The hood loosened, and I might have been surprised by the long blonde hair that was now visible if I hadn't been distracted by the white bandaging around the male's upper chest.

"Sigan, look at this," I said. "It looks like he was previously injured. Perhaps that is the cause of the infection?"

Sigan moved forward and studied the bandaging. "I do not see any blood or smell any signs of infection."

He reached into his pocket and produced a pair of small, sharp scissors as Krey returned with the gallberry serum. Sliding the scissors between the bandaging and the human's flesh, Sigan carefully cut his way upward. He snipped the last bandage, and the material slid down to pool on the table.

The breath whooshed out of my lungs in a harsh rush, and I heard Sigan's grunt of surprise.

Krey leaned over my shoulder and stared at the unconscious human. "Krono, is that..."

"Yes," I said as I stared at a set of small, pert, and utterly perfect breasts. "The human is female."

ABOUT THE AUTHOR

Elizabeth Kelly was born and raised in Ontario, Canada. She moved west as a teenager and now lives in Alberta with her husband and a menagerie of pets. She firmly believes that a person can survive solely on sushi and coffee, and only her husband's mad cooking skills prevents her from proving that theory.

For more information about Elizabeth, check out her website at

www.elizabethkelly.ca

facebook.com/EKellyBooks
instagram.com/elizabethkelly_author
amazon.com/Elizabeth-Kelly/e/B00EOHZ0MS
bookbub.com/authors/elizabeth-kelly

ALSO BY ELIZABETH KELLY

Tempted Series

Tempted

Twice Tempted

Forever Tempted

Breathless

Tempted Trilogy (Books 1-3)

Red Moon Series

Red Moon

Red Moon Rising

Dark Moon

Alpha Moon

Pale Moon

The Recruit Series

The Recruit (Book One)

The Recruit (Book Two)

The Recruit (Book Three)

The Recruit (Book Four)

The Recruit (Book Five)

The Recruit (Book Six)

The Shifters Series

Willow and the Wolf (Book One)

Ava and the Bear (Book Two)

Katarina and the Bird (Book Three)

Porter's Mate (Book Four)

Bria and the Tiger (Book Five)

Rosalie Undone (Book Six)

The Dragon's Mate (Book Seven)

Rise of the Jaguar (Book Eight)

The Assassin and the Bear (Book Nine)

Elora and the Crow (Book Ten)

The Draax Series

Reign (Book One)

Rule (Book Two)

Rebel (Book Three)

Surrender (Book Four)

Survive (Book Five)

Salvation (Book Six)

Harmony Falls Series

Sweet Harmony (Book One)

Perfect Harmony (Book Two)

Forbidden Harmony (Book Three)

Redeeming Harmony (Book Four)

Absolute Harmony (Novella)

Beautiful Harmony (Book Five)

Reckless Harmony (Book Six)

Seasoned Romance Series

Bet Your Heart on Me (Book One)

Take a Chance on Me (Book Two)

Place Your Trust in Me (Book Three)

Individual Books

The Necessary Engagement

Amelia's Touch

The Rancher's Daughter

Healing Gabriel

The Contract

A Home for Lily

Saving Charlotte

Shameless

The Fairy Tales Collection

Broken

An Unlikely Seduction

Holiday Romance

The Christmas Wife

The Christmas Rescue

The Christmas Nanny

The Christmas Boss

Sordid Games